CRYPTO-CRASH

Ian McKinley

CRYPTO-CRASH

DOUBLE DRAGON

Acknowledgements

Thanks to Linda for putting up with me when I'm writing, Denis & Susie for review and Jim for producing the cover.

Part 1: Dramatis Personae

Chapter 1 - Andy

Andy lay on the paddleboard that was gently bobbing on Lago Maggiore while the adaptive acoustics of the microphone remained fixed on a window of the penthouse apartment about a kilometre away. Unfortunately, active counter-measures were in place and all he was picking up was white noise. He glanced up just as a flash from the terrace coincided with explosion of the surveillance kit, along with the front end of his board. He automatically rolled off into the lake, struggling to avoid gasping from the chill of the water while he slowly sank below the surface and swam for a couple of strokes before forced up for a gasp of air.

This was just in time to see the remaining part of the board blasted into fragments, as he would have been had his reflexes not kicked in. *Fucking military-grade chemical laser.* He grimaced and submerged just before the heat and a pressure wave indicated a hit where his head had been a moment before. Thirty seconds underwater and he could see the hull of a yacht above him, allowing him to raise his head for a couple of quick breaths out of the line of sight of his attacker.

Andy was scanning the other moored yachts and motorboats in his vicinity, trying to work out a swimming route to shore without exposure to further fire, when he picked up the characteristic whine of an approaching drone. *Could be police, responding to these explosions, but more likely the fucking Russians.* He quickly flicked through menus on the smartpad attached to his left forearm and selected the option of an intense electro-magnetic pulse. Immediately the whine died and was quickly followed by a splash. *Although the range is only a couple of hundred metres, better clear out of here fast before bystanders realise all their electronics have been fried.* He checked his route again and then duck-dived, stroking towards his next cover twenty metres distant.

Ten minutes later, Andy cautiously clambered up the ancient granite steps leading from the harbour, conscious of looking out of place in his dripping swimming trunks and t-shirt on this cool May morning. Nevertheless, he attracted little attention due to the chaos caused by e-cars and -bikes abruptly stopped in their tracks, further amplified by the fact that all mobile phones and other electronic devices were completely dead. As he walked along the promenade in the direction away from Locarno town centre, he slipped the nuclear-hard pad around his arm so that it was not obvious that he possessed the only e-communication in the immediate vicinity. *Got to get back to where my kit is stashed and then decide what to do.* His rented apartment was actually two floors below the one he was trying to spy on, this being clearly more heavily defended than he had expected. The question was whether to go back there or, if this was too dangerous, decide if it would be prudent just to drop – or, at least, postpone – the entire mission. Of course, having spotted his attempted surveillance, it was possible that the Russians would just up-sticks and move on, but he was fairly sure that would not happen. Retreat could be seen as a sign of weakness and that was death to these gangs, who could operate with ease only when all their competitors feared them. *Explains the fucking Ruskie overkill. Anyone else would have just been happy that their eavesdropping counter-measures were working or, worst case, used some focused weapon to fry my equipment. Not these bastards, though. They'd rather blow everything to buggery, including me.*

Andy's rucksack hung from a tree at a small beach towards the limits of the community of Minusio. *Good old Switzerland, where you can still leave stuff lying about without some bugger nicking it.* Hauling off his soggy t-shirt, he towelled himself down and then pulled on a shapeless hoodie. Ignoring the few passers-by, he stripped off his trunks and dragged on cycling shorts. He then uncoupled the trailer used to transport his board, replacing his name tag with a scrawled invitation for anyone to take it. *Might even be a useful distraction if someone takes it soon.* Thus unburdened, he cycled quickly back to Locarno, selecting a route passing further up the hill, through Minusio, in order to avoid the continuing confusion along the lakeside caused by his EMP.

After a lot of thought on the matter, he decided that returning to the *Vivian* apartment block was the best option. Apart from all the equipment he had stored there, Beat and Heidi would probably still be asleep and, if there were going to be any problems, he could hardly just abandon them.

Andy dropped off his bike in the underground garage, took the lift to the 5th floor and let himself into the apartment diagonally opposite. The large, modern flat had three bedrooms: a master with a large ensuite where the ladies would be, a further double bedroom that he had taken for himself and a third bedroom which contained 3 single beds, all of them currently covered with piles of equipment. The door to the master bedroom was open and he stuck his head around the corner, looking into the bathroom where Heidi was soaking up to her neck in bubbles. "Fancy jumping in?" she asked, raising her eyebrows suggestively.

"Love to, but I need to get sorted out first. You want anything for breakfast?"

"Glass of Champagne would be just the thing. Hair of the dog, you know."

"I can guess," he smiled. "And what about your better half?"

"She's still snoozing, but best bring a glass for her too as she was drinking even more than I was last night. Of course, if she doesn't wake up soon, I'll just drink both glasses."

"Fine, I'll get that now. We can chat later, but I guess there's nothing special to report from last night?"

"Nope, still no coconut. How about your early morning exercise, feel the better for it?"

"Well, the water's a bit cooler than I expected," he replied vaguely. *It could certainly have gone a hell of a lot better, but anything I walk away from unscratched can't be considered complete failure. If anything, a warning like that will certainly ensure that I'm even more careful in the future.*

The capsule coffee machine growled while Andy opened a bottle of Veuve Clicquot and filled two large flutes with the sparkling wine. He returned to the bathroom and passed one glass to Heidi and set his small espresso on the ledge at the opposite end of the bath. In the bedroom, Beatrice was still snoozing, the sheet thrown back so that he could admire her smooth, olive skin and generous breasts, with their small brown nipples. He set the flute on the bedside table beside her and returned to the bathroom, where he peeled off his top and shorts.

Andy grimaced when he caught a sight of himself in a mirror. His head was shaved to minimise the evidence of advanced male-pattern baldness, but the stubble on his chin, once black, seemed to be getting greyer by the day. He kept fit, but his belly certainly wasn't as flat as it had once been and almost blocked out the view of his dick when he looked down. *Then again, the water had been cold.*

"Mmm, that's good," Andy groaned while he eased himself slowly into the scorching water, sliding his legs outside Heidi's until he was sitting upright with the woman's feet touching his groin.

Heidi had raised herself a little to make room for him, so that her breasts were, tantalisingly, just level with the thick layer of bubbles. She sipped her Champagne while Andy slurped his coffee, this warming him from the inside while the heat of the bath removed the chill from his legs and lower

11

torso. "That's good too," he grinned as the woman's toes began to stroke his penis.

"So, is Beat awake yet? There's space enough for her to squeeze in with us," she mirrored his grin.

"Nope, the beauty is still sleeping. Maybe just as well, as it'd be a tight squeeze to get anyone else in here."

"Tight squeezes are part of the fun," her toes squeezed his dick to illustrate her point. "Anyway, what's on the agenda for today?"

"Much of the same, I'm afraid. My cunning plan to get more information on our target came to nothing, so we're still focusing on the honey trap approach."

"Can't beat a classic. So, we laze about all day and then head to the Casino again this evening. It's a hard life! Maybe we should book a massage. There's a Thai place that was recommended by a couple of working girls we met in the Casino last night. Apparently, they do a great *happy ending* for female clients. Maybe also for males, if you want me to check?" His penis was again squeezed, beginning to recover from its immersion in cold water and respond to her dactyl manipulations.

"Fun though that sounds, I'll have to pass as I've got work to do. I could maybe fit in a swim though."

"Not in the lake, I hope. It must be fucking freezing."

"A bit cool," he admitted, "maybe around 18 or so. But that'll be nice to cool off in as, according to the forecast, it's going to be sunny and into the high 20s."

"Not a chance. If you want some exercise, we could have a threesome workout when my partner emerges from the land of Nod."

Andy could hardly claim to be uninterested in this offer, as he was now fully erect. "Well, we can make a decision about that later. Let's just enjoy the bath for now."

Heidi took a large gulp of her wine, then tossed Andy a bar of soap. "Okay, you're paying for all of this anyway. One enjoyable bath coming up." She squirmed around until she was sitting on his lap, squeezing her bum against his erection. "You wash me, and then I'll wash you." She pulled his hands around to cradle her breasts.

Well, this can't help but be an enjoyable bath. He smiled while he silently acknowledged how this woman made it impossible to feel stressed-out when in her company.

Chapter 2 - The team

The cyber-team was originally formed after Andy, Jay, Lou and Su graduated from university and completed their Swiss national service together. This involved the usual military desensitisation, focused on mindless obedience to designated superiors and training in *useful* abilities such as shooting assault rifles, driving trucks and building pontoon bridges over rivers. However, a new exercise on cyberwar defence was included.

Only Lou and Su were friends at this point, but Jay and Andy quickly teamed with them after the Q&A session introducing this project. It was clear that they were the only recruits in the class of twenty who really understood the fundamentals of internet security – and its inherent weaknesses. The aim of the exercise had been to assess the capabilities of a recently identified virus that was attributed to foreign terrorists and list possible defences against it. Within eight hours, Andy's team had traced the source of the virus and initiated a denial of services attack on the Chinese computer centre that was responsible for its production – to the great amusement of their instructor and dismay of the experts responsible for developing the exercise.

Despite very generous inducements to continue on for officer training, the group bonded together and held out for a contract to independently support national cyber-defence. They established a small company, Network Security GMBH, usually abbreviated to NetSec, which contracted to various Swiss government departments. Given that many of the private institutions under threat – banks, insurance companies, pharmaceuticals and utilities – had allocated major funding for such defence, this turned out to provide a huge additional market. Early successes against ransomware hacker gangs brought in big commercial contracts from large multinationals. For such contract work, an extremely low-profile, virtual company, WhiteHatz, was set up. This was decoupled from, and hidden beneath, NetSec operations.

Although a few attacks were launched by the caricature solitary geek living in their mother's basement, most were run by hacker teams within established criminal gangs. The key reason for the decision to bury WhiteHatz in the dark web was primarily to protect the team from potential retaliation. The risk of personal attacks increased as their modus operandi for counter-attacks was established: destroying the hardware used by the hackers and, more importantly, clearing out their bank accounts.

To keep security tight, WhiteHatz comprised only the original team, expanded only after 10 years to include Georgie when developments in quantum computers made someone with focused knowledge of this field indispensable. For many jobs, larger teams of geeks were required, but work was split up before sub-contracting to specialist agencies – mainly based in India – who worked quickly, cheaply and without any knowledge of where their efforts fit into the projects involved.

Successful ransomware gangs could generate incomes of many millions of Euros per year, and potentially much more in special cases. Their vulnerability often resulted directly from this income and the problems of transferring and managing huge funds without coming to the attention of either the authorities or their competition. The usual approach was to focus on payments in crypto-currencies, due to the inherent difficulty in tracing these. Indeed, many believed that such tracing was impossible. However, it was merely very difficult and certainly doable with the right skills and access to powerful enough hardware.

Although quantum computing had emerged only slowly, reminiscent of fusion energy in constantly showing promise but always a large step away from practicality, it offered a shortcut for the very specific task of circumventing crypto-fund security. This allowed the team to seize ill-gotten gains – as anything in such accounts was presumed to be – under the conditions of a *gentlemen's agreement* which allowed 20% of the amount recovered as a "finder's fee", while 80% went into a black account in the Swiss National Bank administered by the Nachrichtendienst, the Swiss intelligence service.

WhiteHatz then had the same problem as their opponents in terms of hiding a suspiciously large income. However, aware of the problems of crypto-currency held on the dark web, another company was set up, ostensibly to manage Swiss ex-pat retirement funds by investing in property – an extremely robust, even if not high-paying, option.

As all the clients were bona fide and all relevant taxes were deducted at source, there was no reason for anyone to carry out the detective work needed to spot the differences between the actual amount they had invested and that held in their names within the company accounts. The company also invested in advanced computing infrastructure, which was supposedly leased out as a service for those needing major number-crunching capabilities, but actually used mainly for their own projects.

From the beginning, NetSec was set up by the founders as a cooperative, with equally shared ownership and split of all income. At that time, none of the team members were in fixed relationships, so there were clear tax benefits in renting a large 8-room villa that provided both accommodation and shared working space for the company.

Even a few years later, when finances were not an issue, the team decided that living close together was something that they all enjoyed. After Georgie joined, the company bought a luxury terrace residence, which stepped up the hillside high above the town of Wettingen. This included 6 apartments that were retained as accommodation, and 4 apartments which were converted into offices and common areas. In addition to a large underground garage and several basement rooms and cellars, including a gym and swimming pool, the block included a typically Swiss Luftschutzkeller – a large, completely overdesigned bomb shelter. This last was converted into a well-shielded server room containing all key computer hardware.

Chapter 3 - Hyo-Jin

In Locarno, Andy's operations were focused on a new Russian Bratva gang that had recruited a top North Korean hacker, Park Hyo-Jin. They had helped her defect and set her up in Switzerland, apparently her dream land of residence. WhiteHatz had already determined that Park was the probable brains behind a couple of ransomware attacks on smaller reinsurance companies based in Bermuda. In both cases, the companies paid the ransoms, but made the attack details available via an international database of financial cyber-crime. This allowed forensic analysis, showing that the Trojan virus involved shared signatures with known Chinese spyware and a search of the CIA's *persons of interest* database identified Park as being now linked to Russian gangsters.

This was part of normal monitoring of developing cyber-threats. However, the next target was one of the major players in the reinsurance business – Munich Re. This led to WhiteHatz being contracted to remove this threat as quickly as possible, while the company stalled on paying the specified ransom of cryptocurrency with a value of 100 million Euro. The team's first priority was eliminating the threat. This could be either done directly, which was especially challenging due to the short time available to identify and neutralise the virus, or by hacking the hackers: breaking into their computer system and stealing the release code from them.

Hyo-Jin had been trained in the Chinese cyberwarfare group of the Ministry of State Security, before returning to the DPRK to join their elite *Lazarus Group* of state-sponsored cyber-criminals. It appeared that she had been tempted away by a combination of both a huge cash payment and the opportunity to use it to experience a lifestyle available only in the West. Deeper assessment indicated that this also provided her with a chance to escape from the prejudice resulting from her lesbianism. This was compounded by her refusal to hide her sexual proclivities within a marriage of convenience to one of her many male admirers within the Lazarus Group, which contained many frustrated bachelors who had little chance to contact the opposite sex, either inside or outside work.

As the aim was not only to defeat this attack, but also to prevent anything similar in the future, a parallel effort was initiated to trace and confiscate all funds belonging to this Russian gang. The great thing about theft from criminals was that there was very little that they could do about it: they clearly could hardly go to the police and, due to intense competition between gangs, could not work together with other victims to mount an integrated response. Indeed, after their accounts were cleared out, gangs were equally vulnerable to both the authorities and fellow pirates.

For this operation, WhiteHatz split the work along the usual lines. Su, as their best programmer, focused on direct debugging; Lou searched for the cash trail; Jay chased links to known organised crime groups; Andy attempted to hack into the computer system used in the attack; and Georgie provided general support for any jobs where her quantum computer could provide an edge.

Chapter 4 - Heidi & Beat

Having identified where Park's team were located, Andy rented a flat below their penthouse as a base for the operation. Based on the background of her sexual predilections provided by the CIA database, Andy chose to bring the Beat and Heidi along with him on this jaunt. Apart from anything else, a group of three renting a 3-bedroom apartment was less likely to cause notice than a single man. A hack of the Locarno CTVs had already shown that Park was a regular customer of the casino, combining a typical Asian fondness for gambling with the opportunity for her to pick up one of the prostitutes who could be readily found in this location. She also had a small rental apartment nearby that was set up only for any resultant liaisons. At all times, she had at least two heavily-built Russian minders, who remained in her vicinity even during her visits to this love nest. She generally spent only a couple of hours there, before being escorted back to the Vivian penthouse.

Park's only other regular departures from the penthouse were daily walks to the nearby Lido, where she swam and took advantage of the wellness area, enjoying a massage a couple of times every week.

After they arrived the previous day, Andy had treated the ladies to an excellent dinner in the old town, before leaving them to enjoy an evening in the casino. Back in the apartment, he tried the usual approaches to hacking into any computers in the penthouse. Andy wasn't surprised to find that there was no use of Wi-Fi detectable in Park's flat and a more subtle search for signals carried over the building power supply also came to nothing. *Probably a Faraday cage around any sensitive areas and an isolating transformer for any charging of electronic devices, which are probably switched off during the process. Nevertheless, cable links show lots of dodgy, pay-to-view, hard-core porn being watched, especially in Park's absence. Guess that keeps her minders amused.*

This lack of progress led to Andy's abortive attempt to check on possible hints available from any acoustics picked up by laser scanning of the glass doors of the penthouse lounge, which led onto the terrace facing the lake. This pretty well exhausted the options for passive monitoring of whatever was going in this apartment. So, the question was whether or not more active options came into consideration, especially given the risks of Russian over-reaction should any such attempt be spotted. This assessment was especially tricky as his friends would be on the front line here and the threshold on what was an acceptable risk had to be set much lower than if he had been doing everything himself. *Maybe one more try at the Casino tonight and then drop this option if we don't get a bite.*

***

Heidi and Beatrice referred to themselves as *hobby prostitutes*. Beat was independently wealthy, having inherited the fortune that her father amassed by clever investment in property throughout Switzerland. He had regularly anticipated trends in

22

the most desirable locations: buying ramshackle old buildings, doing them up and selling them at a huge profit. Her wife, Heidi, was originally a property manager. However, since marriage, both had effectively retired and now spent much of their time travelling or providing volunteer support for a number of charities. As both women were bi, their love life was regularly spiced up by their participation in the local swinger scene, always as a couple.

They were also very keen burlesque performers, often participating in reviews organised by private clubs that focused on the erotic end of the spectrum. From this, they branched out into occasional prostitution, which they did for the fun of it, with all proceeds being donated to a charity supporting abused women and children. Here, they took on jobs only as a couple, particularly specialising in mild BDSM. They openly admitted that both burlesque and BDSM were linked to their fascination with kinky clothes: tight leather and latex suits, exotic underwear and extremely high heels. The prostitution side was also an obvious way for two dommes to find the subs that they were looking for. They insisted that all action took place in a special dungeon constructed in the basement of Beat's villa, a converted farmhouse above Baden, which provided security and privacy without being excessively remote.

Andy initially met Heidi when she was in a relationship with his business partner, Su, a year or so before she met Beatrice. During this time, he and Lou, another business partner, had often made up a foursome with the couple for dinners, followed by cinema, concert or theatre. Despite clear interest from Heidi and Lou, they had never ended up together in bed, mainly because Su, despite a history of bi relationships, was then going through a straight lesbian phase. Although Andy's contact with Heidi diminished considerably after she split with Su, they met up once or twice a year for a drink and a chat. Also, after Heidi linked up with Beat, he would occasionally attend one of their burlesque shows and have a few drinks with them afterwards.

When they developed their prostitution side-line, Andy was easily able to talk Lou into giving it a try. Typically, Lou had a great time but Andy did not feel comfortable in his sub role, although freely admitting that the action was extremely erotic. Lou had been back to the dungeon a couple of times – either alone or with one of their other business partners. Jay, despite claiming to be 99% gay, was typically prepared to give any form of perversion a try. She also took Georgie along once when she was going through a girl / lesbian phase and, apparently, the booked two-hour session extended to an all-nighter.

The happy hookers were also game to support Andy in some of his operations – in most cases providing a distraction for targets when this was needed. Certainly, when the well-endowed couple were in their wildest leather-domme rigouts, any man or woman who could keep their eyes off the pair would need to be dead from the neck down.

Chapter 5 - Georgie

Georgie woke alone in bed, momentarily disorientated until remembering that Andy was in the field, somewhere in the Tessin. *Yes, definitely a boy today*, he grinned, aware of the discrepancy between this acknowledgement and the piss-erection lifting up the thin sheet that was his only bed covering, which existed in his imagination only. *And hetero, perhaps with just the slightest traces of bi. Pain in the arse that Andy isn't about or, more accurately, no pain in the arse for the moment.* George, as he was today, masturbated slowly without any feeling of an associated disconnect. He was aware of being born Georgina and that this was the reason for the lack of a penis, but this did not mean that he was not a real man: at least not today.

At school it had been different, the pressure had been to identify as female – whether hetero, homo or bi – as this would have made things easier for simple logistics such as which toilet or changing room could be used. An alternative option was to go trans, with surgical and hormonal intervention as required to be identify as male, and then select a lifestyle preference on that basis. At this time, homosexuality was slowly becoming more acceptable, but gender fluidity, although a defined term, was often considered more a fad rather than a fundamental aspect of some personalities. Indeed, this was the entire basis of Georgie's identity. He, she or he/she – it mattered not a jot what the pronoun choice was – as long as it wasn't it or them. *It* was applied to inanimate objects and *them* was a term to be used for psychopaths with multiple personalities as far as she was concerned. Georgie was never more than an individual: if anything, more of an individual than many of those regarded as normal.

Throughout university it wasn't much better but, there, defaulting to an asexual mode was an easy option. Although her studies led to a diverse range of contacts, her shyness and rather androgynous appearance, with small breasts, a thin face and short, dirty-blonde hair, led to few friends and little intimacy in any of her relationships. This may well have helped her reach the extremely high academic levels that she did. Maybe it was her self-enforced isolation, but the double-think that she saw her friends and family going through as they struggled to fit her into a single personality profile seemed rather pathetic. A reflection of their lack of individuality rather than a statement of it. Acknowledging that a single person could fit into more than one box – rather than there being a box for such outliers – was the key. There was a term that her bog-Irish grandfather used, *happy in myself*, that hit the nail directly on the head.

Georgie was convinced that her nature meant that she was destined to end up in the quantum computing field. Binary people wanted everything to be zero or one, male or female, and hence were unhappy when something, somebody, was both at the same time. Georgie was completely happy with this – existing in a male-female superposition until the wave function collapsed. But, being more

26

complex than an elementary particle, after a period of collapse, superposition was re-established until the next time. And that was just gender, her proclivities were also variable over a very wide spectrum. She often wondered whether her queerness was quantised or truly continuous, but it was certainly not binary, that was for sure.

It was only after Georgie met the rest of the NetSec team that she blossomed. When they started working on technical shit, regardless of what it was, they really came together as a unit. There was no interest at all in gender or lifestyle preferences, it was all about the job. She was good, they respected that and, occasionally, admitted that she was *really fucking good*. This recognition went to her heart, as she was also aware that this was a dream team, the best of the best.

It was Andy who started calling her Georgie, when her own personal world began to overlap with his. Boy / girl, hetero / homo, vanilla / kinky: the team just didn't give a shit. Who cared a fuck if they used the wrong pronoun, as long as they loved him for himself, herself, whatever-the-fuck-self.

Andy was maybe the nicest guy – person or whatever – that Georgie had ever met. He was a fair bit older, now in his forties, but lacked the hang-ups so typical of oldies. They first had sex while she was a girl, and rather pissed into the bargain. Waking up in bed with him the next morning as a boy tending towards gay could have been awkward, but turned out as a pleasant surprise because this did not seem to bother him in the slightest. He simply followed instructions, leading to the version of wild, sweaty, boy-on-boy sex that she was looking for at that moment. *But now, no Andy, nobody at all. Just as well that masturbation is one of the key characteristics that's common to all primates of whatever sex.*

This musing was cut short when Georgie remembered the last tests run on the new hardware, which promised to completely revolutionise the way that NetSec operated. Despite hating hyperbole, this really seemed to be justifiably termed a technological singularity. The starting point was a neural network tailored to hacking into secure servers, which took full benefit of the knowledge base provided by the semantic web. This was complemented by mathematical tools tailored to breaking symmetric, asymmetric and hashing cryptography, which took full benefit of the latest quantum computing developments to increase the speed of this process by orders of magnitude. Although this concept had been presented to the team several times, he suspected that only Andy realised what a paradigm shift was going to be involved.

Chapter 6 - Su

Su Fong started her morning in the common gym area, as usual wearing only a small black sports bra, miniscule tight shorts and trainers. This provided minimum cover of the ornate tattoos covering her body and showed off her toned physique. Her Chinese ancestry was unmistakable, despite two generations of the family living in South England after leaving Hong Kong. Her almond-shaped eyes and small nose and mouth, gave her an almost elfin appearance – which contrasted with her musculature and short-cut, black hair.

She set the treadmill to a fast walking-pace on a 5% gradient and the computer interface automatically switched to default oral command mode. "Munich Re ransomware debug, display status." A virtual screen appeared in front of her and she first checked the estimated time to the hackers' threatened triggering of the virus. "Fuck, only 5 days," she muttered. "Need to have another chat with Georgie and see if quantum could speed up any part of identifying and defusing the Trojan. Also need to stop talking to myself!" She grimaced and upped the speed to a medium running pace.

"Okay, assessment of infection mode." The display changed to show the back-tracing of the spread of infection through Munich Re's intranet. For operational purposes, complete isolation from the internet was clearly impossible and, even if this was ringed by state-of-the-art firewalls, 100% protection was never possible. In most cases, initial

29

infection was caused by a naïve employee opening a dodgy email or website link. However, there was no trace of this here – as had also been the case for the other re-insurance firms targeted. *Very strange.*

Su glared at the argumentation model summarising the tracing work. *There's something here, something from past North Korean hacks.* "Historical records of anything with actual or possible links to North Korea, ransomware attacks, display by infection method." As expected, mainly email and websites, with a few inside jobs and contaminated data transfer media: discs and sticks of various sorts. *Not what I'm looking for.*

"Expand records to include all cyber-attacks." This greatly increased the number of cases and slightly increased the percentage of insider and infected media, although a few cases classified as *other* emerged. She ignored an included comment pointing out that many attacks, such as denial-of-services, corruption of open websites and focused distribution of fake news, did not require any infection of the operating systems targeted.

"Expand class other, break down by type of crime." Su upped the treadmill speed a bit more as she pondered the complex map of information presented. *There's definitely something there, but I just can't see what it is.* "Slow scroll, with summary of the cases covered for each category." She increased the speed yet again, now running hard.

After fifteen minutes and one further increase of running speed, Su was panting and struggling to maintain the pace, almost unaware of the information passing in front of her eyes. "Thank fuck," she gasped and hit the auto-cooldown button on the training machine. "Freeze there! Focus on raids on accounts in banks, ordered by size of bank."

While the treadmill slowed to a fast walking pace for a 5-minute cooldown, Su scanned the list. Starting in the early 2010s, there was a series of raids on national banks, making use of weaknesses in the inter-bank transfer protocols. But for a bit of bad luck on the hackers' side, an audacious raid on the Bank of Bangladesh would have resulted in theft of almost a billion dollars, transferred from the US Federal Reserve Bank. The international banking community had learned from this and introduced both improved transfer processes and checks to quickly capture any suspicious activity, so such raids no longer occurred.

There's definitely something here: the Lazarus group almost pulled off a heist that dwarfed all the biggest conventional bank robberies, but then backed away after the defences were strengthened. It doesn't look right. Su extended the cooldown for a further 5 minutes at a slower pace. "Present a summary of the Bangladesh Bank raid."

The attack was cleverly planned, with a very slow build up after the bank firewall was first penetrated. The challenge was to ensure that a vast credit transfer wouldn't be spotted quickly enough and then to effectively launder the money before it could be traced back to the raiders.

So, what if the hackers learned from this and turned things around – using the money transfer protocols as a vector for virus infection and

31

targeting users of this system other than the banks themselves? Su frowned as the implications of this scenario became clearer. *With a focus on long-term gains, a virus could be allowed to spread for years, burying itself in key internal operating systems in all of the organisations infected. Then all that's needed is a trigger, which would be impossible to determine as a threat. Something like an enquiry email from a specific address or even a telephone call or text message from a defined number. With a ransom paid in cryptocurrency, the entire money laundering problem becomes much easier to handle.*

Su was still pondering this possibility when the machine slowed to a stop, allowing her to step down and head off to the shower. "Maybe it's just my active imagination," she muttered, while putting her trainers on a rack and dropping her clothes into the laundry basket in the changing room, "but if this is any way right, we could be in very deep shit."

*** *

In her office, Su placed her mug of coffee and a plate heaped with breakfast goodies on a side ledge specially designed for this purpose, then settled into the huge, wrap-around, leather chair and moved it forward until she was surrounded by the displays of her work station. She was wearing only a semi-transparent leotard and had been conscious of Lou's eyes following her after they exchanged good mornings. *Lou's a complete nympho, but she's also a big fan of tattoos and piercings. Especially intimate ones.* As the system booted up following biometric identification, Su couldn't help smiling as remembered highlights of a past encounter with

Lou, when the chubby woman had spent hours exploring the outlines of every tattoo with her tongue. *That's the wonderful thing about women, they take their time and focus on mutual pleasure, rather than just trying to reach orgasm as quickly as possible.*

Su engaged voice controls that allowed her to complement virtual typing and hand movements in her complex user interface. "Resume session," she commanded in a voice that was so quiet that it was almost sub-vocalisation, but was more than sufficient for the combined image analysis from the minute cameras and the array of pinhead microphones facing her. "Overview Munich-Re operating system, display left. Internet connection protocols for fund transfers centre, with associated links to OS highlighted. Firewalls for all external links to intranet, right." Her hands blurred as she expanded OS components and traced the links involved, descending to the coding level and, occasionally, the machine code below that.

The intranet OS is based on old EnGarde Secure Linux, so that's a good starting point. "Start from the virginal OS and note all changes, list by date," she saw that there were hundreds of thousands and the counter was still blurring. "Exclude updates from the software supplier and show only those from last 10 years." Still tens of thousands and counting. "And also exclude anything without any kind of links to external access," using her hands, she refined the interpretation of this rather vague command. As a result, she had reduced the list to just over 500 entries. *Now the donkey work,* she sighed and expanded the first edit on her list.

Chapter 7 - Lou

Lou towelled herself down after her usual morning swim, glanced in the full-length mirror and grimaced. Her face did not show her age, she acknowledged, thick hair still a natural brown without a trace of grey, creamy complexion and the only wrinkles around her hazel eyes being the laughter lines that resulted from her cheery nature. Her breasts were large and firm, topped with prominent pink nipples, and were always well appreciated by her lovers – men and women. *But my belly*, she pinched a roll of fat, *just has to get tightened up. Okay, thighs and bum are also on the heavy side*, she turned sidewise to the mirror, *but that's not a bad combination with my rather delectable tits.*

It's just not fair! Su eats like a pig and she's thin as a rake. Georgie the fucking same. Jay does fuck all exercise – apart from buggering young lads – and he looks seriously ripped. It's just me... well Andy and me... who can't keep trim despite diets and exercise. And, at least in my case, a very energetic love-life. She grinned and squeezed her nipples, feeling them harden. "Ah well," she sighed aloud, "no sex on the menu until at least lunchtime, so I guess I need to put that completely out of my mind".

With some reluctance, she released her nipples and rummaged in her locker, located in the large lounge area set between the 25-metre pool, the sauna and the gym. She finally selected a minuscule black tanga and stepped into it, pulling it up and settling the string into the crack of her bum before adding a translucent blouse which was just long enough to cover her groin. *Fine, that's me dressed for work. Let's just pop up to the office for a coffee and croissant and find out what's going on.*

The lift to the office floor opened into a large kitchen / dining area in which Brigit, one of the service staff, was setting out a small breakfast buffet. This led into a spacious central common work area, surrounded by individual offices and meeting rooms. The offices appeared to be empty, so Lou settled down at the large dining table with a tall glass of grapefruit juice while she chatted to Brigit and considered the attractions of the sensible breakfast of fruit and cottage cheese as opposed to one of the large schoggi-gipfelis – the Swiss version of pain-au-chocolat.

Although Lou had her own office, she usually worked in the open area as it maximised her interaction with the others. When she approached the work station that she usually used, its biometric sensors identified her and woke up the huge curved screen that provided a 180° workspace, which she preferred to holographic displays. This displayed her *hunk of the day* wallpaper, today a black, completely hairless bodybuilder with a truly huge erection. *So much for keeping my mind off sex,* Sue could feel her nipples hardening. *I wonder if Brigit might be in the mood?* She laid the large mug of coffee into the holder in the arm of her seat and licked the last crumbs of gipfeli from her fingers.

36

It's exercise, after all, and I've got a few more extra calories to burn.

"Down girl!" she muttered under her breath, settling into the large leather chair and swinging the inbuilt keyboards into place. The fingers of her left hand called up the finance management cockpit while those on her left pulled up summaries of searches that had been running overnight. She was aware of Su entering her office, but already her attention was being caught up in the flow of financial data that she was accessing. *Not quite as good as sex, but something that occasionally comes close.* Her expert system had already cracked one of the cash flows from their Russian target, tracing it to the nightclubs-cum-brothels that they ran in the Canaries. This was an inherent weakness of cryptocurrencies: in most countries you still couldn't use them directly for most normal purchases. When you were stocking up a bar or paying staff salaries, a conversion to hard cash – Euros, dollars or whatever – was often needed. Grab that cash flow and trace it back, then you find the crypto-wallet. She smiled. *After that, it's a head-to-head challenge: us against blockchain cryptography. Not easy, but something that we can eventually crack given the computing power at our disposal and, what is often forgotten, the smarts to make most use of it.* Here Georgie was NetSec's ace in the hole.

After 3 hours, Lou had determined that the Russians had at least three other wallets, probably holding different crypto-currencies. It would be necessary to raid all of these, preferably simultaneously, if the gang were to be effectively wiped out. *So, a bit of work still to do here. But, definitely time for lunch.*

Georgie was in the kitchen, picking at a plate of salad and sipping a glass of white wine. Dressed entirely in black: t-shirt, jeans and trainers. *Ah, George today.* Lou gave him a quick hug and kiss on the top of his head as she passed on the way to the fridge. "All well with you today, love? How's the wine?"

"I'm great and the wine's fine – a nice, crisp Chablis." Sue could feel his eyes follow her as she poured herself a large glass and set about making a cheese and salami sandwich. "I've been working on hardware upgrades this morning and think we're getting close to the point where conventional computer cryptography can be consigned to the history books."

"Let's hope that the bad guys don't realise that, as I should soon have a bunch of wallets for you to crack." While turning to the side, Lou surreptitiously opened two buttons and then turned back and bent forwards to offer a clear view of the Grand Canyon. She smiled as her colleague's attention was immediately drawn to her breasts, which were close to escaping from the thin fabric. *Works every time – or almost. For Jay, I'd need to be showing off my bum.*

"Um, well, I can set things up to get going if you send me through the target specs."

"I've got the first one nailed down, but we'll have to wait until we have the full set before we start anything. We'll also need to check in with the others to ensure that draining the accounts doesn't compromise anything that they're up to."

"Andy's down in the Tessin, so he's probably still in bed with his hooker pals…"

"And Jay will probably be shagging whoever he picked up last night…"

"So, I guess we're not in a rush," George leered at her in a theatrical manner.

"Not at all, my love. We can just finish lunch and then have a relaxing shag." Lou peeled off her blouse to fully display the goods on offer.

Lou never ceased to be fascinated by the way Georgie's nature changed along with her orientation. George was the archetypal brash youth, ready for any experience, especially if it pushed boundaries: drink, drugs, dangerous sports and, of course, sex. No way that he would pass on a quick shag, especially of an older woman. Of course, as their genius was more than a little autistic, there had to be a ritual to this. This was especially the case when fitting the complex strap-on that Heidi had produced to allow him to perform his chosen hetero male role.

She grinned while she remembered her last session with bi-Georgina – a truly different experience. The girl was shy, hesitant about sex with either men or women, and seemed especially reserved with Lou, maybe due to the contrast between such Rubenesque voluptuousness and her own androgynous body. Nevertheless, as a natural sub, she responded rapidly to rough foreplay and became quite a fox when her blood was up.

When not George or Georgina, Georgie was much more complex and might be completely asexual or focused on some kind of strange kink involving one or more partners of different persuasions. G, as often refereed to then, often gravitated towards Su, this leading to some kind of BDSM session with a role as dom, sub or simply as a voyeur. Not usually Lou's kettle of fish, but she could usually be talked into it if no other options were available.

After a very pleasant session in his bedroom, Lou left Georgie in a post-coital doze and returned to the office. She realised that Su was still working and, based on past experience, probably too caught up in her work to even notice that she'd missed lunch. *Time to be a Good Samaritan and make her take a break.*

Su jumped when she was lightly touched on the shoulder, twisting to bury her face in a large soft breast.

"Sorry, did I startle you?" Lou backed off quickly. "I didn't want to interfere with your work, but you've been at it now for 5 hours solid. Time for a break, love, and maybe something to eat. If you want, I'll make you up a sandwich or something."

"Shit, 5 hours, really? Fuck, I suppose it is." Su pushed her chair back stood and stretched with a groan. "Bugger it, yes, a bite would be good. And a brew, I'm dying of thirst. I also need to chat about this to somebody, have you got time?"

"Always time for you, lover," Lou kissed her lightly on the forehead, rubbing her massive tits

40

against Su's comparatively flat chest. "I already had lunch an hour ago, but I'll happily join you for a drink. Just a little one: a dry white wine. Almost no calories there..." This couldn't help sounding like wishful thinking.

Lou sat silently, sipping her wine, while Su summarised her findings, between bites of a cheese and ham toasted sandwich and swigs from a can of craft lager. "The good news is that I've identified the infection vector: a backdoor created four years ago by a hack masquerading as a security update for the interbank fund transfer protocol. It's actually very cunning, as it was introduced just before a real security upgrade that closed the vulnerability utilised. If anyone was to check, like I did, the original attack is flagged as blocked by the new upgrade. There would also be little cause for suspicion, as the access point was then unused for a year, certainly as far as insertion of malware is concerned. Very careful passive monitoring of the victim would have been possible, however, without leaving any traces that I've been able to detect."

"Playing a very long game, then," Lou commented with a wry smile.

"Definitely, which is the bad news. Not all internal operating systems will be vulnerable, but this targets very old source code that'll be found in a lot of them. I'd guess thousands of companies will be compromised, maybe tens of thousands."

"Shit, that's going to cause a panic if it gets out. In any case, we've got to let the national cyberwar team in on this. With finance being such a big sector, Switzerland could be particularly vulnerable if this is just a prelude to a more concerted wave of attacks." The women looked at each other as they pondered the implications, Lou topping up her wine glass and passing another beer to Su.

"If it was intended as a cyberwar weapon, why risk exposing the threat with these ransomware raids?" Su started slowly, clearly thinking out loud. "And why involve the Russian mafia? I think the tool is based on something from a cyber-attack arsenal, but it's fallen into the hands of a gang who're interested only in making as much as possible from it."

"That kind of makes sense," Lou agreed, "but why not just go for diversion of funds to access cash directly? They seem to be especially familiar with the transfer system."

"Ah, that's the bit I do understand. Since early raids using this approach, suspicious account transfers are much easier to spot using machine learning tools, while laundering the money stolen is a vulnerability that can allow the hackers to be traced and, possibly, funds recovered. A ransom paid in cryptocurrency is much easier to move and hide."

"Clever, indeed. So, how can we fight this?"

"That's what I'm now trying to get my head round. I have to put myself in Park's place, think how I would run the operation. The real problem is that the virus is now sitting passively in a huge number of operating systems and can be triggered at any time by an activating command that would be almost impossible to block. Even worse, it would be possible to build in trip-wires, so that any attempt to eliminate the virus actually triggers it." Su frowned and looked into the eyes of her colleague. "What do you think?"

"Off the top of my head, I'd say that it looks like we're fucked. However, let's get all our evidence sorted out and we can bring the rest of the team in on it – and maybe also the national defence lads if required."

"I guess so. There's a lot of stuff to be organised and I need to make sure that I'm not exaggerating the problem. Anyway, it might get a bit clearer if Andy manages to snag the Korean. Let's wait until tomorrow and then we'll have a team meet. Maybe somebody will pick up something I've missed." *But, somehow, I very much doubt it.*

Chapter 8 - Jay

Jay slowly came awake, opening his eyes and peering around in the faint light penetrating the drawn curtains, gradually making out a very small penis about a centimetre from his nose. *Fuck, I must have pulled Michael Angelo's David last night.* He struggled to contain a laugh, which came out as a kind of snort, while he strained to remember what had actually occurred. *Lots of alcohol and drugs would be a pretty safe guess.* He looked closer. *Not a trace of pubes, entire skin smooth as a baby's bum. Shit, don't let this be a schoolboy!*

He drew his head back a bit and slowly lifted the sheet that was covering his bed-mate's torso. *Well developed, anyway, nice flat stomach that goes well with those powerful looking thighs.* As the sheet rode up a bit higher, a pair of medium-sized, but very well-shaped breasts were revealed. "A transvestite," he whispered in relief, this beginning to trigger recollections of the previous night. *Olga, Helga, or something like that, maybe? That's the problem with gathering intelligence in a fucking Bratva club, the bastards all drink like fucking fish. It's amazing that I can remember anything at all: must have been a lot of brain cells lost last night.*

Didn't remember it being so small, though. Jay examined the mini-penis closely before peeling back the foreskin and starting to slowly suck on it. After a couple of minutes, he felt a mouth close on his own organ and Jay could feel his rapid response while the object of his attentions slowly engorged.

Okay, not the big, black, mega-stud that it could have been, but there are worse ways to wake up. He grinned and concentrated on his fellatio, sure that this would burn a lot of the remnant alcohol out of his system, and hopefully the developing hangover along with it. With a bit of luck, by the time they had finished, he'd be able to remember exactly where he was and what the hell he was doing there.

***

Maspalomas, that's the place. Post-coital relaxation seemed to have rebooted Jay's brain. He remembered his father talking about this area of the Canaries when it had been newly developed: a totally synthetic holiday destination in the sun for northern Europeans, especially Germans, Scandinavians, Dutch and Brits. In the early days, a welcome gay-friendly resort that, as general acceptance grew with time, expanded to cover most of the alt-sex spectrum. Inevitably, however, this also brought in those who exploited the darker end of this spectrum. In particular, the Russian gangs.

Olga was a Belarusian prostitute at the top-end of the market, servicing well-heeled clients who fancied a bit of strange during their holidays. As such, she was much better off than the hordes of girls and boys lower in the food chain, who were effectively slaves for rent, at prices for an evening less than that of a bottle of local wine. Although strictly illegal, the authorities turned a blind eye to a market that encouraged specialist tourism in a time where global climate collapse was destroying this entire industry, along with the economies of many countries that depended on it.

After a long, shared shower and the inevitable sex resulting from it, Jay watched Olga dress, transforming herself from obviously trans to a confusingly prim-looking, but well-developed schoolgirl, without even the artifice of makeup. Clearly this was the basis of her popularity, hitting all the bi buttons in one trim body. *Not at all my normal taste in partners, but a shame that this is only a one-night stand nevertheless. From our pillow talk, which I can now remember to some extent and which was all recorded anyway, it's clear that Olga's club isn't the one I'm looking for, the one compromising clients as a way to obtain access to company intranets. Well, tonight it'll be a different club and a different prostitute – life's tough on the front lines of the cyber-security business!*

***

Despite rising sea levels, the Maspalomas dunes still provided a long beach with surfers at one end and safe swimming in a sheltered bay at the other, near Playa des Ingles. In the middle was an area long regarded as a haven for nudists and, especially in some parts, the queer component of this community. Jay had already walked the entire length of the beach once, noting that, in the areas most popular with gays and lesbians, it was predominantly old fat guys with tiny dicks that were parading about near the path along the shore, while the more interesting young guys were further back, closer to the dunes proper. Apart from the usual fag-hags, there were quite a few trans and lesbian couples, also closer to the path. They tended to be much fitter and well-toned, so this had the feel of being more like a market place than a beach, which would fit in well with the bars and clubs that provided nightlife for this part of Grand Canaria. Jay selected a spot a little bit further from the path, between a cheery, if rather chubby, lesbian couple and a threesome of two dark-skinned bodybuilders and a pallid, thin, but well-hung transvestite. He took a towel from his backpack and stripped off, aware of the appraising stares from his neighbours. *May as well get into the mood of things while killing time before the clubs open.*

Part 2: Crashing crypto

Chapter 1 - Capture of the Golden Goose

After dinner, Andy walked the ladies to the Casino and then returned to the flat to monitor their progress via hacked security cams. Park was playing poker and doing very well. Later, one of her bodyguards cashed in her chips, while Park chatted to the working girls at the bar, at least three of whom he knew to have been her partners in the past. Just as Andy was beginning to think they had failed yet again, Park caught Heidi's eye and there was a clear indication of interest on both sides. Beat waved their target over and called a waiter for a third glass, so that Park could share their Champagne. From the gratuitous touching, which came just short of outright groping, it was clear that Park was keen to make up a threesome.

Video of the action in Park's love nest was comprehensive, due to cameras that Andy had already secreted there as part of his initial stake-out of the Russian operation. Heidi and Beat knew about this, but being aware that they were being videoed did not seem to inhibit them in the slightest. Immediately after entering the apartment, they started off with deep kissing, gradually undressing Park en route to the bedroom, subjecting more of her body to kisses, touches and playful bites. The hookers, in turn, stripped down to their signature tight corsets and thigh-length, long-heeled boots and removed dildos and red silk bondage cords from over-sized handbags.

When the ladies eventually returned to the apartment, Andy had a bottle of Dom Pérignon opened for them. The plan had gone well, with the pill slipped into Park's drink in the Casino. "So why did you go back to the flat with her afterwards?" he wondered aloud.

"She was a very nice woman and clearly in need of a bit of relief," Beat replied, "so it seemed like the kind thing to do."

"She also picked up our drinks tab," Heidi added, "and was happy to pay 500 for a couple of hours."

"Isn't that a bit cheap for your specialist services?"

"Well, we hadn't discussed that and we weren't quite sure if that would be her thing," Heidi smiled. "Although, as I'm sure you noticed, after she got over her initial surprise, she got well into the mood."

Andy smiled back and looked at his watch. "Yes, well I'll be moving ahead with my plan in about an hour and, all being well, will then head directly back to Wettingen. This place is booked until the end of the week, so stay as long as you like."

Heidi's grin widened. "We don't want to know what you're up to, but we'll certainly be having fun. We've promised shibari lessons to a couple of the Casino girls and one very handsome young gigolo, so that'll keep us busy. I don't suppose you've got time to sample some of our tricks?"

"That's a very tempting offer, but I'll need to take a rain check on that. Possibly we could fit it in when you get back to Baden. Oh, while I remember, was Park pierced anywhere interesting? Image quality wasn't great, but I think I could see nipple rings."

"Yes, indeed, those were the obvious piercings apart from ears and belly-button," Beat giggled, "but there was also one that you might not have noticed…"

"Unless she was sitting on your face!" her partner added.

"Indeed, a Princess Albertina. You don't see those often and that woman has really large labia, so hard to spot…"

"Even when she's sitting on your face, unless her legs were wide open," the women burst into a fit of giggles.

"A Princess Albertina…" Andy was sure that he'd heard the term but couldn't quite remember what it was.

"The female version of the Prince Albert," Beat explained. "You know, through the urethra like the ring Jay is so happy to wave in your face!"

"Ah, sounds painful."

"Not at all, and can really increase urethral stimulation, if that's your thing," Heidi grinned. "I quite fancied one, but don't have the anatomy for it. Su has one, though."

"There's so much metal through Su's parts, that doesn't narrow it down much. But I think I now know what you mean. Anyway, I've got stuff to prep, so help yourselves to the rest of the sparkly."

50

Andy had evidently diverted the ladies' minds onto the topic of piercing, which seemed to allow for some fairly exotic options in their BDSM scenarios. Interesting though these were, he tore himself away from the couple and retreated to his work room before he ended up getting talked into something that would divert him from his carefully laid plans.

***

It was almost 2 am when his tap into the emergency services hotline picked up and intercepted a cell call from the penthouse. It was clearly one of the Russian guards, struggling to ask in broken English for immediate medical assistance. Andy's expert system mimicked that of the helpline, working its way through automated questions that identified the problem as a woman with acute stomach pains. Using a voice synthesiser just in case the call was being recorded, Andy then broke in to say that a doctor was in the immediate vicinity and could come by within a few minutes. He would provide any support required until an ambulance arrived.

Andy was already wearing a paramedic uniform and double checked the contents of his case before donning surgical gloves, injecting himself with a counter-agent to the anaesthetic he planned to use, and then taking the lift first down to the ground floor and then up the penthouse. One of the guards was waiting for him in the hallway and took Andy through the open door, which he noted was equipped with a terahertz scanner manned by a second guard. This would, however, show only a

51

normal range of medical equipment in his bag. *Just as well I decided against carrying a gun.*

As soon as the door was closed behind him, Andy pressed the trigger that released odourless gas from the reservoir built into the handle of the case, relieved to note that this was completely soundless. He continued a series of questions about the emergency without eliciting responses while following his guide through a sitting room and along a corridor with a number of rooms leading off it. He was shown into a bedroom where a fully-clothed woman was curled in a foetal position, groaning while she clasped her stomach. He started to approach her just as the two accompanying Russian heavies began to stagger. One of them made an effort to draw a pistol from his shoulder holster, but then both dropped heavily to the floor. Andy noticed that Park had also stopped writhing, so he moved to her side and quickly injected an antidote to the poison that was responsible for her intense stomach cramps.

Andy then cautiously peered back into the main sitting room, where he could see another guard slumped on a settee in front of a widescreen television showing a football game. However, from here he could also see the back on another man who was standing on the terrace. This was clearly outside the Faraday cage as he was talking on a mobile phone. *Fuck! Just what I don't need.*

Returning to Park's bedroom, he injected both men with an almost undetectable potion that caused cardiac arrest and then removed their heavy pistols, pleased to see that both of these were equipped with silencers. Andy walked back into the lounge just as the door to the terrace was opening. The man entering had a startled look on his face as he tried to pull his gun, forgetting that he had his mobile in his hand. It wouldn't have helped anyway. Andy's machine pistol was set to automatic and pumped a full load of 18 bullets into his chest. While his target crashed backwards through the door, Andy fired a burst from the second gun into the head of the thug lying unconscious on the sofa.

He was fairly sure that all his opponents were dead, but quickly checked the other rooms to ensure that nobody else was present. *Bastards deserve to die for attempting to murder me this morning, but this is actually a mercy. If any were still alive after the gang discovered that they had lost the Golden Goose, their death would certainly be slow and very painful.*

Andy returned to Park's room and saw that, although still unconscious, her body was less tense, indicating that the antidote had done its job. He returned the guns to the mobsters' shoulder holsters, just to add some further confusing evidence for whoever discovered the bodies first, whether the police or other members of the gang. He then stripped Park of all clothing, noting that she had lost bladder control at some point. *But could have been worse,* he grinned while peeling off her sodden knickers. "Well, that's taken care of any tracers that might be secreted in her clothing," he muttered, "so now the other obvious possibilities..." He removed earrings, the rings from nipples that stood proud from her small, sagging breasts, the ring from her

53

belly and then opened her legs wide to search for her other piercing.

After a bit of fumbling about, distracted by the smell of urine, Andy found the ball closure ring and eventually managed to force it open. *Very unlikely that this is a tracker, but better safe than sorry.* He threw the jewellery onto the heap of clothes and then struggled to wrap Park in his medic jacket. It wasn't very subtle, but enough for a quick trip down the elevator at this time of the morning.

After Andy gathered up a couple of top-end laptops and crammed them into his bag, he set an EMP burster to maximum output, on a timer to ensure that it went off only after he left. This would ensure that all electronics within the Faraday cage, including any hidden video capture, would be completely fried – but this without impacting the other residents of the block.

Andy hefted the strap of his bag over one shoulder, the supine Park over the other, and then staggered out of the penthouse into the elevator lobby, setting the door to lock behind him. *Shit, she's quite small, but bloody heavy! Either that or I really need to spend more time in the gym.*

***

With his prisoner strapped into the back seat of his electric Range Rover, the trip back to Wettingen via the Gotthard Tunnel went smoothly, the little traffic on the road mainly cruising at the speed limit under autonomous control. He arrived just before 6 am, driving into the spacious underground garage and plugging the car in to charge before he called Su. As long as she hadn't ended up in bed with someone after a wild BDSM session, this was about the time she usually got up.

Andy had clearly wakened her, but she was happy to come down and help out with his prisoner. More than that, she was evidently very keen to meet the enigmatic Park. Andy wasn't sure if he should wait for Su before going further but, in any case, applied a patch with a dermally-active counter to the knock-out gas. *It'll take ten minutes or so before she's fully compos mentis, but that'll get us moving along quicker and I can then get to bed. I'm bloody knackered.*

Su still hadn't appeared when, about five minutes later, Park's eyes began to flutter and she started to mumble something in what was probably Korean. After about another minute, her eyes opened in shock and she ran her hands down under the jacket draped over her, confirming that she was completely naked. Andy received a hate-filled glare and she started to shout at him in broken Russian, while struggling to wrap the jacket tighter around her body.

"Look, I'm sorry about that…" Andy started, just as the woman detected that her nipple-rings were gone and then frantically clawed her groin.

"You fucking, raping, pervert, fucking bastard," she spluttered while she tried to squeeze as far away from him as possible. "What the fuck are you doing and where the fuck am I?" Andy could determine a trace of what Su referred to as a Hong Kong English accent. "You have no fucking clue what trouble you're getting into. When those Moscow fuckers find you, you're fucking dog food."

"My goodness, you do swear a lot, my dear," Andy put on a posh English voice which, in some bizarre way, seemed to reduce the stress in such situations. "In any case, I'm afraid that your Ruskie colleagues are pushing up daisies at present…"

"Daisies! What the fuck's that to do with anything?"

"Oops, sorry, a bit colloquial there. They've gone to meet their maker, sitting together around that big samovar in the sky…" she was looking like him as if he was screaming mad. "Or, to cut to the chase, they're all fucking deceased. I killed them all. So, you might want to bear this in mind when thinking about screaming at me again."

Luckily, at that point the elevator pinged and Su strolled across the garage, smiling as she picked up the vibes of conflict. "Ah, Miss Park, it's a real pleasure to meet you. I hope my colleague here has been treating you well." Park seemed shocked into silence, as this greeting began to register. "Anyway, I'll take you upstairs, where you can get freshened up and we'll find you some clothes. Andy will just finish up here and join us for a debriefing over breakfast. How about that?"

Park turned, looked Andy in the eyes and held his stare while she lifted up the jacket and pissed on the back seat of his car. *I don't think I've ever seen a look that said "fuck you" more clearly. Thank God I've leather seats, but this is just after I've finally got rid of the smell after Georgie vomited in the back after a very heavy session of night club drugs. Still, I suppose it could have been worse…*

***

Su led Park to her bedroom and into the large en suite bathroom. "Hyo-Jin's your name, isn't it?" she asked while helping the woman remove the jacket that was her only covering. She openly inspected the exposed body while Park stood in front of her, unbothered by her nudity. *No oil painting, but certainly keeps herself fit and certainly not body-shy. More importantly, mega-smart – my kind of woman.*

She gently stroked Park's breasts, feeling nipples hardening under her fingers. "Yes, my name's Hyo-Jin," the Korean slowly responded, "how did you know?"

"Oh, I know a lot about you" Su grinned lasciviously.

"And that's why that mad fucker kidnapped me? You're in fucking deep shit, you know. They will come to get me and everyone that was involved in that attack will fucking die, very fucking painfully."

"Well, we'll see about that. I suspect that your Bratva gang won't last long enough to even think about revenge. But we can talk about that after I've got you cleaned up." Su started to strip off her own clothes, aware of Park's gasp as she saw the extent of her tattoos. "So how about if we share the shower, as I haven't washed yet."

Park let herself be led into the shower, gasping as the first cool jet hit her before the water quickly warmed. She looked Su straight in the eyes: the two women were almost exactly the same height and two pairs of hardened nipples rubbed against each other. "So, first you kidnap me and now you want to fuck?"

"I've actually wanted to have sex with you for quite some time," Su whispered in her ear before couching down to lick the engorged labia that still retained a trace of the smell and taste of urine. "Consider this as part of the softening-up process before your interrogation."

***

The foreplay in the shower ended up with an extended Sapphic session on Sue's huge bed. Although tempted by the idea of a post-coital doze, her body's demand for caffeine drove Su to get up, dragging the small Korean off the damp, rumpled sheets and back into the shower. Despite temptation to go further, she restricted herself to a quick but intimate rinse of her new lover, although helping her fit a ring into her Princess Albertina piercing took her restraints to their limits. Hyo-Jin could easily fit into a pair of Su's tight shorts and training vest, while Su herself dragged on matching clothes. In the empty kitchen, Su filled a huge mug with freshly-brewed coffee and then hunted around until she found green tea, which she then prepared for someone she could not quite categorise as either a captive or a potential girlfriend.

***

After breakfast, assembled from the buffet laid out in the kitchen area, Su led Hyo-Jin to the main meeting room where Andy, Lou and Georgie were already gathered. The Korean hacker glared at Andy, now dressed in conventional shorts and a Japanese microbrew t-shirt. She was clearly bemused when she was introduced to the others. Lou was, typically, wearing a translucent smock that clearly showed that she was wearing little, if anything, beneath it. Georgie was in girlie mode – dressed in a pink, Hello Kitty mini skirt with matching t-shirt and slippers – looking anything but a top-end quantum computer whiz.

"Is this a fucking joke?" Hyo-jin glared at the team who had kidnapped her.

Su put an arm round her shoulder, attempting to reassure the bemused super-hacker. "You should be aware that looks can be deceptive…"

"Yes, you don't judge books by their covers," Andy added.

Hyo-jin closed her eyes. "Fucking books now. That rapist fucker is mad as a really mad fucker!"

Chapter 2 - Cyber-harakiri

Andy was amused when Su and Park entered the meeting room, hand in hand and clad in matching tight shorts and t-shirts. His colleague had clearly managed to calm down the Korean hacker, and he had a very good idea of how she had done it. Nevertheless, when he caught Park's eye she gave him an unmistakable death-stare. *Not a happy bunny, that one.*

Andy had already been updated by Lou and Georgie on developments while he had been busy kidnapping the Russian gang's prime asset. He was immediately aware of how serious the threat posed was and, like his colleagues, at a loss to see how it could be addressed. In any case, it was critical to get as much background as possible from the Korean – so he decided to stay in the background and leave interrogation to the women. *It's clear that Park hates my guts and wouldn't piss on me if I was on fire. Even though she'd no problem pissing on my bloody car seat.* He couldn't help grinning at the thought.

As previously agreed, Lou took the lead. After introducing herself and Georgie, she provided a concise overview of what the team were all about. Park was clearly sceptical. "You are just a fucking private company and not Government? That cunt," she glared at Andy, "fucking kills Russian Mafia hit men and rapes me with his hands. This is your business model? I think you all must be lying bastards."

"Calm down, Hyo-Jin," Su squeezed her thin shoulders. "Do you think I'm a lying bastard?"

"You are a good shag, okay, but maybe also a lying cunt. How do I know the truth?"

"Well, dear, why don't I tell you what I know about you and what you've been doing with those Ruskie bad-boys? Then you can make up your mind." Lou smiled in a reassuring manner. She then put their cards on the table, listing up all the accumulated evidence on the cyber-ransom attacks and the bigger picture of the vulnerabilities of the financial institutions that they had discovered.

"So now we come to the bottom line," she concluded, "you either help us or we will need to turn you over the Nachrichtendienst, the NDB. This is the Swiss version of something like the US NSA. They will subject you to much more extreme interrogation than we would consider and, if that didn't work, would pass you on to either Interpol or the CIA. If the latter, then a long period of torture is likely and, if they managed to break you, they'd probably then try to swap you with some asset of their own held in North Korea." For the first time, Park's resolute image seemed to crack for an instant and a look of fear crossed her face before she recovered her normal belligerent mien.

"But we don't need to go in that direction," Su squeezed her arm. "The threat here is global and I'm sure that, if you help us a bit, we can get some kind of deal for you."

"What fucking deal? There's fuck-all you can do. I am here because Switzerland will probably be less fucked than most shit-holes on this planet. You

61

think you know what is happening, but my work for those gangster bastards was only to set up my Swiss refuge, so I am not so fucked by the apocalypse."

"What apocalypse is this?" Very unusually it was Georgie who asked and Andy noticed a strange look on her face, almost fear. When the Korean didn't respond, she continued. "The attack is going to take place soon and it seems like you're jumping the gun, escaping before its worst impacts kick in."

"Fucking right! It's the Kim dynasty suicide weapon. Fucking cyber-harakiri!"

The meaning of this was slowly dawning on Andy when Su spoke. "You were pushed from smaller scale attacks to going for a big payoff because time was getting short. North Korea will launch a cyber-attack that'll effectively destroy international finance. This will be devastating as global trading will collapse …"

"But how's this possible?" Andy interrupted. "The cyber-ransom I can understand, but…" He ground to a halt. "Wait, the Trojan has been in place for years, probably infiltrated through most key finance management tools and databases. If it's activated to cause all the systems to self-destruct, the entire house of cards collapses."

"Cyber-harakiri," Park nodded her head. "DPRK is fucked, but it was a fucked-up shithole already. But all now are equally fucked, even the capitalist fucking paradises."

"Let me try to get my head around this," Georgie spoke in such a low voice that Andy had to strain to hear her. "The North Koreans are going to trigger a virus that'll wipe out international commercial infrastructure, inevitably causing global chaos. Because of the current strains on the system due to over-population, global warming and pollution, this could reach a tipping point leading to famine, civil unrest, wars. Together these would cause millions of deaths…"

Park rolled her eyes while she shook her head. "Not fucking millions, bastard modellers say hundreds of millions, maybe a fucking billion or two."

"You can't be serious!" Su gasped, looking in horror at the woman that she had just bedded. "Nobody in their right mind would do that! It's genocide on an unbelievable scale!"

"Fatherland's ruling cunts also mad as mad fuckers," she shook her head, looking a little sad. "Anyway, it is all done already, set up before I even joined Lazarus. I can access the backdoor, for the ransomware stuff. But the virus is on a timer, so fuck-all you can do about it."

"A timer?" Andy interrupted. "So, do you know how long we've got before it's triggered?"

"Ten days. So, fuck-all to do but build bunkers fucking fast."

The NetSec team were shocked to silence. This was an actual EOTWAWKI scenario: the end of the world as we know it.

***

Despite the time difference, it was clear that Jay needed to be brought into the discussion. A video link was set up within ten minutes and he eventually appeared, looking somewhat bedraggled, wiping sleep from his eyes. He was linked though his palmtop, which clearly showed his bedroom in the background, with his head-and-shoulders format not quite blocking out the naked boy who was sprawled face-down on his bed.

Jay's sleepiness vanished while Lou summarised what had been learned from Park. As she put it, "we need to see if there is anything at all that we can do to counter this threat but, if not, construct a parachute to protect us from the worst-case impacts."

"Well, being in Switzerland will certainly help. I guess I'd better get my well-used arse in gear and book a flight ASAP. The Bratva gangs must be very low priority now."

"Definitely," Su contributed. "It looks like Hyo-Jin… Park, the Korean hacker," she expanded in response to Jay's frown. "Anyway, she was using the Russians, not vice versa, so we can forget about them. So, any ideas about what we should do now?"

"Pass it all on to the NDB," he suggested.

"I'm already drafting a brief summary of the situation that'll go to them," Lou responded. "It suggests that we keep Park with us while we focus on trying to find a phage that'll counter the Trojan."

"Fuck-all chance," Park muttered in the background.

"The one chance we might have involves technology that didn't exist when the virus was developed," Georgie contributed, softly. "We've invested a lot of our ill-gotten gains in a quantum computer that's one of the most powerful in the world and, even more importantly, tailored for crypto-cracking. If Hyo-Jin will work with Su, Lou and me, it might be possible."

Park did not look convinced, but said nothing.

Jay scratched his head, clearly deep in thought. "Mmm, that leaves myself and Andy," he spoke his thoughts aloud, "so I guess we can focus on developing a strategy for the case that things go totally tits-up."

"Fuck that," Park interrupted. "I will help you useless cunts, but on one fucking condition. You find the beloved bastard leaders and fuck them in the arse. My country will be complete shit, but top bastards always have escape plan. Find them and fuck them up: then I will help."

"Don't you think we can worry about that later?" Su was clearly trying to calm things down.

"No! Fuck-all we can do later. Do it now and then I help you, to give you a little fucking chance."

"I don't think we have an option, lads," Lou looked unusually grim. "You guys can cover both these jobs, but focus on finding *bastard leaders* and giving them a good fucking."

"It's what I do best," Jay grinned, causing the first smiles seen this morning. "Maybe revenge isn't what we really should focus on at present, but the crimes here are so heinous that we can't risk these bastards getting off with it."

Andy saw heads nodding around the room. *Okay, now we know what we need to do. The really tricky bit is how?*

***

Park agreed to start working immediately with the ladies on potential anti-viral approaches, despite

65

being clearly unconvinced that quantum computing could contribute to a solution. Additionally, she provided a link to a dark-web server that held background on the North Korean group that she claimed were responsible for initiating the attack. While the others went off for a tour of Georgie's domain, Andy remained in the meeting room, downloading Park's file and sending a copy to Jay. "What do you think, start with really screwing these fuckers or on preparations for surviving the apocalypse if Georgie can't pull off a quantum miracle?"

Jay was clearly distracted by something happening in the background. There was movement on the bed and it was evident that at least two young men were slowly writhing about on it. "Oops, sorry, I've got some other screwing to sort out here before I get to work on anything. Remember it's two hours earlier here," he raised his eyebrows and gave a cartoonish, lascivious grin. "In any case, you'll need to run Park's info through the big server to mine for cross-references so that you can flesh it out. There's an app I use for that, called *context*. You'll find it in my shared toolbox. It includes the decryption and translation routines that'll be required for intelligence service material on North Korea. Even with the Exaflops that you have, it'll take a couple of hours and I'll be back in touch by then."

"Totally shagged-out, I assume," Andy grinned.

"One can but hope." Jay was already rising, inadvertently showing a substantial erection, before the video feed cut off.

Andy sighed and initiated the search as instructed. *While I'm waiting, I can start thinking about apocalypse scenarios and how to survive them – which could well be a much trickier job. Although, I really need to catch forty winks first.*

Chapter 3 - Quantum game-changing

Hyo-Jin was very impressed by Georgie's hardware. "All this shit and no fucking Government control. Fucking unbelievable!" She scowled at Georgie. Evidently the disconnect between Hello Kitty themed clothing and quantum super-computers was proving a bit much for her.

"We're contracted by the Government, and also private companies, to take down hacker groups, many of whom are stealing a lot of money", Lou explained. "Some of them end up in jail, but others can't easily be touched by the law. So, part of our job is to confiscate all their finances, completely gut them. It depends on our target, but raids on their funds are often enough to finish off those involved, because criminals regularly prey on weaker criminals. It may be harsh, but it can act as a deterrent."

"Those fucking Ruskie cunts in Locarno, your fucking hitman murdered the bastards."

"As Andy already pointed out, the heavies protecting you were guaranteed death as soon as you were taken. The only question was how drawn out and painful it would be."

"Fucking bastards deserved being fucking murdered anyway. Had only interest in fucking football and arse-fucking, bondage porn."

"Yes, well, this is the hardware," Georgie interjected to avoid any possible digression into bondage porn. "There are two parts, a conventional Mega-qubit supercomputer and my pet – a flash-hypercomputer."

"A flash hypercomputer, what's that?" Park's gratuitous swearing vanished and her English suddenly improved and became more colloquial, while Su and Lou exchanged looks of surprise.

"It's experimental at present, but could... actually will... completely revolutionise the computing business. In particular, all conventional cryptography is now dead in the water. Even the Kyber variants developed with quantum computing in mind."

Hyo-Jin frowned. "That's a big claim to make. How many qubits then?"

Georgie grinned as the question she was waiting for finally came up. "It's difficult to tell. You might remember Feynman said that *if you think you understand quantum mechanics, you don't understand quantum mechanics*: the same thing applies to quantum computing. If I had to put a number on it, maybe in the order of Peta." She laughed aloud at the Korean's look of shock.

"Ten to power of fifteen, that's not possible! Mega to Peta in one jump: that's what you're saying? All in this tiny box?"

"Exactly! The workings are completely optical and limited by the speed of light, so I need to keep it small. Of course, that's because qubit coherence can be maintained for only very short times. I'm now somewhere about a microsecond but, if I pull out all the stops, I think a millisecond would be doable."

"And you think that one millisecond will be enough to solve this problem?"

"With Peta-qubits available, I could solve just about any problem given an appropriate quantum algorithm. Fundamentally, I have a form of generative AI that would involve a neural network on a conventional computer. But quantum neural is a completely different kettle of fish as all possible network connections can be sampled simultaneously. Also, you have to remember that I can utilise quantum time-flip resonance to get a lot more out of the short coherence times. Best to consider it a black box that needs only the algorithms that relate network inputs to desired output."

"Fuck!" Park gazed at the machine with a look of awe. After a minute or so of silence, she spoke up again. "So, where do you get the algorithms from?"

"Ah, that's the hard bit. You, Su and Lou have now ten days to produce the right one for me."

***

Andy took a sleeping tablet that knocked him out for 2 hours but, thereafter, felt as if he had enjoyed a normal 8 hours. He got up, threw on a robe and headed for the basement. There, he switched on the swim flume, which he thought of as an aqueous treadmill, and set it for 20-minute kilometres. After getting his pace settled down, he let his mind wander. In terms of public opinion, bankers generally rate alongside lawyers, accountants and politicians as being considered self-serving, over-paid and untrustworthy. A banking crash might be seen as natural justice, denying them the outrageous bonuses that they regularly awarded themselves, whether they did a good job or not. But, of course, it wasn't as simple as that. There would be the direct impacts of disappearance of e-banking at a time when very few people used cash; loss of pensions and sources of loans; crippling of international commerce when almost every country depends on it. This then snowballs when famine hits, with civil unrest leading to regional conflicts and wars. Even before this latest global threat, climate change, pollution and environmental degradation were already leading towards a tipping point when civilisation would collapse. From such a perspective, this could well be the final straw.

I'm just rephrasing what Park already said. Describing the apocalyptic scenarios that the North Koreans have already modelled. This is just the global overview: what does it really mean for we lucky few who are wealthy and based in Switzerland? Well, transactions are about 90% cashless, but does having folding money in circulation help at all? Whether a bakery or a brothel, goods or services need to be exchanged for a token that allows other goods and services to be obtained. Barter just can't work in any but the most primitive societies. The problem is that we've created a hugely complex financial edifice that's become increasingly esoteric. It's bloated with instruments and tools, such as futures, derivatives and autonomous high-speed trading, which are becoming totally disconnected from the real world. Just a single rogue trader, whether human or electronic, can lose the equivalent of the GNP of several small countries in an instant. It's an accident waiting to happen and I'm sure that prudent nations like Switzerland will have counter-measures in place to handle a large banking crash. But probably not anything like this, where the entire financial infrastructure is wiped out. Anyway, note to self: get the NDB to check this out.

Andy glanced at his watch and saw that only thirteen minutes had passed.

Okay, got to get more concrete. What are our priorities if we want to get through any plausible crash with minimal damage? We can safeguard wealth by ensuring that it's in hard commodities. Luckily, we already have a lot invested in property. This is a pretty secure investment in a Swiss context, but the top-end accommodation that we've purchased would probably have less real value than farms or operations producing essential products, such as dairies, bakeries, butchers, etc. We also have gold, as protection against currency fluctuations. But this is virtual, as it's in a bank vault somewhere rather than stored in our basement. Even then, gold has no real intrinsic value: would a better investment be in small, high value equipment? In any case, we need to reconsider this. Something to check with Lou.

Our location is very convenient for us, but maybe not optimal if things start to fall apart. But with only 10 days, there's nothing we can do about this. The main thing, really, is to take all possible funds from bank accounts or any kind of financial investments and turn them into something real. Like wine, for example. Our huge wine cellar isn't even half full, so I can take the job of filling that to the gunwales.

With thoughts of fine vintages filling his head, Andy noticed in a mirror that he was smiling as he entered the changing room, *I suppose every apocalypse has a silver lining, but I really hope that we don't have to test if that's actually the case in real life.*

***

Jay had shooed-out his playmates-of-the-night and was now projecting the preliminary results of the search carried out by Andy. The hold on power by the Kim clan had been weakening for some time as the previous Supreme Leader, Jong-un, became increasingly eccentric with time. His successor was a cypher, apparently a cousin, Young-Ju, who stepped into the power hiatus following of Jong-un's surprise heart attack. Since then, several purges of top military were undermining his position and the country's already fragile economy neared total collapse as global warming impacts added to the impacts of sanctions on the rogue regime. It was an open secret that the Lazarus hacker group were state-sponsored and one of the country's few sources of foreign currency. However, its leadership and core teams were much harder to trace.

The great thing about the vast volumes of information available on the internet is that, although many find it overwhelming, if you have the right tools then you can extract much more than is immediately obvious. Jay grinned as he unleashed his tailored inference engine. *We've a load of speculation and rumour, which superficially seems useless. But focused assessment of likelihoods, based on advanced sematic analysis, reduces the challenge to one of determining the highest probability solution to the problem.*

As a tree of key argument linkages built up on his holographic display, Jay noted with surprise that a number of links to Switzerland emerged. It seems that generations of the Kim dynasty had been educated in secret in Swiss private schools. Bearing this knowledge in mind, he immediately wondered if, in some way, this was linked to Hyo-Jin's decision to make her bolthole there. Even though the traces were well hidden, three ultra-expensive properties seemed to be owned by Young-ju's even more secretive wife, Gaeun. One of these was in the centre of Geneva, one on Zurich's "Gold Coast" and the last a huge chalet in Zermatt. Further traces of emails and e-transfers during the purchasing process provided a lead to a younger sister, Dam-Bi, who had, in turn, a range of obscure links to the Lazarus group. Nevertheless, the Kim clan was so secretive that other family members could well be involved and even the names identified could be incorrect due to the inconsistent representation of Korean names in English.

The question now is whether this attack is run from the top or is something cooked up at a lower level, without the knowledge or consent of the leaders. I can use my NDB links to access records of all those entering Switzerland over the last month who are declared to be, or could be, Korean and then run a match against everyone identified to play

74

a significant role in Kim's dictatorship. And their families, of course.

At a loss for anything further to do, Jay logged off and rummaged around his room for something to wear for breakfast, wondering idly if the boys might still be lingering in the hotel restaurant.

***

After lunch, the team assembled to review progress and prepare for a formal video-meeting with the head of the NDB, Petra Zürcher, who was going to coordinate Swiss national response to this threatened attack and also act as liaison with the major financial organisations that were in the firing line.

As always, Lou kicked off as soon as Jay's secure video link was established. "We should keep this short, but need to check that we're not missing anything critical – or overstating risks – before we chat to Frau Zürcher."

"Impossible to overstate fucking risks..." Park muttered under her breath.

"In any case, Georgie's quantum computer offers a ray of hope, although we need to make it clear that this is a novel application of an emerging technology, so we can offer no guarantees that it'll work. Do you think that's a fair summary, lass?" she twisted around to face their incongruously-clad quantum guru.

Georgie frowned and tapped her lips before responding. "From speaking with Hyo-jin this morning, it seems that the key vulnerability of this Trojan is the trigger and its associated timer. We need a code package that'll reset this to remove the

75

immediate threat, moving the trigger date by fifty years, say."

"Why not just delete the trigger completely?" Andy enquired.

"Ah, that's the clever bit with this virus," Su responded while placing a hand on Parks shoulder, possibly to prevent her interrupting with her usual string of profanity. "The trigger acts as a dead-man's handle, blocking activation of the operating system kill routine."

"Well, then, why not simply disable the kill routine?"

"Fucking trip wires," Park glared at Andy.

"Yes," Su broke in, "I don't think there's anything that we couldn't break through given time, but the risks are high if we rush things. Only one minor slip and the entire target OS is gone, along with all associated databases and backups. This is further complicated by buried links that also communicate to any other infected systems, so that any interference with one then triggers all of the others."

"Auto-fucking-catalytic," Hyo-jin nodded. "Turns everything to total shit, absolutely fucking everything!"

"Yes, there seems to be little doubt about the capabilities of this bug," Lou shook her head. "It's the ultimate cyber-weapon, as it leaves no chance of recovery after it's been triggered. Our focus has got to be on stopping it being triggered in the first place."

"So how is setting the trigger date different to disabling this this bug?" Andy frowned as he struggled to get his head around this problem.

"Ah, that's where we have a break. To make reset of the date easier for the bad guys – so they can tailor the initiation of the apocalypse to meet their specific goals – this involves only a digital authorisation signature. As this is based on the old SPHYNX+ system, we can certainly crack this."

"Okay, so how do we do that?" Andy took his usual role as Devil's Advocate.

"The safest option is to hack into the threatened systems and reset the triggers in parallel," Su answered.

"And how many can you handle?"

"All of them," Georgie responded with a grin.

Andy scowled in disbelief. "Hack into thousands of systems? That'll take months, if not years. We've only got ten days, remember."

"Actually, it's hundreds of thousands – maybe a million or so. Just putting together the hit list will take a while, but we've got the tools to do it."

"But hacking into them all, how long will that take?"

Georgie's smile widened. "That'll be done in the blink of an eye if my flash computer works as I think it will. Of course, if it doesn't, then, as Hyo-jin would say, we're totally fucked!"

Andy had no response to that.

***

The session got more technical as Georgie and Su went into more detail of how the hacks would work. Although the flash hypercomputer could easily manage all the decryption tasks in the fraction of a second during which qubit coherence was maintained, this time was far too short for the interactions involved in resetting the timers in the targeted system. There was also the practical side of the internet bandwidth required to run hundreds of thousands of hacks simultaneously. Together, Su and Georgie had developed a scheme in which their quantum supercomputer coordinated the hacks and compiled the decryption jobs. These were then passed together to the hypercomputer, which handled them effectively instantaneously. The trigger reset would then be implemented using internet access via the entire NDB intranet, which Lou had responsibility for setting up.

"We've got all the hardware in place, assuming the hypercomputer comes up to scratch, but we still need the software," Lou summarised the situation. "I can cobble together the linking and communication tools needed from material to hand, but the algorithm to control the hack and reset the timer needs to be developed by Su and Hyo-jin, while Georgie needs to develop the protocols for implementing it using the super-hypercomputer hybrid. Whether that's possible or not in the 10 days that we have, we'll find out only when we start working on it."

"And, if it's impossible, what then?" Jay asked.

Andy shifted uncomfortably in his seat. "If the entire global financial system collapses, things will be dire even for a country as inherently stable as Switzerland. The NDB already have a heads-up, but I doubt that they've got any contingency plans for a threat of this magnitude. The hard decision they have to make is the extent to which they inform others. There are two big risks here. The first is that, if the Lazarus group learn that we know about the virus, they will probably trigger it early. From what we've just heard, it's clear that they have the capability to do this – especially given the autocatalytic nature of activation." He received a grunt and a glare of acknowledgement from Park. "The second is that the threat becomes common knowledge, resulting in a panic. This could do huge amounts of damage, even if we do manage to defuse the virus."

"Anyway, that's all out of our hands, I'm glad to say. For us, as a group, there are a number of actions that we can take that reduce our vulnerability in the worst-case scenario. Primarily this involves converting resources that we hold in the financial marketplace – accounts, pensions, shares and stuff like that – into tangibles. Luckily, we have invested a fair amount of our profits in hardware and properties, but both individually and as a company we still have many millions that are at risk. I've drafted a list of options that you'll have received by now, but we need to move fast on some of these. For example, pensions and insurances will take a bit of time to sort out."

"And what is the downside if we do all this but Georgie's miracle machine works?" Jay asked.

"There will certainly be a small cost if we have to reverse everything, but not much, as we'll know what the situation is in less than a fortnight. We might, however, want to spend a bit more time reconsidering here. As this threat to global stability isn't unique and reflects inherent risks, some form of defence-in-depth could be a good financial strategy in any case. Anyway, something to consider in the future."

"Hyo-jin, what was your plan?" Su asked, causing everyone to focus on the small Korean. "You certainly must have had a lot of time to think about this."

"The deal was not finalised due to bastard rape cunt," she gave Andy a death stare, "but was set up to buy a block in the centre of Lucerne. This was a large apartment for me and rent from shops and other apartments."

"You won't be able to get rent after the financial crash," Andy pointed out.

"All barter, fuckwit," she spat back at him. "If no money, then rent is paid in things. Baker, supermarket, liquor store – all these are in this block. Also, a brothel in one apartment."

"It rather exploits the tenants, though. They have to work out a way to survive without money, while you just cream off what you need as rent."

"How come the women here are smart and this cunt is so pigshit thick?" Hyo-jin chortled. "Any system only works if both sides accept it: we know this in the DPR. The renters will be happy to pay, because then they are sure they have a place to live and, anyway, payment seems less than cash paid before. If you can't pay rent, how do you know what happens in the future? Maybe you're kicked out."

Andy noticed that again Park's English improved and cursing disappeared when she was making a technical point. "Actually, Hyo-jin's correct: this would be a win-win situation. If banking services disappeared, assuring that you keep a roof over your head would be a major concern for anyone who didn't own a property outright. Although it's certain that some system would eventually be put in place, if you've lost all the buffers provided by savings, pensions, insurances and the like, you'll be feeling very vulnerable."

"That's okay for shops, but how does it work for normal salary slaves, who're then without any kind of income?" Lou asked.

Andy could see that Park was thinking over a response, but he could already imagine how this would work. "If not goods, then services. I guess that, for the hookers, this would be clear. But almost everyone has something to offer, be it only cooking, cleaning, running errands... I'll have a look to see how we could take over some parts of this into our overall backup strategy."

"So, this rape guy takes my idea and I get butt-fucked? That's how you work, you cunt..." Park seemed ready to physically attack the much larger Andy.

Lou, with a bit of help from Su, managed to pull the irate Korean back into her seat. "Calm down, love, nobody at all is getting butt-fucked if we can possibly avoid it. Given that you were part of the team responsible for this attack, and would have let it happen if we hadn't intervened, you can't expect too much sympathy for your plight. However, this gives you an incentive to work with us. I promise you that, if we can implement Georgie's counter-measures, we'll release you and won't touch your cryptocurrency wallet. So, you can do with it what you will. Does that seem fair?" She looked around at her team, who were all nodding their heads. "Fine, that's unanimous. Are you happy now?"

"What if I help you and it still doesn't work?"

Lou grinned, showing a side that was rarely seen by her teammates. "Then, my dear, you are penniless and on your own. Probably totally fucked in more than one sense of the word."

Chapter 4 - Financial crash risk reduction

Before breaking to produce the briefing documents for Frau Zürcher, Jay presented a quick overview on his findings on the likely escape strategy for whoever was responsible for ordering the attack. To the other team members, it seemed an unlikely coincidence that Switzerland emerged as the prime location of their expected havens.

This was quickly explained by Park. "It is supposed to be secret, but all North Koreans know that the best places in the world are USA and Switzerland. The States has Las Vegas, Disney World, California, basketball and all that shit, but full of massacres and crazy rednecks with machine guns. Switzerland has Alps, Heidi, neutrality and no crime – so it is the best choice. Also, we have an embassy in Bern, which makes it easier for leader's family and friends."

"A bit simplistic," Su grinned, "but I can see your point. Anyway, this should make it a bit easier for us, especially if everything goes via the embassy."

"Not everything," the Korean shook her head. "Too dangerous to move money through the embassy, so that is the job of a private bank. Bank owner is big friend of the Supreme Leader"

"That's not a problem, we can even access a bank like that through the NDB."

"No point, account is cleared out already."

"So, the Kims already knew to move into tangibles?"

"For some of account, maybe. But I took the rest."

"Bollocks!" Su frowned. "So, how much did you steal?"

"It was all Euros, but now mixed cryptocurrency in my wallets. Worth about a hundred million, I guess."

"Bugger me!" Su looked at the hacker with a new respect.

"That was my main plan. The ransomware shit was just to get Bratva fuckers to move me here to Switzerland and provide protection. Payment is always uncertain, as victims may grow balls. But I got what I needed. You know, property in Lucerne is fucking expensive."

Subsequent discussion quickly drifted off to assess how unlikely such a private bank attack might have been in the past and how inevitable it would be in the future

"Anyway, this is good and bad news," Lou summarised to bring them back on topic. "It's good in that loss of such a large sum will cause problems for whoever is escaping to Switzerland, bad in that they now know someone is targeting them. Anyway, this'll give Jay and Andy more to work on. We should stop now and get the briefing material sorted out for Frau Zürcher. Who wants to be in on that meeting?"

"Definitely not me, I need to get a flight back to Kloten, ASAP," Jay responded immediately and then logged out of the meeting.

Su and Georgie looked at each other and raised eyebrows but, before they could respond, Lou cut in. "Okay, girls, I can read your minds. You've a lot more important things to do, solving a nigh impossible problem with only Hyo-jin to help. Fine, Andy, it looks like you and me. And, anyway, don't you know this woman?"

"Petra, yes, I overlapped with her at college," he replied, rather evasively.

"Good, that'll help. Okay, we meet back here at 14:00 for our video call."

Andy felt as if he should speak out, but decided against it. *I don't think anybody needs to know that I went out with Petra for a few months, but it ended badly when she found out that I was shagging her young sister. She's older now and a senior civil servant, so shouldn't let an old peccadillo come between us. Or is that just wishful thinking?*

***

Petra Zürcher was a trim, dark-haired woman in her forties, who would be described as handsome rather than beautiful. For the meeting, she was supported by two colleagues, pretty young blondes, who were so similar in appearance that they may have been twins. All three wore atypically-formal charcoal-grey jackets, white shirts and black ties, which gave the appearance of a uniform of some kind. Andy idly wondered what else they would be wearing out of the view of the camera. Maybe short, form-hugging skirts or skin-tight trousers. Whatever, despite greater concerns, he hoped one of them would stand up during the meeting to provide a further fodder for his, admittedly puerile, fantasies.

Zürcher was known also to Lou, so thanked them for the meeting and then introduced her colleagues – Ursi and Vicky. Andy scanned virtual business cards linked to the video, indicating that they were coordinators of cyber-defence and communication, respectively. *Rather powerful positions given their apparent youth, but probably indicating that these are very smart cookies.*

Petra looked grim while she skipped over pleasantries and moved to the topic of concern. "We've gone through the material you provided, which certainly supports the case for an unprecedented threat. The first point to be clarified, though, is whether you're 100% sure of this. Is there any possibility that it could be a false alarm?"

Lou had anticipated this question. "Although absolute certainty doesn't exist in real life – and this is especially the case when considering anything to do with computers – I've no doubt that this threat is real. We've been able to find traces of insertion of the sleeper Trojan in every financial system we've looked at. This includes not only big boys like the Swiss National Bank, UBS and the Zurich insurance group, but also Cantonal tax and budget offices. There's always the chance of a flaw in the coding of either the trigger or the autocatalytic, operating-system burner, but I think the sophistication of this threat makes such hopes extremely unlikely, especially given the pedigree of the Lazarus group."

This was clearly the answer that Zürcher expected. "Yes, that was wishful thinking. Your assessment matches that of our team." Ursi nodded in confirmation. "So now the tricky question: how confident are you that you can defuse this threat?"

Lou was also expecting this question, but paused before answering. "That's harder to answer. We've identified only one possible defence, but it relies on a novel application of unproven technology. It's feasible in principle but, to be honest, we'll know if it works only when we try it."

"And, if it doesn't work?"

"I believe the technical term is that we're *truly fucked*."

Zürcher looked grim as she thought this over. "Is there anything that NDB or any of the other agencies – national or international – could do to help?"

"Apart from providing the access bandwidth for implementing our hack, I don't see anything specific that you can do here."

To Petra's evident surprise, Ursi spoke up at this point. "I've been thinking over this since you mentioned that the approach is feasible in principle but untried. What about if we set up a small-scale analogue of the problem in order to test your proposed hyper-supercomputer setup: would that help?"

"You've got access to a Peta-qubit machine?" Lou sounded sceptical. "Su said that her lash-up was at the cutting edge here."

"Well, maybe not Peta, but probably somewhere about Giga. In any case, it's an experimental flash quantum computer."

"PSI," Andy muttered.

Ursi evidently heard this. "Exactly, the Paul Scherrer Institute. We could simulate the virus on a thousand or so encrypted-access operating systems and then try out the algorithm you're going to use on them."

"That's a great idea, Ursi," Lou smiled, "we just need to get our fingers out and produce the algorithm."

"Of course, you could also set up a parallel NDB team to work on this," Andy pointed out, seeing the opportunities that this approach offered. "Any algorithms they developed could be compared against ours on the PSI simulator and then we can implement the attack with the best-performing variant."

"Yes, that's doable, but we'll need to be careful how we set this up. It'll have to look like a theoretical exercise," Ursi looked at Vicky.

"Yes, this is a hot topic that we haven't developed a policy on yet," Vicky looked to Zürcher for input.

"Indeed, the threat is held as top secret. Presently it's known only to a small team within NDB and the responsible Bundesrat." Lou and Andy knew that this was the cabinet minister with responsibility for the military. "Because of the risks that will certainly result if this potential disaster becomes more widely known, as yet we haven't informed our partners in the international intelligence community. We can't put this off much longer, but it's so sensitive that it'll require a decision by the entire Cabinet. I'll brief them tomorrow morning. Have you any thoughts here?"

Lou looked at Andy, who had anticipated this topic and prepared a response. "We've discussed this issue, but mainly listed problems rather than develop solutions. The first problem is technical: if more agencies learn about this threat, each will start developing counter-measures. Rather than complementing our efforts, we're likely to step on each other's toes, greatly increasing the chance of hitting a tripwire and setting off the cyber-crash before we've had a chance to implement our plan. It's true that the big agencies have much greater resources than us but, due to their size, they're notoriously inefficient and, in a number of areas, best described as chaotic. Overall, I think they'd be more of a hindrance than a help." He noticed that both Ursi and Vicky were nodding their agreement.

"The second problem is social. If the financial collapse occurred, it would hit everyone at a very personal level. Being aware of this risk, it's inevitable that individuals will start to take precautions, building parachutes in case the worst comes to the worst. But few would look after only themselves: they have family and friends that they'd want to protect also. Even if one person informs only five others and each of them, in turn, informs another five, it's exponential growth and the cat will be out of the bag within a day or two. This'll certainly result in massive socio-economic disruption, whether or not our counter-measures succeed."

"And what about your team... and mine for that matter? Are they immune to this very human trait?"

The NDB ladies seemed on tenterhooks, waiting for an answer to Petra's question.

"Of course not. We've already started developing a strategy for the protection of our company and the members of our team."

"And not informed anyone else? Not even parents, children, siblings...? That's hard to believe."

"No, not a peep to anyone else yet. We have, however, an information package that'll allow all close family and friends to minimise impacts if things go tits-up. This will, however, be distributed only an hour before our hack is initiated. Even an hour will be enough for it to spread a bit, but this'll be inherently limited, especially if the hack occurs late night or early morning."

"That's quite clever, actually," Vicky smiled warmly in Andy's direction. "We should set up something like this for our team and the Bundesrat. It's a good way of avoiding the temptation to leak information. Could you send us the package that you've produced?"

"It's still a bit rough, but I'm sending it through to you now," Andy accessed the link on her virtual business card. "We could iterate on it if you like, as it would be good to have independent feedback on it."

"Great. I'll set up a one-on-one chat after I've had a chance to think over this draft."

Despite this positive development, Frau Zürcher still looked unhappy. "We're still left with building a defence strategy at a national level for this worst-case scenario. This also needs to be coupled to something at a global level", she grimaced at the thought. "Although we may be an island within the EU, we're completely dependent on international trade. You proposed some options... I guess this was you, Andy... could you go through them for us?"

"Sure, no problem. The Swiss internal bit is easier, as you have more control there. Best would be if the Bundesrat orders all relevant financial institutions to improve back up of their key databases. This could be coupled to the recent ransomware attacks. They would need to set up a completely isolated intranet on new computers. These could just be standard desktops, so no great cost there. Then scan in the databases."

"Scan in?" Petra frowned.

"Exactly, absolutely no electronic data transfer from the contaminated system," Ursi explained to show she had picked up the critical issue here. "It would have been tricky in the past, but we should be able to sort out a cheap and cheerful system using webcams or even smartphones to scan the databases as they scroll on a display screen. It's slow, but very secure."

Andy nodded. "Yes, that's the key. The new intranet can include any commercial database managing software, but take a basic one from academia rather than one tailored to financial applications, just to be on the safe side. The database can then be copied onto transfer disks if the main system goes down."

"The infected computers can't be saved?"

"The computers themselves are fine," Ursi answered Petra's question. "If the bug trashes their operating systems, we simply purge the entire network, returning the hardware to factory default machine code. We then load an archive of the complete system from before the virus was introduced and update it with our scanned database. It'll take some time and be clunky with such old software, but it should work."

"Why not update the operating system with something newer? The old system won't have some of the functionality that we now expect. Things like handling the wide range of electronic currency available."

"Actually, that's a good thing," Andy intercepted the question. "Georgie's hypercomputer is the final nail in the coffin for cyber-currency. The block chain should now be considered dead and gone."

"In fact, it's worse than that," Lou added, "flash decryption effectively removes all protection from electronic financial transactions or any other confidential communication."

"That's good to know, but not critical at the moment," Zürcher forced the discussion back on topic. "The key thing is that we can start now to avoid losing everything if an OS crash occurs. Implementing that in Switzerland is doable, especially as we can put pressure on Swiss organisations to act quickly. But what about our international partners?"

"We can let them know what we're doing, without explaining exactly why we're doing it. We can focus only on reducing risk from system hacks, which this will certainly do," Lou suggested.

"We could easily do that, but very few are likely to see this as a critical threat, so won't move fast enough."

"Even if we let them know the entire story, do you think that they'd be able to move fast enough? A small, high-tech country like Singapore might, but the bigger the country, the more inertia in the system."

"Mmm," Petra was deep in thought and spoke slowly as she worked her way through this problem. "We can issue a general warning as soon as I've clearance from the Bundesrat. This will require immediate backups to be generated in the way that Andy specified. Then we need to focus our efforts, with the EU being a priority from a Swiss perspective. There are at least two of the Bundesräte with good personal contacts to the Central Bank president, so we can work through them."

"That sounds like a sensible way to proceed." Lou looked at Andy. "Is there anything further from our side?"

"I don't think so."

"And from your side, Petra?"

"I think that's all for now, but you'll have to keep me updated on how preparation for the hack is progressing."

"I'll give you daily progress reports," Lou promised. "In terms of the technical side, especially setting up the analogue test case, it'll be easier if Su from our side liaises directly with Ursi."

"I know Su Fong," Ursi noted, "so that'll work fine."

"Excellent, so we're done for now," Petra concluded. "We can let these folk get back to work, as I'm sure they've got plenty to do."

While goodbyes were being said, the link was terminated.

***

"Well, Andy, how do you think that went?" Lou stretched, which strained the fabric covering her bosom almost to bursting point.

"I'm bloody glad we live in Switzerland! I think Petra's crew are on the ball and we might just be able to pull off Georgie's quantum miracle with their help. Even if it doesn't work, we have a chance of putting a safety net in place."

"A safety net for Switzerland," she reminded him. "I can't see this working for anywhere else."

"I think Petra's plan for the ECB could work."

"Even if it does, that would cover EU-level financial institutions at best. I can't see that trickling down to the level of the member countries in time."

Andy smiled as Lou peeled off her blouse and struggled out of the bra that strained to contain her massive tits.

"God, I hate these bloody things," she chucked the bra casually onto the conference table, sighing in relief while she gave a little shimmy to set her breasts swinging. This naturally held Andy's attention and forced him to see that her large nipples were erect. "The meeting didn't last as long as I expected, so maybe we've got time for a bit of stress relief before we get on with our work. What

94

do you think?" She lifted her boobs to make it completely clear what was on offer.

"Good grief, woman, you're a nymphomaniac! We're discussing apocalyptic scenarios and you want to shag?"

"Well, if the world as we know it is about to end, we should get as much shagging in as possible before it does." Lou stood and unzipped the short skirt that she was wearing, revealing a minute, completely transparent tanga. "I'll tell you what, you can think about those tasty twins while you screw me – and I'll do the same." She giggled lasciviously.

Seeing it was the easiest way to escape, Andy began to undress while Lou stepped out of her knickers.

"You've had your wicked way with the big boss, Petra, haven't you?" Lou grinned while she lay back on the table and opened her legs.

"How did you know that?" Andy could feel his erection harden as he looked into his colleague's open vagina.

"I can always tell," her grin widened. "Maybe I'll have a think about giving her a good seeing to while you dream about the young nubiles. There's a lot to be said for a more mature woman.

Andy silently agreed as he entered her, reaching over to squeeze her hard nipples. *The combination of experience and completely uninhibited enthusiasm is one that's difficult to beat.*

Chapter 5 - Pillow talk

It was only 10 o'clock when Andy realised that his searches were gradually producing less useful input. *Using drugs to replace a good night's rest can only work for so long.* He stretched and waved his hand to switch off his workstation. *Of course, the work out with Lou could also be a contributing factor.* He grinned and then headed for the suite that he shared with Georgie.

Georgie was already in bed and, from the bedware alone, Andy could see that he wouldn't be sleeping with either George or Georgina. The former would be nude and the latter wearing some kind of baby doll rigout. As his partner was wearing black silken pyjamas, this probably indicated asex, so at most a cuddle before sleep. *That, at least, I'll be able to manage.*

Noting that his bedmate was staring at the ceiling, Andy stripped off and slipped quietly into his side of the bed in an attempt to avoid disturbing their resident genius. He could now make out the soft muttering that was so typical of Georgie working on a tricky problem. Suddenly she went quiet and closed her eyes for almost a minute.

Her eyes opened again and she spoke clearly, still staring at the ceiling. "What do you think of Park?"

"Well, I wouldn't turn my back to her if she was carrying a baseball bat."

In this fugue state, Georgie was impervious to humour. "Of course, because you raped her." He also seemed to have forgotten Andy's protestations of innocence here. "But how good is she really, as a hacker? The backdoor into the operating systems is clever, but conventional. Could their tripwire be smarter and sensitive to our crack of the access signature? For example, you can simulate quantum coherence on a conventional computer, which makes an attempt to get around it virtually impossible."

Andy thought for a moment, trying to work out just how such a function could be emplaced during the original hack. "I don't know details, but I would guess that nothing so sophisticated would have been attempted, because it inherently increases the chance of the introduced backdoor being spotted. If it was me, I'd just go for a bog-standard, simple-as-possible dead man's switch – something that wouldn't let loose in case of a perturbation such as a power cut."

"That's a good point, I hadn't thought of that. I guess our counter-attack is perfectly doable then." With that she closed her eyes and immediately started gently snoring.

Andy sighed as he turned on his side to face away from his partner. *With anyone else that would have been very weird but, for Georgie, par for the course.* Within a couple of minutes, he was also fast asleep.

***

Lou hated sleeping alone but, unfortunately, was a light sleeper and easily disturbed by any partner who snored, fidgeted or even breathed heavily. This effectively eliminated all of her work colleagues but, through the wonders of internet contact sites, she had a list of bed-mates that she could call on when her need was great. Although many of these were commercial escorts or prostitutes, a few were similar to herself and in relationships with partners that they simply couldn't sleep with. As she really felt in need of a good night's sleep, she was in bed with a young gigolo who, apart from being very pleasing to the eye, went out like a light after he had performed his duties. On the negative side, he talked a lot – both before and during sex.

Unlike Jay, who often tended to have young lovers that only just passed the crossbar of legality, Lou generally preferred more mature partners. She made an exception in Romeo's case, not only because he slept like a corpse, but also because he was hung like a bull. *A very well-endowed bull*. Lou grinned while she played with his erection, trying to filter out waffle about the latest movies, music and television soaps. Once he was on the job, the topic would change as he seemed to think that talking dirty would help to get his clients into the mood.

Lou was well aware that, even without foreplay, she needed no encouragement to get ready for sex. Nevertheless, she was happy to play along after he helped her roll onto hands and knees in preparation for some doggy-style.

He entered her well-lubricated vagina with a sigh and began to hoarsely whisper into her ear in his exaggerated Italian accent. "So, my love, you can feel me inside, getting deeper, getting you hot. Who would you like to have with us, for a ménage à trois, or even à quatre?"

Lou surprised herself when she answered without thought. "There's two of my colleagues, twins, I'd love to have them here with us."

He growled, thrusting harder. "Another two men, joining me together in your pussy, your mouth and your ass. You'd like that, wouldn't you?"

"Mmm, two more men would also be good, but I'm thinking about twin girls. They're quite beautiful and I've always had a fantasy about having sex with sisters."

Romeo's pace dropped off while he considered this, then built up again after he gently nipped her shoulder. "The two sisters, what would they be doing to you? What would they do to me?"

"Let me think about that. I would have one below me – soixante-neuf – licking both me and you. You'd lick the other one until she comes, then they'd swap places."

"You're a very dirty women, I like that."

"You have no idea," Lou groaned as she felt herself approaching the edge, the thought of group sex with the NDB girls making it even harder to hold back. "Then I'd swap places with Ursi and let you shag her tight little arsehole. I'd lick her until you both come together and…" She shuddered with pleasure as the orgasm hit and the narrative continued only in her head.

A few minutes later she was beginning to doze, the shagged-out boy already out cold by her side, when she suddenly remembered that she'd given the name of the twin in her fantasy. "Should remember not to do that in future," she whispered to herself before she also dropped off.

***

Jay smiled at the young man posing at the foot of his bed. Robert was a recent contact who he met through his preferred pick-up site – *wildbucks.ch*. Bob advertised himself as a bi-curious consultant, but Jay had already ripped his full profile from the internet and knew that he was actually a schoolteacher, recently married with a young baby, which probably explained the tired look that he tried hard to conceal. He was free for the night, he admitted, due to his better half visiting her parents in Northern Ireland. "Okay, lad, stop preening and get your bare arse into this bed."

"Then what, you old bugger? I think it's time for me to go on top."

Jay grinned. The lad was really asking for a serious shagging, but it was clearly going to involve some foreplay. "Well, give me a good blow-job and then you can choose: top or bottom."

Although not very experienced, Bob was nothing if not enthusiastic. "Well, that's a good start," Jay stroked his partner's short blond hair, "but what does your wife think about this? If she also wants to swing a bit, you should arrange to bring her along with you some time."

The young man looked up as he reached for the lubricant spray at the side of the bed. "It was actually her idea. She still hasn't got into sex the way it was before the baby and I think that her idea is that me having sex with a man is less of a threat to her than if I was with another woman."

Jay stretched his head back in pleasure as the fluid was massaged onto his growing erection and

100

balls, before a couple of fingers slipped into his anus. "So, what do you think? Would you fancy us sharing her? What about double-penetration, that can be extremely intimate for all involved?"

"I've never really thought about that, but it could be fun. I've looked at loads of group porn, but hadn't really thought about it with Ally." He grunted as he impaled himself on Jay's prick.

As Jay started to pleasure his lover with his hands, he couldn't help thinking about double penetration scenarios with Bob's wife, who was quite delectably androgynous. *Good grief, maybe I'm closet bi.* He was smiling at this idea before his approaching orgasm drove all thoughts from his mind.

***

Su lay in bed with Hyo-Jin's head on her shoulder. "You were surprised when we had wet fucking in the shower, weren't you," the Korean said in a low voice that was almost a whisper. "You knew I was a lesbian, but you didn't know about that."

Su ran her fingers through the woman's hair. "Well, it's not so unusual, especially in bondage games, but I didn't know that you'd be into that."

"I was held in a special school for top girls, ages from 12 to 17. It had women staff and teachers, except for occasional visiting male professors and coaches. The girls slept together in dormitories, one for each age group. So, I had twenty girls to fuck every night. Lesbian fucking was encouraged by the teachers, who were mainly fucking dikes. The bathrooms had common showers, baths and open toilets – no stalls like you have here in the West. There was one teacher in particular, very fucking ugly and very fucking fat, who regularly came in to shower with the girls and she introduced us to piss play. Some of the girls hated it, but I thought it was fun."

"You know," Su murmured, "you swear a lot, especially when you're annoyed or discussing sex."

"Those fucking Ruskies are to blame," her hand slipped down over Su's groin. "I learned English at school, of course, as I was a fucking mathematician and aimed towards computer sciences. For further training in Beijing, I learned a little Chinese, but only a very little, as we were hacking mainly US software. But when I decided to get out, then I was only speaking English with these fucking Russian bastards. The only English I heard spoken by natives before that was in the fucking porn sites I hacked into."

"I thought it was tricky to access western web sites from either North Korea or China…"

"For normal fuckers, maybe, but not genius-level programmers.," she stated without any pretence of false modesty. "When I was 12, I had already secret access to a TOR server that gave me everything I wanted, without any chance the fuckwit teachers would spot it. I was the go-to-girl for all porn fiends, even the 17-year-olds. They all wanted fuck-porn, big black guys fucking the arses of little oriental whores, the dreams of girls not straight lesbians. Some of the lesbians were also customers for similar stuff, looking for perverse videos of black women with fucking huge tits."

"Jesus, your life has been weird beyond belief."

"School was fine for me – maths, computing and sex – but hard for some other girls. The top athletes were all on drugs to enhance performance. I had close friends who were gymnasts; even by 17 they had no tits, no pubes and not even fucking periods... Although that's not so bad, I suppose."

"I thought sports bodies like the IOC were very strict about stuff like that."

"Fucking useless! Our medics were always far ahead of them. The West calls this abuse, but most girls were happy with their luxurious life. Well very good by our standards. Also, they had good opportunities for the future. Some missed their families, but I was an orphan, so no problem for me."

"I suppose that, for a lesbian, there are worse places to experience puberty than a girls' school." Su playfully stroked her lover's breasts.

"Yes, school was good, but afterwards was a bastard. There are very few women in Black Hat groups in Korea and China, mainly just fucking male geeks. I liked the work, but was chased all the time by the guys and pressured by bosses to get married. I was fucking raped twice: once in Pyongyang and once in Beijing. Not a good idea to attack a top hacker like me. I really fucked up those cunts, big way. The Chink committed suicide and the Korean has a lifetime sentence in work camp, so maybe worse than death."

"Christ, you're not someone to mess about with. I guess we need to keep you happy." Her hand slipped lower, rubbing the Korean's clitoris and causing a moan of pleasure.

"And what about you, when did you discover that you were a lesbian?"

"I'm not," Su felt a quiver of surprise pass through her lover's body. "I'm bi, at least as far as sex is concerned. I have very close male and female friends, and have had occasional sex or even deeper relationships with some of them. The most important part for me is that they've got to be smart, as I need some kind of soul mate. So, I guess you might fit the bill here." Her fingers now slipped into a very wet vagina while her partner reciprocated the move.

"We need to talk more about this, after the fucking." Hyo-Jin threw back the single sheet covering them and squirmed around into a soixante-neuf position.

Su smiled before getting to work with tongue and fingers. *Blunt and to the point – but that works for me. Seems to have been a lot of domination in that school of hers, so maybe we've got even more in common than I thought.*

Part 3: ...and the shit hits the fan...

Chapter 1 - Testing quantum toolkits

After a week of intensive effort, the basics of the hack on the trigger of the OS-killer were nailed down. This was facilitated by taking over the financial transfer network of a recently bankrupt trading house and isolating it completely from all external communication links. A forensic analysis of the Trojan could then be carried out without risk of a mis-step leading to an autocatalytic cascade. Even with access assured, the trickiest part was actually resetting the timer, as this was incorporated into the trigger and directly linked to the clock that is a fundamental component of any operating system. Resetting was based on a strict protocol, with any slip leading to instant initiation of the virus. However, the timer, which was connected to numerous tripwires, had a single direct connection to the trigger, which was an inherent weakness. Simply excising this connection would effectively render the Trojan inert, allowing the tripwires to be completely ignored.

In parallel, Ursi had set up a group of NDB cryptographers to work with the PSI quantum physicists on the analogue test system. Even the definition of the test case caused a bit of friction, especially after Georgie had suggested that PSI run Su's decryption algorithm on their flash hypercomputer with the aim of cracking two operating systems simultaneously. The NDB guys were offended that their own algorithms were considered inferior, while the physicists considered the challenge well below the capabilities of their machine.

Ursi explained this in a video meeting before the first test run. Despite Georgie's recommendation, this test would use a NDB algorithm and aim for ten simultaneous hacks. "Surely, this'll be a better test of your approach?" she concluded.

Georgie, once again with a Hello Kitty theme for a rigout that appeared to consist of only a long, very baggy t-shirt with pink fluffy slippers, shook her head in despair. "It's not going to work – not a chance. You don't have close to enough power for that."

"But you've now got your hack outlined," Ursi looked unconvinced. "How many systems do you intend to crack simultaneously?"

"We don't know yet, as the list of targets is still being refined. The limiting factor is bandwidth between the super- and hyper-machines – and the coherence time, of course. With the ten microseconds that I'm sure of, we'll be able to handle a hundred thousand, which could go up to ten million or so if I can crank this up to a millisecond."

"But PSI have a Giga hypercomputer that they have already held for a millisecond, so this seems to me like a hundred simultaneous hacks could easily be on the cards."

Georgie again shook her head and sighed. "Firstly, these problems don't scale linearly and thus the basis for your calculation is incorrect. Secondly, PSI has shown coherence for longer times when the computer was running a system check, but not while running an algorithm that pushes performance to its limits. Thirdly, the NDB algorithm is simply taken over from one designed for a quantum supercomputer, so it's clunky and only about 10% as efficient as Su's. Anyway, it's up to you. I predict, however, that you'll fail completely."

It was clear from the expression on the NDB coordinator's face that she could not take Georgie seriously. "Fine, let's just see how we get on."

"I bet you don't even get one OS cracked."

Ursi glared at the younger woman. "OK, what do you bet?"

"If I'm right, you wear a Hello Kitty shirt at the meeting tomorrow."

Ursi looked unsure, but clearly couldn't back down. "Okay, it's a bet."

"Excellent, I'll get the shirt couriered over to you now," Georgie giggled.

"And what if I win?"

"If you win, I'll attend the meeting clad only in a layer of chocolate."

"Well, it seems that we've covered everything critical and we should finish up before any further silly bets are made." Lou waved and closed the link before anyone had an opportunity to respond.

In the NetSec meeting room, Lou raised her eyebrows. "Are you sure about this, Georgie?

Chocolate would make an awful mess of your chair."

"Don't worry, I'm absolutely certain. I'll tell you what, if I'm wrong, you can eat the chocolate off after the meeting."

"Well, that would be a win-win situation for me," Lou licked her lips. "I must say that I'm really looking forward to tomorrow's meeting."

***

As Georgie had predicted, the PSI test failed miserably. The supercomputer delivered the ten decryption tasks, but received no output from the hypercomputer before coherence was lost. It was repeated immediately afterwards with eight tasks, then six, then four, then one – without receiving a single solution to the problem. Finally, to test that it wasn't a hardware problem, a much simpler decryption problem was input, which was solved just before decoherence occurred.

At the meeting, Ursi was gamely wearing the lurid Hello Kitty t-shirt in place of her usual shirt and tie, but also her usual grey jacket which served to reduce its impact. Probably to emphasise the victory – although always difficult to tell for Georgie – today it was George in gay boy mode, wearing a copy of the NDB uniform, which contrasted with his over-the-top makeup, earrings, nose-rings and blue-dyed hair.

Ursi grimaced before conceding defeat. "I know that we've been proven wrong, but don't see how we can set up any test on the PSI system. Maybe your gender-fluid guru can help us." Georgie's only response was a smile.

"Yes, whether lad or lass, our Georgie's smart as they come," Lou smiled possessively. "What do you think, love?"

"As I mentioned before, the first move is to switch over to Su's algorithm. That should increase efficiency by a factor of about 10. In addition, increase the number of physical connections between the super- and hyper- computers to four, separating input and output for each of the two tasks. That doesn't give you a lot, but every little helps."

"So, out of interest, how many connections do your machines have?" asked a chubby young man, one of the NDB cryptographers.

"Presently a hundred with most for input, as the problem specification is larger than the solution. With a bit of luck, we'll be able to double that within the next couple of days if we can source the required optical fibres and lasers in time."

"Doesn't that make the coding hellish complex," he enquired further.

"Not really, the entire architecture is set up for parallel computing, so all that's needed is to specify the input and output selection process for each task."

He smiled his thanks, but seemed rather unconvinced.

"Well, that's it from our side," Ursi concluded. "It'll take a bit of reprogramming and hardware modification, but we should be able to try a double hack tomorrow. We'll pass results on to you as soon as we have them. Any progress from your side?"

Lou displayed a flow chart of the hack components. "I think we've got the essence of the operation nailed down now. For each OS, we need to decrypt the Korean's key that gives top-level administrator access, then bypass the trigger timer and simultaneously disconnect the link from the over-ride to the trigger. The system is complicated by the tripwire feed, which goes through the over-ride and gives us the instant that we need to isolate the trigger before it can fire."

"And you've got to get this right, every time, for a wide range of OS architectures..." Ursi looked worried.

"Well, there is no 100% in this game," Su admitted. "It's inevitable that we'll screw up a few times."

"But then we're screwed, surely. As soon as we miss one hack, the autocatalytic cascade starts."

"That's why we've prioritised our targets by geographical location: starting in Switzerland and working outwards. Although we perform the decrypting simultaneously on the hypercomputer, implementation is steered by the supercomputer using the NDB slave network. This is effectively limited by the length and number of connections, and, of course, light speed in the optical cables. It's then a direct race between autocatalytic initiation, which runs through the same functional unit as the tripwires, and our hack, which disconnects the trigger directly. I reckon we'll win in most cases."

"But we will probably lose some systems..."

"Of course, it's inevitable. That's why Andy's backup plan is so important. It should also be clear that the risk of failure due to autocatalytic initiation will increase as the action proceeds and could be significant for systems that are physically close together but distant from us – for example, in Australia or South America."

"I realise that this is beyond your control, but it'll be tricky to explain this to our partners."

"Don't," Andy interjected. "There's no way anyone outside of our core group needs to know about this hack. If we don't succeed – or if we don't do anything at all – all key systems are burned to the ground. Anything at all that we save has got to be a bonus, but it would be asking for trouble to publicise this success. Whatever happens, just bury this entire action as deeply as possible."

"Is that in your company's best interest?" Petra enquired, having been a silent observer until this point. "Surely a win here would be fantastic bit of advertising."

"Not at all," Lou smiled. "Our main selling point is complete confidentiality and a focus on serving the best needs of our clients. Here we're working for the Swiss Government, so that's where our priorities lie."

"You don't actually have a contract for this work," Ursi reminded her.

"We have a flexible call-off contract and will bill you in the event of a success. If we fail, then no bill. Of course, for that scenario, you'd be unable to pay it anyway."

The meeting went silent as this message sank in.

***

Andy's searches of North Korean properties in Switzerland were constrained by the high security in place, but his tools indicated that the Zermatt chalet contained only the staff who maintained it, while there were a number of individuals who had arrived on diplomatic passports in the Geneva and Zurich villas. The names on the passports were clearly bogus, but this was normal practice for senior members of the Kim dynasty travelling to Switzerland.

By the evening, Georgie was girlie lez in a short black leather dress and knee-length boots, indicating a high likelihood of ending up as a sub in one of Su's BDSM fantasies. Andy was thus unsurprised to be alone when he finally got to his bedroom. He was just in the process of drying himself after a shower when there was a knock on the bedroom door and Lou entered without waiting for a response. "I saw kinky Georgina heading off with Su and Hyo-jin, so she'll probably spend the evening in the basement and then end up in bed with them. So I thought you might fancy a bit of company."

Andy smiled at this offer, knowing that *company* was Lou-speak for a session of wild bonking. "Well, that's a good idea. I could really do with bouncing some ideas on how to nail the North Koreans with somebody. What do you think?"

Lou smiled back while she peeled off the negligée, which was evidently her only item of clothing. "That's perfect, it's great to have a topic for pillow talk afterwards. Hurry up and finish, so we can get to it. Any preferences – heads or tails, front or back? Maybe try one of Georgie's toys?"

Andy quickly finished drying and jumped onto the bed, lying on his back with his legs open. "Lucky dip: I'll leave it up to your imagination."

"A good choice, although I'm sorry now that I didn't come better equipped. Let's see what our gender-fluid comrade has in her love box," she rummaged around in the carved oak chest at the bottom of the bed.

"Um, nipple clamps. They'll do for a start." She grunted as she tightened these onto her large, already-erect nipples. "And a pair of butt-plugs, I'll have the larger one as my bum certainly gets more use than yours does."

The buxom woman clambered onto the bed until she was kneeling above her partner's face. The large plug went first into her gaping vagina, then into his mouth before she lay forward to give him a better view of her anus. A drawn-out groan of satisfaction followed the process as she slowly inserted it, moving it backwards and forwards until it was fully in place. "Now for the fun bit," she chuckled as she first jammed the other plug into her vagina, noisily slurped on it and then jammed it hard into his arsehole.

"Fuck, do you need to be so brutal?" He then grunted when it was pulled out and pushed back in even more roughly.

"Just getting into the mood for tonight, as it seems the girls are in need of a domme." She nipped his scrotum with her teeth causing a squeal of surprise from her victim.

"I'll do it. I can do dom…"

"No chance, girls only tonight. So, get your laughing gear in action for the foreplay and then we can get to the main event. I'm going to ride you into a greasy spot."

As the oral sex proceeded, Andy struggled hard to avoid premature ejaculation, being sure that his bossy partner would have already planned some form of punishment for this case.

***

"I would say that you achieved your aim, I am indeed now little more than a greasy spot." Andy sighed contentedly, playing with the now unclamped nipples of the woman who lay by his side.

"Not the worst shag I've ever had," she smiled, "and it put me right in the mood for a bit of bondage and hanky-spanky. But there was something you wanted to talk about, wasn't there?"

"Aren't you needed in Su's dungeon?"

"It'll do them good to wait, as anticipation is half the fun. In any case, getting all three of them dressed up will take an age. Sue told me it's going to be a leather and latex theme, so there will be loads of straps and buckles to be sorted out. Just tightening corsets to get them right is a job that'll take the best part of an hour for those three."

"Probably best if I don't think too much about that, or I'll have to tie you to the bed and leave the lesbians to their own devices," he squeezed a huge breast hard and was rewarded by a groan of pleasure. "The problem is that, now Jay and I have located the Koreans, what do we do about it? I'm

114

sure Hyo-jin would insist that we torture them to death: men, women and children. Given the potentially genocidal nature of this attack, this could possibly be argued to be appropriate punishment for the perpetrators. Personally, though, I can't accept such treatment of uninvolved family and members of staff who are only doing their jobs."

"A tricky one," she agreed, casually stroking his slowly recovering erection. "I'm sure some kind of compromise will be needed. This should show justice has been served on the guilty parties, thus minimising the chaos that could result if others pile in seeking revenge."

"Anyway, the first task is to identify who is where and what their links to the Lazarus group are. Then we can work out how best to hit them."

"Why us?" Lou asked, twisting to look Andy in the eye. "We're supposed to be hackers, not direct-action folk. Shouldn't we leave this to a police or military special unit?"

"Arresting those at the top will only open a political can of worms for little Switzerland. There need to be bodies on display, but we don't have black-ops units like those found in many other countries. I'm sure one judicious leak would encourage one of our partners to do the job for us, but I don't like the idea of any of those nutters running loose in Geneva or Zurich. Any slip-up at all and the collateral damage could be hellish. I also thought about sicking the Bratva on them, but it's the same problem. They'd probably just blast both villas to smithereens."

"Well, we don't have to worry about this until we've sorted out the targets."

"Yes, that's a hacking job and what we do well."

"There are other things we do well," Lou slid down to take his dick in her mouth.

Andy rapidly forgot about his worries thereafter.

Chapter 2 - Apocalypse jump-start

Two days before the deadline, Georgie was ready to run first simulation tests of defusing the Trojan. PSI had now managed five simultaneous decryptions using Su's algorithm and pushing the hardware to get coherence times close to the theoretical maximum for their hypercomputer.

Petra and Ursi were present in person in the control room along with Su, Lou and Hyo-jin, while other key members of the NDB team were linked in by video. Tension was already building up when Andy broke in on an intranet link. "Fuck! Autocatalysis has been triggered somewhere around Beijing."

"Christ, we're fucked," Ursi groaned.

"Initiate the hack now, forget the tests," Lou shouted.

"It'll take too long," Petra sighed. "We haven't even tested this system and the OS collapses are spreading towards us at light speed. Everything in Switzerland is probably down by now."

"How could this happen?" Su wondered aloud, her face ashen.

"There's no shortage of high-level hackers in China, so I suppose they also spotted the threat and have attempted to neutralise it." Petra's hands were shaking. "Clearly this attempt was unsuccessful."

At this point Su noticed that Georgie, today a hetero boy, devoid of makeup and wearing a black tracksuit, seemed less concerned that the others. Actually, he seemed to be trying to hide a sly smile.

"Georgie, what are you so happy about, you little bugger. You're up to something, aren't you?"

The sounds of panic in the room died away as everyone waited for an answer. "Well, we always knew that there was a risk of others finding out about this virus, either on their own or due to a leak from our side. I actually thought it would be the Yanks, but I suppose that the Chinks were also prime candidates."

"Stop pissing about, lad" Lou glared at him. "Cut to the bloody chase!"

"Okay, I've a monitoring routine running that detects evidence of a hack being initiated by others, whether successful or not. In such a case, my hack is automatically triggered."

"Shit!" Ursi shook her head. "This is without the system being tested at all."

"I was pretty sure it would work and all key components have been in place for a couple of days. Of course, I'm constantly upgrading and so the capability today would be much less than I could have managed in a couple of days." He looked at a small palmtop. "It should have the potential to save around a half a million systems."

"Good God, you did this all off your own bat," Petra was shocked by the very idea.

"It was just a prudent action to set up. I hoped that we wouldn't need to use it, but clearly it was a smart move."

"Maybe, but that's assuming that it worked," Lou pointed out.

"Oh, it worked, no doubt about that," Georgie's grin became even smugger.

"And how do you know that?"

"Records are scrolling up now," he initiated a holographic display, "but the fact that Frau Zürcher isn't already besieged by panic calls from every bank in Switzerland shows that it's worked perfectly for the local systems. I never doubted that. The only question is how much we've lost on a global scale."

"Do you have any idea about that?" Su enquired, struggling to get her head around this sudden reversal of their fortunes.

"You can just imagine two wave-fronts travelling around the globe towards each other. The one centred on Shanghai started earlier, but the Swiss-centred one is more efficient and moves faster. I'd hazard a guess that we've lost about 50% of global financial infrastructure, with the Far East taking the biggest hit and Europe best protected."

"Hell's bells, how do we recover from this?" Petra wondered aloud.

"That's your problem," Georgie smiled. "I've pulled your chestnuts out of the fire, so the ball is now with you, if I can mix my metaphors."
***

After Petra and Ursi left, the full team, including Hyo-jin, assembled in the main meeting room. Lou opened a magnum of Dom Pérignon while Jay set up an array of flutes. "I know it's just coming up for lunchtime, but we need to celebrate dodging a bullet here. I know Su and Hyo-jin contributed the critical algorithms..."

"With a bit of help from you also, Lou," Su interjected.

"Anyway, George was the mastermind behind averting a complete catastrophe. Grab a glass and we can toast his success."

"No, it was a team effort," Georgie insisted, blushing while he raised his glass. "To us!"

"To us!" Glasses were raised, clinked together and the fine Champagne sipped.

"But, why didn't you let us know what you were setting up?" Lou asked the question that was on everyone else's mind.

"It didn't seem worth mentioning," he answered shyly. "The virus had been in place for years, so the chances of it being triggered in the next few days seemed remote. I'm just paranoid by nature, I suppose."

"Well, thank fuck you are," Andy grinned. "In our line of business, you just can't be too paranoid."

"Interesting, though, Georgie's point about low probability of this occurring," Jay mused aloud. "Either they've known about the virus for some time and, like us, are forced to rush because they know that the timer is about to trigger it…"

"That needs a leak from fucking Lazarus team," Hyo-jin pointed out. "It would be the only way to know that."

"Indeed," Jay continued, "but that's certainly possible, given the number of DPRK hackers trained in China."

"Easy for China to do," she admitted, "but it looks all fucked up. The planned attack would also hit China, so North Korea should be a radioactive hole immediately after this was discovered."

"Hyo-jin's right," Andy contributed. "The Lazarus group is biting the hand that feeds them, which would not go down well in Beijing. Maybe, if the Chinese hack had worked, this would be a cloud with a silver lining. China would be okay, but a lot of the West would be crippled. And, in that case, the blame can be firmly placed with the DPRK. Now they're hoist by their own petard, but some form of retribution will be essential to save face."

"Rapist cunt is correct," Hyo-jin's glare seemed less severe than usual. "Maybe in a few days, but then homeland is getting fucking nuked for sure."

"This is getting worse and worse," Lou sighed. "I was feeling positive for about an hour, but now my happy bubble is well burst."

"Sorry about that," Andy apologised. "But what Jay was saying crystallised something that's been in the back of my mind for a while. We were focused so much on the counter-measures, and parachutes in case they didn't work, that we forgot to think about what the fallout would be even if we were successful. What's certain is that we don't just return to normality as it was defined yesterday. Half of the world's population has lost key financial services, so there's going to be panic and general chaos in the countries most impacted. Even in Europe, the collapse of trading partners will hit, as will public loss of confidence in banks and weak currencies. Switzerland will come out very well, but the value of the Swiss Franc will shoot up, which brings its own problems."

"Um, does this mean that we'll suffer due to moving funds out of our Swiss bank accounts?" Jay wondered.

"I doubt it. Investment in gold and other tangibles will probably inflate by an even bigger factor. Of course, crypto-currencies will also go through the roof."

"Shit!" Everyone turned to face Lou in surprise. "Shit, fuck, bugger, bum! Andy is completely right. We may have dodged a bullet, but that was just the first exchange of fire. The Lazarus group initiated a global cyberwar, which is bound to escalate regardless of the results of their attack. The Chinese will either nuke North Korea or annex it. In either case, probably presenting this as a consequence of an unprovoked attack. The US won't be happy, but won't stand in their way. But this isn't enough, they need some way to recover their formal financial might. This will probably involve cyberwarfare, so we need to prepare for round two, which will be directed at the countries who have suffered least and hence have advanced in terms of their relative position to China. I guess number one targets are the US and EU, but Switzerland is likely to be caught in the firing line."

"Woman with big fucking tits is smart; the bastarding apocalypse is still coming." Hyo-Jin seemed quite pleased by the prospect.

"I really wish someone could prove me wrong," Lou grimaced, "but I guess we need to carry out a detailed threat analysis and then determine if any pre-emptive retaliation is justified."

"Can we assume that China is the only threat here?" Su asked. "Both the Americans and Russians are notoriously sensitive about their position in the international pecking order, so can we ignore them as possible risks?"

"Certainly not," Lou responded, "but this highlights lack of knowledge as a key constraint on any assessment. We just don't have a clear picture of either the damage that has been inflicted on the infrastructure of key countries and trading blocs or how those impacted are assigning blame for the attacks. This we need ASAP."

"I've got a toolkit that can mine most of this information from the internet," Jay contributed. "This could be combined with a bit of judicious hacking into intelligence service intranets, which I'm sure that Su can help me with,"

"With George's decrypting capacity, we can hack into anything, the main limiting factor will be what effort is needed to cover the traces of these hacks," Lou frowned. "Security agencies are going to be on hair triggers now, so we certainly want nothing that can be traced back to us."

"Fine, so I can get started on that immediately after lunch." Jay rubbed his hands together in anticipation of the challenge.

"There's something else," Andy smiled at Lou apologetically, as if unwilling to further spoil her day. "Remember that Hyo-jin doubted that the Chinese got the knowledge needed to counter the threat from Lazarus. This means that we have to consider a possible leak from our side to explain the coincidence of their action being so close in time to ours."

"Shit, I'd forgotten that," Lou admitted. "But is this critical at the present moment? For such a complex operation we needed to inform a much larger number of participants than we do for a normal op. I suppose a leak was almost inevitable. It was only a matter of time."

"The timing is one aspect, but did the Chinese know about the autocatalytic destruction mechanism?" From the confused looks, it appeared that only Su had an inkling of the point that Georgie was making. "If they didn't know about it, they'd work one by one, starting with their most valuable asset and working downwards from there. If they did know about it, then, like us, parallel hacks are the way to go."

"I feel like I'm missing something really obvious here" Jay confessed.

Georgie looked at Su and was clearly relieved when she took over. "If your hack algorithm is crap, the result is the same in both cases, you lose everything. But, if your hack is good and it's just bad luck that you set off one trigger, in the one-by-one case you lose every system after you get one wrong. Just to illustrate the point, say you have a 10% chance of screwing up. Then, with a bit of luck, you manage to protect about nine systems and then everything else is gone. If you simultaneously hack ten thousand systems, you would have protected nine thousand and lost the rest. If you focused entirely on your own systems, which I'm sure they would, that's a big difference."

"Yes, that's one of the points I wanted to make," Georgie smiled her thanks at Su, "and this is something that Jay's input should be able to determine. The thing is that, if they've cobbled together linked super and hyper quantum machines as required for the simultaneous hacks, either on their own or based on hints leaked from our side, they've certainly got the potential to up the ante in this cyber war."

Andy slapped his forehead. "Of course, if they have that capability, I know exactly what they'll do…"

"Hit the blockchain," Georgie completed the sentence for him.

"Damn right, it's what I'd do in their position. If they have access to any operational banks at all, even if they aren't in China, they immediately convert all their cyber assets into cash and / or tangibles. Then, directly afterwards, they wipe out the value of all crypto-currencies by flooding the market with Bits or Tokens or whatever produced by their quantum hypercomputer. They also have the ability to decrypt anything running through a blockchain, so that the financial collapse that I predicted happens faster and to a greater extent than would have otherwise been the case."

Georgie nodded. "Right, so, first task for me is to take input from Jay and use it to reconstruct the Chinese hack, determining what Q-power was needed to implement it."

"So how do we do run with this?" Lou asked.

"We've always stayed well away from cryptocurrencies, as the writing was on the wall as soon as powerful quantum machines began to be developed," Andy answered. "For our own purposes, we have encryption routines that are inherently un-crackable, based on the electronic equivalents of one-time pads, but I'm not sure that these can be scaled up for international commerce. In any case, I guess you're just going to have to contact Petra and ruin her day."

Lou inelegantly gulped down her glass of champagne. "Bollocks! Well, I suppose if we're going to share our misery with NDB, we're as well doing it as soon as possible."

Chapter 3 - Sharing misery

Mid-afternoon, the team re-assembled with a video link to Petra and Ursi in order to go over the preliminary results from China. The evidence was clear: the propagating front of system collapse left twenty-three banks and five insurance companies untouched, but none of these were major financial institutions on a national scale. A map of the locations of the surviving institutions plotted them all in a small region in the outskirts of Beijing, effectively showing the location of the cyber-war unit that had initiated the action.

"What is certain now is that this was a simultaneous hack, similar to ours, and thus with full knowledge of the autocatalytic kill function," Su pointed out. "The target must have been to protect thousands of systems within China, but this failed either due to an inefficient attack algorithm or lack of quantum power. We suspect the basic hack coding was effective, as indicated by the successes, but that coherence was lost during the 29th hack, triggering the propagation of the system killer. Seems like a case of over-confidence in the capabilities of their attack, so I guess heads will roll."

"Fucking right, they are useless cunts," Hyo-jin confirmed.

"There's something strange here," Lou frowned. "Why rush into this if they knew they still had a couple of days? Why not more fully test their system?"

"I suspect that this again points towards leaks from our side," Jay pointed out. "If they knew that we were getting close to implementing our hack, they'd be under pressure to jump the gun and get in before us. As we know, our hack poses greatest risks for systems spatially distant from us. Even if they knew that we aimed to protect systems globally, which their hack probably wasn't set up to do, the resulting economic disadvantage for China would be unacceptable. And, if not for Georgie's amazing jump start, even the failure that we've seen would have left China with 28 intact systems and all other countries with none. That would be a win of some kind."

"Jesus, I don't want to even think about that scenario," Petra sighed. "The bottom line, though, is that we need to beef up security and limit the number of people in the circuit. It'll be tricky, but from now on only Ursi and I will be involved from the NDB side and I'll even switch out the Bundesrat overview committee. It's probably the weakest link here, as such committees are inevitably key targets for foreign spies. We regularly find attempts to bug offices and meeting rooms, which are often traceable to partners like the US and UK who are fairly blatant about their activities in this field. The Chinese are probably also active, but tend to be much more subtle. Anyway, I'll initiate a major disinfection action in Bern to be on the safe side."

"Say you're correct, and the Chinese target cryptocurrencies," Ursi spoke up hesitantly, indicating that this was something that she was unsure about. "What can we do about it? These are now such a fundamental part of the global economy that their elimination would be devastating."

Andy sighed and rolled his eyes theatrically. "Cryptocurrencies have passed their sell-by date and that's a simple fact of life. They're going to go down the toilet one way or another but, if this is as part of a cyberwar attack, we come off really badly. If we were to pre-empt this attack, however, we can guide the collapse and minimise its impacts. Indeed, if we're clever about it, we could even benefit from such a collapse."

"How is that…?"

"There's no way…"

Petra and Ursi were talking over each other and then both abruptly stopped.

"I think our NDB colleagues can't follow your line here," Lou broke in. "I know this is a bit of a bugbear of yours, so I'm sure you've got some kind of cunning plan that you can outline for us."

"A cunning plan, that a good term for it," Andy smiled. "It starts with us raiding all cryptocurrency wallets and converting tokens into hard cash…"

"Are you joking?" Petra raised her voice in annoyance. "The total value held in these wallets is a good proportion of Global Domestic Product – in the order of tens of trillions of dollars!"

"Yes, that's why we don't want the Chinese to wipe this out, which they can't do if we've already stolen it."

"So, your cunning plan is to steal tens of trillions of dollars?" Petra was clearly shocked at the concept.

"Well, not on my own. Georgie and Su will do the heavy lifting."

"That's insane."

"Rapist cunt is off his fucking head," Hyo-jin agreed with Petra in her typically colourful manner.

"Yes, well, there is indeed madness in my method, which is why I think the Chinese won't think about it as long as this plan stays tight. We start off by using Georgie's hybrid machine to break into and remove the contents of every crypto-wallet."

"There are now many hundreds of millions of those since some countries started adopting crypto as national currencies," Ursi pointed out.

"Yes, but unlike the Lazarus Trojan, we don't need to do them all simultaneously. We start with the Chinese and all other big wallets where the losses will be kept secret. This includes any with the slightest hint of a link to organised crime. The stolen tokens are then placed in a series of accounts that we create in any banks around the world that are still functional, immediately being converted into local currency, dollars or euros. This is a lot of work, but can be readily handled by the supercomputer. Georgie, how long does it take to re-establish coherence in the hyper after it's been lost?"

"A couple of hours."

"And how many wallets could you decrypt in parallel?"

"Effectively this is the same work as the bank hacks and so, with the current setup, about 5 million or so."

"Excellent, so we move ahead in blocks of about 5 million, ripping about 60 million per day, and the job is done in a week or so. If we plan it properly, we'll have 90% plus of the total value of holdings in the first few blocks. Also, as news of this action spreads, the smaller holders will clear their wallets by themselves."

"Right, let me see if I can get my head round this," Petra sighed, clearly still not convinced. "You're going to steal all this crypto and then bank it as real money: tens of trillions of dollars of it. You'll have wealth beyond comprehension, but this has still been lost from the global economy. How does this help?"

"Well, of course, it depends what we do with it…"

"Stop being a tease, Andy," Lou sighed. "Let us know how this works."

"That's the easy bit, we just give it back to the original owners."

"Cunt is a really mad fucker," Hyo-jin nodded wisely to show that this answer clearly confirmed her original suspicions.

***

There was a shocked silence, then Petra coolly attempted to summarise Andy's proposal. "We kill cryptocurrency by stealing it all and converting it to hard currency. We then give it all back to the original owners so that, even if the crypto business then disappears as an option, the global impact will be negligible. Is that it?"

"Well, maybe not give it all back. We would deduct a handling fee, say one permil of the value.

That seems fair, as nobody should be silly enough to think that crypto is a good idea, A lot better than losing everything, which is what would happen if the Chinese scenario went ahead."

"One permil is still tens of billions of dollars!" Ursi pointed out.

"Yes, it's crazy, but not totally insane," her boss noted. "But how do you actually find out who you've stolen it from? I thought the entire point of such currency was to make this difficult."

"Yes, that's actually the clever bit. Can you see it now?"

"Come on, you smug bugger, stop pissing about and answer the lady's question," Lou commanded.

"Okay, anyone who has had their wallet raided will have to contact us and provide evidence of ownership of what has been stolen. By us, I mean the NDB of course. When the NDB authorises it, we arrange the fund transfer and the Swiss Government does what they want with the handling fee."

"Fucking mad as a mad fucker," the Korean muttered.

"That's very generous of you," Frau Zürcher looked unconvinced. "Why do you need NDB involvement at all?"

"That's because the clever NDB team managed to outwit the thieves and have taken charge of their ill-gotten gains."

"Ah, that's not daft," Lou acknowledged. "If the mysterious hackers actually had the funds that they had stolen, they'd be the number one target for all other black hats around the globe. This was something that I worried about."

"It's actually more serious than that. There will be huge amounts of the booty that won't be claimed. I suspect 10% or more, as this corresponds to black funds hidden away by criminals, terrorists, dictators, tax-averse billionaires, dodgy politicians and the like. They can't admit ownership, but will move heaven and earth to try to recover their money. We can set up a dummy account in the Swiss National Bank that can be the focus for anyone silly enough to try to get access."

"Mmm," Petra looked suspiciously at Andy. "You said a dummy account, didn't you," she waited for a confirmatory nod, "so where will the funds actually be?"

"Oh, we're going to keep them. Seems only fair, doesn't it?"

"So, NDB gets billions and you get trillions, is that how it works?"

"Remember we're doing all of the work. NDB is simply paid to provide a figurehead."

"We get trillions, do we?" Lou was evidently waiting for the punchline. "What on earth do we do with so much money?"

"We give it to charity," his grin widened. "There's going to be a lot of suffering caused by the disruption to date and even more to come. I'm sure there's a lot we could do with a few trillions, especially if it's focused on those who have suffered from the fundamental unfairness of current global wealth distribution."

"We're actually giving it all away?" Jay asked.

"Well, we take a one permil handling fee." Everyone smiled at this with the exceptions of

Petra, who was still frowning, and Hyo-jin, who continued pointing out what a mad bastard he was.

***

While the ladies assessed the practicalities of ripping-off cyber-currency on a global scale, Jay and Andy assessed results from the hacks on the two DPRK-owned properties. Although both villas had at least one room isolated within a Faraday cage, they were both set up as smart houses with services that could be controlled remotely. This provided an easy access point, from which all video and audio equipment present could be hacked into. In particular, top-end computer interfaces were widely distributed throughout the properties, allowing extensive coverage via the cameras and microphones designed to allow verbal and gesture commands to be used.

They had now a full list of both guests and staff in these properties and, especially due to TVs in bedrooms, a good overview of the relationships between them. Two of the Kim clan, identified as Dam-Bi and Gaeun despite the pseudonyms they entered the Schengen zone under, were in Zurich together with their staff, reflecting senior positions in the Government. The relationship between these two women was evidently very close and, especially after they had been drinking, they often ended up in bed together. Given the DPRK's opposition to homosexuality of any form, this indicated that the staff were picked to keep any such dalliances secret.

Su had passed on a summary of Hyo-jin's background and Jay had been particularly amused at the way in which, as a girl, she had used access to

134

pornography as a tool to gain status. This fit well with the record from the Kim ladies' boudoir, in which viewing hard core porn seemed to be the usual accompaniment to foreplay. There was a preference for lezdom dungeon action involving very large-breasted black women, with the occasional addition of enormously hung black men, always playing a humiliated sub role. This seemed to be simple voyeurism, with action between the Korean women restricted to what Su would term *vanilla lesbianism*, with a focus on energetic oral sex.

The four senior Government staff in this house were assistants to the Kims, young men who seemed to form two gay couples, although there seemed a lot of mixing when it came to sex. "Makes a lot of sense, if you want to ensure silence about your own homosexual activities," Jay noted.

All logged audio had been translated and assessed by Jay's expert system to determine degree of knowledge of the Lazarus Trojan. This was a common topic in conversations logged between the Kims and their assistants, so they were clearly well aware of the plot. Deep semantic analysis indicated that Dam-Bi and her senior advisor were directly tracking activities of financial markets, so were probably more directly involved than the others. In hundreds of hours of recoded audio, there were no indications that anyone else in that villa was aware of the threat.

Jay summarised the findings and concluded that there were six here to be included in the retribution hit list, but nothing to support actions against any of the others. "Well, Andy, you've been silent up till now. What do you think?" he finished.

Andy pondered for a bit before responding. "There seems no doubt that those six are complicit and should probably leave the villa in body bags. Even though we're not sure that other family and staff are involved in any way, they can't be seen to be benefiting from this attack. I think we'd be justified in confiscating everything we can find and extraditing them all back home to Korea with only the clothes on their backs."

"That's a bit severe. Even in the best case, that's exiling them to a country that's going to be a complete hellhole by the time the dust settles."

"Tough titties! We'll also have to include the other scions of the dynasty attending private schools in Switzerland. They also get the boot back home."

"You're a hard man," Jay sighed, "but I guess you're right. They've all been living well on wealth ripped off from North Korea, so they deserve to end up there. It'll be bad enough for staff, but I don't give much for the chances of family lasting long back home."

Andy shook his head. "Just think of the atrocities that this crowd has been responsible for over the last century. We really should be worrying more about the victims than those who benefited from this hereditary dictatorship."

"Okay, fair enough. The Geneva house is maybe a clearer case, but the links are probably best shown visually." Jay presented a map of relationships between the five senior directors from the Ministry of State Security residing there, together with their families in three cases and either concubines or prostitutes in the other two. Together with seven assistants, this group were intimately involved with the Lazarus group and regularly discussed different scenarios that could emerge after global financial meltdown. There was no indication of a trace of remorse when discussing decimation of the populations of hardest hit countries due to famine or breakdown of service infrastructure, or even as a result of military retaliation against North Korea. In contrast to Zurich, conversations between other staff indicated some awareness of the Trojan, even if not all aspects of its likely impacts.

"A total bunch of heartless bastards," Jay concluded. "I'd put them all onto the hit list, with the twelve at the top tortured to death in a really horrible way. Well, all the adults anyway: the kids could sort themselves out in the streets of Pyongyang."

"These buggers are the ringleaders, no doubt about it. I wouldn't be surprised if the Kims authorised the action, but these are the guys that carried it out. Is there any chance that we can find out a bit more about what they've got planned for surviving the chaos in Switzerland?"

"Ah, that's a bit trickier as I probably need to integrate the audio analysis with everything that we can extract from images and video."

"Do you have anything from the Faraday cage in the basement? If it was me, that's where this would be planned and documented."

"You're really paranoid, Andy," Jay laughed. "I doubt that others would be so worried about being overheard in their own property. Anyway, I didn't hack the cage because of the small risk of this being detected. They have a large computer inside it, but have screwed up security by powering it directly from the mains, so I can hack my way in via that."

"How long do you reckon that'll take?"

"Bandwidth is very limited, so I'll load a smart bot that'll search the memory and transfer out only material that's likely to be of interest. It's the option with the highest risk of being spotted, but video-feed indicates that there's nobody in the basement at present, so probably worth the risk. It'll be a trickle feed but, all being well, we should have most key output in about an hour."

***

While Jay was doing his thing, Andy looked further into opportunities for direct action against the Korean safe houses. The first question was what to do about the Zermatt chalet, as this did not seem to contain any of the key personnel currently present in Switzerland. Relatively isolated, but in a prime ski-in / ski-out location, it could be easily seized by the local Kantonspolizei as soon as evidence was provided that showed the purchase was illegal and part of a criminal money-laundering scheme. The question was: would this have a positive or negative impact? The former would result if the Koreans panicked due to this indication of a weakness in their plans, which could then lead to further errors that would help to bring them down. The latter, of course, resulted from an opposite response from these soulless creatures, causing them to go underground and, possibly, escape the dragnet closing around them.

Much though I'd like it to be the case, there's no way that these folk panic. They've the same cultural background as Hyo-jin, which includes a brutal ability to do anything at all required to survive any real or perceived threat. She's actually right, the only way to remove them as a risk is assassination. We can always try to minimise collateral damage, but there'll probably be family and staff caught in the firing line and I guess we just have to live with that.

***

Jay was looking grim when Andy met up with him to review the material hacked from the Geneva computer. He did not beat around the bushes. "We're in deep shit, mate. Those fucking Koreans know all about us."

Andy frowned. "Back up a bit. They can't possibly know about us. It's just impossible."

Jay presented the results of the hack, summarised in the form of a holographic 3D logic tree resulting from associated semantic analysis. "This isn't just a vague hint, it's a fact as you can see," logical linkages were highlighted in red. "There's layer upon layer of evidence. This also indicates how it was done: Hyo-jin!"

"She's in cahoots with these guys? That seems a bit unlikely, given that she's the one who's so insistent that we torture them all to death."

"Yes, but there's a file on her that traces her movements over the last two decades. They knew she was in Locarno and now they know she's here in Wettingen, although they seem to know little about who we are."

"How's that done? Surely, she doesn't report in to them, does she?"

"I haven't been able to extract details yet, but I'm certain that she's being tracked."

"I knew that would be a risk when I extracted her from the Russians, so I stripped her completely and even removed rings from her more intimate piercings."

"We all know about that, you rapist bastard, you," Jay smiled and slapped his colleague on the back. "So, it must be internal: a bioactive implant of some kind, I'd guess. Anyway, we need to have a chat with Hyo-jin and disable this ASAP."

"Definitely. But why have our opponents done nothing about her so far. Surely, she must be considered a threat?"

"Actually, it seems that the Koreans were happy with her to work for the Russians. They've been following her investments and planned to take over her assets during the chaos that would result from the financial meltdown. They assumed that the Russians would kill her but, if not, they're prepared to murder her themselves."

"I'm sure Hyo-jin will love that little bit of information," Andy smiled as he imagined the string of invective to be expected. "But surely it's not just Park that's got such a tracer?"

"No, it seems that all techies anywhere close to Lazarus have these implants. Of course, they're almost all in North Korea, with a few in China. The only other escapee seems to be a guy who managed to take his family with him to the States. He's now settled in Los Angeles, in Koreatown. Clearly a stooge maintaining a low profile, but set up as a fall-guy. They have concocted a lot of incriminating evidence of him playing a key role in the Trojan development, which would be leaked immediately after the attacks are completed. There will also be material to suggest that he was known to, and supported by, the CIA, which will create yet another shitstorm. It's actually quite clever, as it diverts attention away from any traces of culprits that might end up in Switzerland."

"Buggeration! Every time we seem to have a handle on this threat, a new wrinkle emerges. It's a complete can of worms! Do you think we could keep your hack in place, so we can follow how their plans develop?"

Jay quickly checked. "Well, my intrusion hasn't been spotted yet. I can ramp down the search engine I've inserted, which'll decrease the chances of it being picked up. But there's still a residual risk that they'll spot our hack and that might spook them."

"I've been repeatedly underestimating these guys. The entire operation is more sophisticated than simply hiding out and letting the virus do its work. They're still actively managing things and we're now in the firing line due to Hyo-jin's presence. We need to talk to her now and come up with a plan to either immediately divert their attention or go for pre-emptive retaliation: taking out all their Swiss operations."

***

141

Hyo-jin was unhappy about being pulled away from the cyber-cash heist, but was persuaded by Lou, who also came along. Both Hyo-jin and Lou were shocked by the material that had been hacked from Geneva, with the former cursing under her breath for most of Jay's presentation.

"So, first question," Jay finished. "How did you end up with a tracer implant?"

"Fucking, bastarding, cunting doctor at school," she shook with rage. "Before leaving the fucking school to start work with Lazarus, a doctor cunt says I've got a fucking growth in my shoulder. After fucking operation, all is fucking okay."

"That'd do it," Andy nodded.

"So now we need to get that tracer deactivated PDQ," Lou frowned. "We have EM bursters and I guess we could set up a lady-sized Faraday cage in the workshop. That should do it. Oh, as long as you don't have any medical implants, like a pacemaker or insulin pump. Do you?"

Hyo-jin shook her head, while continuing to curse under her breath.

"Hold on a minute," Jay mumbled, deep in thought. "Is this really the best way to go? Remember, this can act as a tripwire. As soon as we fry the tracer, the Koreans know that something's going on. This thing has run for years, why should it suddenly pack-in just as things are getting critical?"

"Good point," Andy nodded. "But the longer that thing is active, the more likely it is that Hyo-jin will be targeted here, so we could all get caught up in a murder attempt. And you can be sure that these fuckers will not for one second worry about collateral damage."

"Could we clone the tracer before we zap it?" Lou asked.

Both Jay and Andy nodded, but Hyo-jin broke in before either could say anything. "Easier if you just cut the fucker out. Get the cunt out; any fucking pain is okay for me."

"That's very brave of you, but we'd need a specialist surgeon to do that," Lou pointed out. "It can't just be a sealed electronic unit, like you might have had in a nipple ring. We'd have picked that up when Andy did a final check on you after you arrived." Hyo-jin looked confused, so Lou expanded. "There're multispectral scanners built into the frames of all doors into the building: it's a standard security precaution. This would pick up any normal bug. It thus has to be something much more subtle, probably bio-organic. Even if we could find it, there's a very good chance we'd kill it during extraction."

"Well, kill the fucker…"

"But this is exactly what we don't want to do, unless we can replace it by a dummy," Lou interrupted to remind her of the key issue involved.

"I think we need to get Georgie and Su in for a bit," Andy said, thoughtfully. "The tracer can't be continuously active, as there's too much of a risk of being spotted. It must sit passively until interrogated and then simply respond with a short ping. If the interrogation was piggy-backed on a GPS, mobile phone network or something else ubiquitous, all that's needed are detectors sensitive enough to allow the ping to be triangulated."

"So how do we clone that?" Jay wondered.

"Not a Scooby," Andy smiled. "But that's why we work with mega-smart cookies like Su and Georgie…"

"You think I am fucking stupid, rapist cunt?"

"No, that's not what Andy meant," Lou put an arm around Hyo-jin and squeezed the angry woman against her ample bosom. "The guys know that they're not as bright as us women, but are too dumb to be able to understand just how mega-smart we are. They just guess."

The small Korean seemed mollified or, at least, diverted by the hard nipple that was poking her cheek. "Just get this fucking thing out of my body. Cut off my whole bastarding arm, I don't give a shit."

Andy could understand her fear. She was already marked for death and, when it was realised that the operating system killer had been defeated, this was likely to be ordered sooner rather than later. *But our risk is almost as high. These lunatics would happily obliterate this entire building if they thought it'd ensure that Hyo-jin was dead. Must remember to ask Jay to put determining their inventory of weapons onto the search list for his hacking tool.*

***

Jay again summarised the situation when Su and Georgie joined the group. To everyone's evident surprise, Georgie simply nodded and grinned. "Okay, I can do that. When do you want it done?"

"Well, ideally as soon as possible," Andy replied hesitantly. "How long will it take?"

Georgie frowned and paused for an instant. "Well, the main time needed will be for assembling the kit: say an hour or so. The hack will be quick and I can then produce the clone. As long as it would work for you, I could load it onto an old smartphone that I have lying about in the workshop. Would that be okay?"

"Unbelievable!" Jay was shaking his head in amazement. "I wasn't sure that this would even be possible, never mind doable in your workshop in such a short time."

"Why so surprised?" Georgie looked confused. "It's actually a piece of piss. You know, of course, that the supercomputer is electromagnetic in essence, not optical like the hyper machine?" Seeing that this did not seem to be answering Jay's question, he continued. "The matrix of qubits in the supercomputer are held within an organic crystal and coherence is established by superconducting nanotubules. Interrogation is then done using squids and I've got loads of spares kicking about the workshop."

"Ah, superconducting quantum interference devices," Su expanded for the benefit of anyone who hadn't picked this up. "So, that's how you intend to analyse Hyo-jin's implant."

"Of course. We put her in a little Faraday cage to prevent the resulting location ping getting out, thus ensuring that our work doesn't tip-off the bad guys."

"I think I get it now," Su frowned in concentration. "You expose the implant to a series of radio signals and monitor responses using a squid. Then it's just a decryption problem, varying the input until the desired output is produced."

"Classic black-box neural network, especially easy as all we need to do is produce an algorithm that will produce the specified ping from the identified interrogation. I already have a routine that does this automatically, so I only need to load it onto the phone and ensure that the signal is also appropriately weak, but that's easy-peasy."

"You're a bloody wonder," Lou leaned over to kiss a bemused Georgie, who was evidently unsure what all the fuss was about.

"Righty-ho, so that's apparently the easy bit sorted out. I guess you ladies can go off back to Georgie's domain and make this all happen. Jay and I will sort out the logistics of handling the cloned tracer when you have it."

"What nefarious plan do you have in mind?" Lou looked at Andy suspiciously.

"Well, our gardener, Lizbet, has a son who was twenty-one recently, hasn't she?"

"Yes, Jason, he's the one who calls you Uncle Andy," Su responded with a smile.

"Cheeky young bugger! Anyway, I was thinking of treating him to a trip to Iceland."

"Iceland?" Lou frowned.

"Yes, great combination of one of the few countries that was hardly hit at all by system failure and so remote that mobile phone coverage is non-existent in many places. I'll send him off business class, all expenses paid with a credit chip and a pile of hard currency. He'll be off like a rat up a drainpipe."

"Isn't that a bit dangerous for him?" Lou still looked worried.

"I can't see how. It'll take a while until the Koreans spot that the tracer is on the move and they'll take more time getting set up for someone to follow it. Even if they get near, the spatial resolution on such a tracer is poor – probably good only to get positions down to within tens of metres. As they think it's still within Hyo-jin, that's who they'll be looking for, not a Swiss youth."

"It could work, but I know young Jason is completely caught up in his love-life at present. An interesting triangle involving a brother and sister," Lou smiled, her eyes sparkling at the thought.

"I don't even want to know how you come by such information," Andy rolled his eyes, "but it shouldn't cause a problem. He can take both of them with him."

"Well, if I was him, I'd go in a flash," Lou seemed satisfied. "Okay, girls, let's get our asses in gear and do the real work while the boys play at being travel agents."

Andy watched them leave, wondering if this was really going to work and, even if it did, what new surprises the Koreans could come up with.

***

Within two hours, the tracer was cloned, Hyo-jin's implant was fried and Jason had picked up the phone and his instructions, ready to fly to Reykjavík with his lovers early the next morning. Andy's story

147

had motivated him: a joke on Georgie focused on a phone that she had recently lost. Jason's specified goal was to hide the phone at Snaefellsjokull, the entrance of the route to the centre of the earth in Jules Verne's novel. Georgie loved puzzles and would have to work out this location based on cryptic clues during a holiday next month. Jason clearly thought that Andy had more money than sense, but was happy to indulge him and promised to send a photo of the phone's final resting place.

After this eventful day, the exhausted group were sitting around the dining table just about to start an early dinner when Jay's expert system automatically switched on a wall-screen monitor to display the breaking news. A stealth attack by China had destroyed all North Korea's nuclear weapon delivery systems just before war was formally declared on the rogue nation. Evidence was provided on the source of the cyber-attack and a list of names published, which were claimed to include all of those involved in the creation and distribution of the virus. The Chinese demanded that all of these be handed over to them for *appropriate punishment*, which was certainly a death sentence. If this demand was not met, they threatened to reduce the entire country to ashes, with use of weapons of mass destruction implied, even if not explicitly stated.

"Jesus, what else can possibly happen today," Andy groaned. "I can't say that I'm surprised, but I just didn't think the Chinese would react so quickly or hit so hard."

Hyo-jin was unperturbed by this attack on her homeland. "Fucking Chinks' banking systems were hit hard, so they must fuck-over fucking People's Republic."

"Well, we just need to see how the buggers in Geneva respond," Jay frowned.

"I now wish we could have moved the tracker away earlier," Lou looked worried. "Do you think they might try to eliminate Hyo-jin now?"

"Well, they now know that they're at the top of China's hit list," Andy called up a display of the details distributed by the Chinese. "I see Hyo-jin also appears, but quite far down, in with the other techies. The question is whether they choose to keep their heads down until the dust settles a bit or if Hyo-jin is considered an important loose end that risks exposing their link to Switzerland. She'd then be targeted for immediate elimination."

"They'd need to be very careful about that," Su pointed out. "If Hyo-jin was killed and her body identified, they'd actually create the exposure of a Swiss that they want to avoid."

"That's true," Jay acknowledged, "Hyo-jin needs to vanish without trace or her body needs to be destroyed beyond recognition."

"Easy as fuck, back home," Hyo-jin observed, "but hard as fuck here."

"Eloquently put," Andy smiled, "but we have to err on the side of caution. What do you think, Jay? Could we provide a distraction that would focus their minds elsewhere?"

"I'm into the smart-house controller in Geneva, so I could produce a power surge that'd black them out and probably cause some fires. However, we'd then lose our hack into their shielded computer."

"I think it's worth the risk," Lou turned to look at Jay. "You said earlier that your hack was running slow to avoid the risk of detection. How about if you boot it up to full speed and then fry the computer with the resulting power surge?"

"Mmm, let's think about how this could work. There's surge protection on all power supplies, but this's electronic, so I can bypass it. The computers have additional protection, but I can bypass that also if I abandon all subtlety in the hack. Yes, it's all doable."

"Okay, get that done ASAP," Lou decided. "I think we can hold dinner for a bit. Personally, I feel the need of a drink. Anyone else for a pre-prandial Fino?"

Jay and Andy each grabbed a glass en route to their workstations, while the rest of the group settled down to sip sherry and watch the antics of the news analysts struggling to interpret the developments of the day.

***

While Jay handled the Geneva villa, Andy checked on the status of the Zurich hack, skimming over a summary of developments provided by the semantic analysis tool. The Kim ladies were now in bed together but, instead of the usual porn, were following the situation in their homeland via reports on a cable TV channel. The Chinese threat had resulted in a military coup and searches were underway for all those listed as responsible for the cyber-attack. Top of the list was the Supreme

Leader himself, who had already been arrested along with many members of his extended family. Of course, with the notable exception of those in Switzerland, who seemed to have vanished without trace. The ladies toasted this news with Champagne and giggled together while speculating what the Chinese were likely to do with their relatives. At first, Andy was shocked by this callous behaviour, but then remembered the Machiavellian power struggles within the Kim dynasty and the numerous assassinations of siblings and other close relatives associated with these. *This kind of behaviour makes it easy to justify us carrying out retribution of any sort against this family of psychopaths.*

Andy then joined Jay, who had completed his attack on the Geneva villa. This had resulted in chaos due to a fire in the basement. As the entire automatic extinguishing system was also knocked offline and the villa blacked out, staff were struggling under torchlight to quench the burning equipment with pans of water from the kitchen while a garden hose was being set up.

"You've done a great job there," Andy grinned, "there's no way that that crowd are going to be thinking about organising assassinations in the near future."

"Indeed," Jay nodded. "Even the big bosses are running about with buckets of water, as they clearly want to avoid bringing the fire brigade in. They can't avoid smoke being noticed though, so they'll have police at their doorstep soon."

"Is there anything from the full-force hack before the power surge?"

"It's being processed now. I think I set off an alarm, but I'm not sure that it'll have been noticed in all the subsequent confusion."

"Any chance of the hack being traced back to us?"

"I doubt it but, in any case, they'll need to sort out all the damage that I've done to their computers before they can even start with a trace."

"That gives us a window, but I still feel vulnerable, even with Park's tracker soon on its way to Iceland," Andy frowned. "I think we need to eliminate them immediately, which is going to be my priority for tomorrow."

"Okay, let's get some dinner now. By the time we've finished, I may have more from the analysed hack to help you on that."

"I'm happy to take any help I can get. These bastards are not only ruthless, but very clever. I'm sure our attack this evening will have stirred up a real hornets' nest and we need to be sure that we get them before they get us."

***

Despite a normal prohibition of television during meals, the team were unable to turn away from the evolving crises around the globe. There had been attempts to play down the impacts of the collapse of financial systems in Europe, but this was impossible in many countries where there was no alternative to e-money and hence all commerce ground to a halt. When it further emerged that records of bank accounts, pensions and holdings of stocks and shares, had disappeared, civil unrest was inevitable. This, particularly in urban areas, led to rioting on a

152

scale beyond anything that had been previously experienced. The Chinese announcement that the financial collapse was a cyber-attack and their declaration of war against North Korea added fuel to the flames. One country after another collapsed into total anarchy, when even declaration of martial law failed to calm the wrath of their confused and frightened citizenry. The feeling of betrayal by politicians, financial institutions and even the military and intelligence services was widespread, regardless of their nation's state of development.

"It really has the feeling of a world's end scenario," Lou sighed as she passed around the bottle of fine cognac serving as a digestif. "Hard to imagine what it would be like without Georgie's legerdemain this morning."

"Even as it is, things'll get worse before they get better," Andy added. "If the Chinese actually wipe out the cryptocurrencies, it'll be the final straw and socioeconomic collapse will spread even further, maybe even to the countries that we've managed to protect best."

"So, does this mean that we go ahead with your pre-emptive attack on token wallets?" Lou asked.

"I don't think we have an option. I've been thinking through this; we desperately need some good news to break this spiral of bad following bad. If we – or, actually, Petra and the NDB – can come up with a win against hackers, this'll contribute a lot. It'll be even better if we emphasise that the bad guys with vast hoards of crypto are being screwed, but the little guys are getting their cash back. Of course, mainly we want to pre-empt the Chinks, but this spin-off will be invaluable."

"So, there's a soft side to you after all, mister tough guy," Georgie giggled in a way that seemed out of place with his current persona.

"Yes, well, showing some wins also leads on to our opponents in Geneva. I had great plans to take them out using the hacks that we've established, but I was forgetting the bigger picture. The best option is to leak their locations along with a few juicy snippets to prove the identities of the key players. We use an untraceable link to transmit this the Chinese Embassy in Bern and let them do the heavy lifting."

"The NDB will be seriously pissed off," Lou pointed out.

"Yes, they'll have to rap us over the knuckles, but they'll see that we're avoiding a diplomatic incident that could get very messy." Andy shrugged his shoulders. "Think about it. If we formally notify the NDB where the Koreans are, they'll have to move and arrest them. After that, China will demand that they're handed over, which Switzerland can't do because they're facing certain death sentences. It's so much easier if China can simply announce that the missing culprits have been captured and are now en route to Beijing. That's also good news for the masses, as they want all those responsible to suffer and an end to nuclear threats in the Far East. A definite win-win situation."

"That's clear enough for Geneva, but what about Zurich?"

Andy looked into Lou's eyes while he considered the options available. "China must have assets in Switzerland to carry out the raid on Geneva and we want them to focus on this, as they're the greatest threat to us. We set this up and, after it works out, leak also details of the Kims in Zurich. Because of their high political profile, the Kims might be assigned priority if we leaked both together. This case also risks tipping off the Geneva crew, which we really don't want to do."

Hyo-jin nodded. "Rapist fucker's idea is not completely crap. Chinks will fucking torture those cunts." She smiled while rubbing the arm with the now defunct tracer, indicating that this was considered justice for what they had intended to do to her.

Lou squirmed in her seat. "That's exactly what is bothering me. There will be collateral damage and I don't think the Chinese will care who suffers and how much before all those involved die. It's death in any case for anyone on their announced list."

"Given the global misery caused by their actions, I've no sympathy," Su announced. "I vote we do as Andy suggests."

Looking at the nodding heads, Andy and Jay rose and headed for their workstations.

"Don't worry lads, this is something that you've been forced into," Lou called after them.

Andy grinned. *I may burn in hell for this, but I'm really going to enjoy totally fucking-up these evil bastards.*

***

Andy headed off to bed early, leaving the others to further analyse the actions of the day and their global impacts. He had already nodded off, sleeping on his side, when a slim form slipped in beside him and spooned against his back. George, he reminded himself, still half asleep but gradually responding to the small hand that was squeezing his balls. He slowly twisted onto his back and brought his arm around the thin naked body pressed against his side. A hiss of pain reminded Andy that his partner, as Georgie, had spent the previous night in Su's dungeon and so was clearly still somewhat tender.

While he hovered on the edge of sleep, Andy thought through his relationship with this distinctly odd person. Born a girl and with no interest in physically changing her body, Georgie's individual characters were a constant source of confusion for him. The gender-fluidity bit wasn't a problem as such. Boy, girl, neither, both; whatever he-she-it-them wanted to be was fine with him. Even when combined with associated sexual proclivities – homo-hetero-bi-asexual – there was nothing that he couldn't handle, even though his head spun every morning when he tried to work out who he was waking up beside. But when you added kinks and fetishes on top of this, covering the entire spectrum of BDSM and weird role-play, Andy really struggled. He could manage what Su called vanilla BDSM, but lesbian Georgie's craving for harder flogging, electro-stimulation, breath play and suchlike took him far outside his comfort zone.

He still struggled to understand how Lou, the most caring and friendly of all the team, took so well to a dominatrix role. He had seen how she tightened nipple clamps to the point that her subs were screaming in agony and then, with a well-placed touch, turned this into a screaming orgasm. *Probably empathy was the key here: understanding exactly what was needed to fill the sub's hidden desires, whether pain, immobilisation, humiliation or whatever. A Domme who is cruel to be kind: a weird idea.*

Andy gradually became aware that the body in his arms was sliding down lower and then his growing erection was being licked before taken into a warm mouth. *Oh, well, no point in overthinking things. Best just to go with the flow.*

Part 4: The female of the species...

Chapter 1 - Crypto clear-out

Next morning, Su had already fit in a training session and Lou a swim before they breakfasted together with Hyo-jin. Shortly afterwards, they were joined by Jay and his lad of the night. Dolf, a seriously ripped, young, black man, was clad in only a minute, translucent posing pouch. Lou was almost salivating at the sight, taking every opportunity to touch him or show off the erect nipples that were well displayed by the diaphanous shift she was wearing. To her disappointment, he was clearly immune to her charms and thus probably straight gay. Or, possibly, completely shagged-out after his night with Jay.

Dolf was shooed off after breakfast and the others assembled shortly after in the meeting room to review overnight developments. Andy and their quantum guru, today asexual G, brought breakfast coffee and croissants with them. As often when asex, G was wearing a long black robe and a matching fez, with no makeup or visible rings.

Jay kicked things off with the status of their major concern: the Koreans in Geneva. After being tipped off, the Chinese had moved rapidly, hitting the villa in the early hours of the morning. The attack was preceded by a directed EMP that blacked-out the premises. Unfortunately, learning from the power surge that had previously been used against them, all locks defaulted to *closed* and thus a shaped charge was required to gain entrance to the building. Jay's system had automatically reset and regained contact to the few monitors in the building which were nuclear-hard, allowing an impression of the firefight therein to be obtained.

The key ringleaders retreated to the basement as soon as they were woken by the attack, locking themselves in this safe-room and leaving their staff to face the incursion. Although the defence was led by a security team, everyone else in the house was well-armed and fought bravely against the intruding forces. Nevertheless, they were outnumbered and out-gunned, so the outcome was inevitable. The door to the basement would have presented a serious challenge to the attackers, but Jay's leak had pointed out that the ceiling was only normal reinforced concrete, allowing it to be quickly penetrated by another shaped charge.

Immediately after access was provided, a gas canister was dropped in, which quickly rendered five of the occupants unconscious, although the sixth had time to take the easy way out by shooting himself in the head.

Thereafter clean-up was rapid. All bodies, whether dead or unconscious, were loaded into vans which departed at speed. There was no attempt to clean up blood within the premises but, to delay detection of the massacre, the main door had been replaced during the incursion and this was locked before the Chinese hit squad left.

"Well, I think we can say that went down well." Jay was clearly pleased with the results of his actions.

"How many dead?" Lou enquired, looking much less happy.

"Eighteen Koreans and six Chinese, with another two Chinks seriously wounded. However, from the video of the fight, I think that there were no innocent bystanders here. Even the cleaning ladies were armed with Uzis and didn't hesitate to use them."

"Mmm, okay, I'll give you that. What's the situation now with the captives?"

"Captives and bodies were driven to a small airfield and flown out in a private jet belonging to the Embassy. I guess they're well on the way to Beijing now."

"And what's our next move?"

"We can now leak the info on the Kim ladies and get the Chinese back into action. I'm not sure if they'd do anything during daylight, but that villa is quite private and surrounded by a lot of land, which made its price truly eye-watering. At a push it might be possible, but the logistics may be tricky. They used just about every free resource that they had for the Geneva attack, which was only seven hours ago."

"Fair enough," Lou sighed, "set that in motion and we can only hope that it won't turn into such a bloodbath."

"I suspect that the Chinese will really want to have the Kim ladies alive," Andy contributed, "so a gentler approach might be adopted. Anyway, Jay and I will work over the contents of our leak to see if we can suggest an option in that direction."

"Okay, now what about preparation for the crypto-heist. Where are we on that, G?"

"Going very well, we've taken over fifteen trillion so far and I think we can actually stop earlier than planned. There are reports of these thefts emerging in the dark-net, so we can expect a rush to escape into normal currency or tangibles, especially since there's a moratorium on trading stocks and shares because so many of the exchanges are down."

Lou looked shocked. "Did we actually agree to initiate this action?"

"I think there was a consensus," Su intervened, "but it was necessary in any case to prevent the Chinese pre-empting us. I've been using Jay's knowledge mining tool and it's clear that their plan wasn't quite like Andy anticipated. Instead of cashing out their own crypto wallets and then destroying these currencies, they've already used their quantum hypercomputer to raid other wallets, with a focus, unsurprisingly, on North Korea and Taiwan. Cashing-out crypto has started, but is greatly limited by the damage that their banking infrastructure has suffered."

"They'd already completed these raids, plus a few on targets in Singapore and Japan, before we then cleaned out their wallets," G continued. "As we can raid very much faster than Beijing, this competition will have minimal impact on our plans."

"I think the message here is that we need to get Petra moving ASAP," Andy suggested. "She should issue an announcement that a Swiss counter-terrorist team have traced the gang of hackers and confiscated their funds, turning them into hard currency to reduce their vulnerability, but will now organise refunding this money to the original owners. This will certainly do a lot to restore public confidence."

"Wait a minute," Lou interrupted, "won't this let the Chinese claim their money back?"

"We would, of course, openly refund the contents of any wallets to bona fide owners. But their own piracy has made this very difficult for the Chinese. Time stamps will show a large inflow of funds matching those ripped off from other countries. So how can they claim anything without making it clear they're also in the cyber-crime business? Taiwan and the others will certainly make claims and we can reimburse these from currency taken from the Chinese wallets. The Chinese will know that Bern has information that would incriminate them and destroy the legitimacy of their de-facto annexation of North Korea. However, if the Swiss say nothing, there's no reason for Beijing to rock the boat. Certainly not when things are as volatile as they are now."

"Great, G, once again you've done a brilliant job." Lou gave the quantum wizard a matronly pat on the head. "So, after this good news, let's have a look to see how most of the globe is in the process of going to hell in a handcart." She then presented an edited overview of news articles, organised by geographical region. "As our base, Switzerland has come out relatively unscathed so far. The situation can only improve when we start to get Brownie points from reimbursing stolen crypto. I'm pretty certain Petra will be guaranteed a good promotion, and could even be in the running for a Nobel Peace Prize," she grinned while Andy rolled his eyes. "We can but hope for something like that, as it'll help keep us out of the spotlight."

"Next, the EU. Again, in good shape due to our hints to the President of the ECB. There are national variations, but the inertia of this trading bloc will certainly allow them to work some way through the short-term troubles. Other non-EU Europe was hit harder, especially the countries with strong links to Russia. Russia, together with the CIS, was vulnerable due to their unstable power structure, with a few oligarchs controlling a significant fraction of total GDP. Individually, they appear to be keeping their heads above water, but they had vast holdings of crypto from dodgy sources, which will have vanished by now and be hard for them to recover. Some kind of internal coup seems inevitable, but this could very easily lead to civil war."

"We managed to shield North America quite well. The USA and Canada anyway, even if it doesn't look so good for Mexico. South America is a zoo. Many regimes there were unstable due to widespread corruption and are now falling apart. The big cities are especially bad. Places like Sao Paulo are war zones, where any hope of maintaining order has been given up and the centre abandoned to the pillaging mob." Video images emphasised how bad the situation had become.

"Of course, other countries are much better off. Australia and New Zealand are so rich in natural resources that any financial system collapses are more annoyances than the catastrophes they were elsewhere."

"They're also pretty laid back," Su interjected. "It'll be weeks before some of the Ozzy beach bums that I know will even notice that anything has happened."

"I'm sure that also holds for my sports-mad Kiwi acquaintances," Lou smiled in agreement. "Anyway, culture certainly plays a big role and will limit impacts in many island states, whether in the Med, the Atlantic or the Pacific. Even Japan, which has a devastated finance sector, has been very quiet. Rather than rioting, there people tend to help each other get by and wait for the politicians to get everything sorted out. I guess a history of major natural disasters helped develop this mindset."

"Now China. During the Chinese period of miracle growth this century, the power of the military was eclipsed by that of extreme wealth, in the kind of parody of capitalism that we already saw in Russia. With the loss of much of that wealth, coupled to the huge loss of face resulting from an attack being made by a basket case like North Korea, the consensus is that a change of regime is inevitable. If the crypto-raids had come off, maybe that could have been postponed, even if not prevented. But, now, I just don't know. I guess collapse of the current regime will happen very quickly, with the result of this depending if it happens by the current leaders falling on their swords to allow fast transition to a new ruling committee, by a military coup, or by a civil uprising. Whatever the case, its superpower status is now well gone. They may have annexed North Korea, but whether they can hold onto it is another question."

"Fucking ace," Hyo-jin mumbled, smiling as she regarded the chaos in China with distinct schadenfreude.

"So, Far East outside China... Again, it varies a lot from country to country, with culture and natural resources probably influencing the consequences more than the extent to which their financial sectors were damaged. So far, serious problems in the Indian sub-continent are concentrated in the mega-cities, but this is being played down by both India and Pakistan, who're engaged in their usual sabre-rattling."

"Then there's Africa," Lou sighed. "Some of the better parts of North Africa are similar to the worst parts of Europe, but the most of the rest has gone down the toilet completely. A few remote farming communities may be okay, but the rest may well be apocalyptic. Due to overpopulation, corruption, tensions between different racial and religious groups, pollution and environmental degradation, this was an inverted pyramid that only international efforts could keep balanced. Populations will be decimated and, although again concentrated in the big cities, almost everyone will suffer to some extent."

Andy spoke softly to break the horrified silence, noting that even Hyo-jin was a bit deflated by this brutal write-off of an entire continent. "It may sound callous, but a lot of these developments were going to happen anyway. Lou's inverted pyramid analogy is spot on. This kind of apocalypse was inevitable for the *business-as-usual* mindset that guided the planet, despite evidence that hitting a tipping point of some kind was inevitable."

"Yes, well, unlike most of the great and the good, we've actually done something to help rather than just lining our own pockets. We're now Robin Hood hackers, stealing from the rich and giving to the poor," Jay grinned as he saw how his words helped break the depressing mood.

"I'd almost forgotten, we're going to have a couple of trillion to fund good works," Lou theatrically slapped her forehead.

"A couple of trillion minus one permil," Andy reminded her.

"Whatever. So, how's this going to work?"

"Not a clue. I just dreamt up the concept, Su and G made it happen and so I think you should be the one to work out how all this dosh would be best used."

"That's a huge job, I don't think I could do it on my own."

"Funny you should say that, I had an idea here," Andy wore his most annoying smile.

"Stop being so bloody annoying, just spit it out!"

"What about Beat and Heidi?"

166

"Don't be so bloody..." Lou hesitated and frowned. "It initially sounded daft, but now I'm not so sure."

"Yes, we don't want them drawn into anything that could be risky, so they can't know anything about what we've been up to. But, say we had a contract to develop a programme to optimise use of Swiss international aid..."

"Um, so this is a scenario that appears to be covering how the Swiss Government manages lots of cash to be used for supporting those most impacted by the cyber-attack. That fits well with the narrative of the NDB being the key player in confiscating hacked funds. The Happy Hookers already know we are Government contractors, so have no reason to expect that it's us who actually have the cash here."

"Why would they, where could we possibly get megabucks from?"

"You're not as daft as you look, lad." Andy was squeezed against a pair of enormous tits and made very aware that there was only the finest of fabrics between him and them.

"Yes, well I'll be happier when we also have the Kims out of our hair. There's a line from a song that keeps going through my mind, *the female of the species is more deadly than the male.*"

"That's because you work with us," Lou pointed out. "Big muscles were good when dinosaurs ruled the earth, but now it's brains that count, so women dominate."

"But G is the smartest of us all?" Andy objected.

"Just proves the point, the bit of woman in that wonderful mix is enough to blow you simple guys out of the water. It's the way of the future!"

"How did I ever think I would win an argument against a woman – or anyone not uniquely male?" Andy quickly covered his bases.

"Because you're a guy," Su responded instantly, causing laughs around the table and even a trace of a smile from Hyo-jin.

"Okay," Lou stood to close the meeting, "you all know what you have to do and I have a vague inkling of how I need to move forward. I don't know about you lot, but I'm just about pissing myself when I think about the situation that we're in. This is the stuff that Governments should be doing, superpowers even, but we're just a wee team of hackers. Bollocks! The positive side is that I'm well primed for wild sex, if anyone's in the mood."

Andy smiled. Nobody but Lou could turn this job from hell into an opening for kinky sex. Then he saw the open interest from Su and Hyo-jin, with even Jay looking a bit interested. *Fuck, am I the only member of the team not scared into impotence by this apocalyptic scenario? They all seem completely turned on – with the exception of G, of course. Which begs the question: are they all fucked in the head or is it just me? And G, naturally, who is certainly fucked in the head in so many ways.*

Chapter 2 - Baiting Petra

The team met again for a brief update before dinner. Lou had a contented, cat-that-got-the-cream grin, a sure indicator that she had been well shagged, almost certainly more than once. Looking around the table it was hard to eliminate anyone as a possible participant. Even G looked less tense than usual. As his asexual phase often included uncommitted exhibitionism or voyeurism, it wasn't impossible.

Lou opened things up as usual, but immediately threw a curve ball. "I know this was planned to be an internal meeting, but NDB would like to link closer to us, so I propose that we bring in Petra and Ursi. Anyone with any problems about this?"

Andy rolled his eyes while everyone else agreed to this proposal. "Okay, it might be petty for me to object, but do we really need Petra in on this?"

Lou frowned in his direction. "You have problems with Petra?"

"Well, not problems as such. But we're doing all the heavy lifting here, so why should we…"

"Petra's proposal is that she attaches Ursi to work directly within our team…" Lou broke in.

"Oh, that's all? Fine, get them in then." At first, Andy relaxed. Then, observing her sly grin, he wondered if he had, as in so many cases in the past, been suckered by Lou somehow or other.

The NDB participants were linked in and immediately Petra went into attack mode. "We appreciate all you've done Lou, but we didn't authorise initiation of the crypto-heist."

Andy wanted to burst in, but Lou placed her hand over his mouth. "There wasn't time for consultation. As soon as the Chinese initiated their raid on Taiwan, we had to react immediately."

"But you didn't even attempt to contact me!"

"Why would I do that? There's nothing that you could have done except to nod your head. In that case, if things had gone tits-up, you're left holding the can. There was no alternative to what we did, but we gave you plausible deniability in case it turned into a shitstorm. It all went well, as you know, and NDB are now the flavour of the month as far as the Bundesrat are concerned. Why are you trying to give us a hard time?"

Petra initiated her response with a death stare. "We haven't had time to prepare for this. There are literally trillions of dollars dropping into accounts that we now seem to control. But we don't have either the plans for what to do with this cash or the staff to implement any plan that we do develop."

Lou responded with her dominatrix look of contempt, which had caused many a sub to wet themselves, whether they wanted to or not. "You realise, of course, that you're bitching about having to manage a huge budget in a world where most countries, large organisations and individuals have been rendered bankrupt. Are we supposed to feel sorry for you?"

Andy struggled to hide a grin. In his wildest fantasies, he had never considered anyone facing up to his ex-girlfriend in this manner.

Petra was struggling to contain her rage. "What-the-fuck-ever, I need to be kept up to date on all this shit. So, I'm going to second Ursi to work with you."

Once again Lou covered Andy's mouth, holding the collar of his shirt to stop him bouncing to his feet. "This is, of course, under our conditions. She works for us, within our organisational system, that's non-negotiable. She reports back to you, of course: there can't be any negotiation on that either. The key thing is that she must recognise and accept the way that we work. It's very Swiss, based on team consensus. Ursi comes into the team, so she has one vote on a decision. You have no over-riding say – or, in plain text, no veto – on any action we agree to undertake.

Petra looked like she was going to explode, but hauled herself under control. "I could sell some of this to my bosses, but I need to have some kind of say in decisions. These have global consequences, for fuck's sake."

"Let's make this clear, so there is no misunderstanding," Lou showed an uncompromising side that nobody on the team had seen before. "We have the lead here and have already prevented the world's entire financial infrastructure going down the drain. We've also blocked a currency heist on a global scale and passed most of the booty to you. You've absolutely no say in what we do, not any, fuck-all! We need you, of course, but that's just as long as you do what we tell you to. Is that clear to you?"

"Now, Lou, there are issues here that need to be handled at a national level."

"If that was the case, why weren't you handling them?" Lou shook her head in annoyance.

"Well, we were – at least preparing..."

"Fuck off, Petra! You were all caught with your pants down. We've run this entire op and the most that you've done is provide support."

"Well, I wouldn't quite..."

"Shut the fuck up, for God's sake!" Lou was now sounding seriously pissed off. "We'll continue to support you, because that's best for everyone. You focus on local, but we do regional, continental, global. You're out of your depth here, so just send us your girl and we'll integrate her completely into our activities. But don't even think about pretending that you have any control on the way that we operate."

Petra was clearly shocked to the core, struggling to find a response.

"Oh, I forgot to mention that Andy thinks that you're a shoo-in for a Nobel peace prize. If that happens, I assume that there'll be a case or two of Champagne heading our way."

Petra was unable to find a response to that, but Ursi was able to sign off on her behalf. "This sounds great, see you guys in a couple of hours."

***

When the link to NDB was dropped, Lou sank back in her seat with an exhausted sigh. "Do you think that'll do it?"

"What?" Andy had finally escaped from Lou's grasp. "That's the most stunning bit of Petra-fucking that I've ever seen! I want to father your babies, dozens of them, just because you're so fucking fantastic."

"A bit of hyperbole there, chum," G pointed out, just before the rest of the team confirmed Andy's impression.

"Hold on!" Lou shouted to cut her way through the babel. "First of all, we do need NDB, even if Petra can be a total pain in the arse at times. Secondly, Ursi would be really useful, as she complements Su's expertise in the hacking area…" she stopped to listen and try to translate Hyo-jin's string of invective.

"Right, of course, we also have Hyo-jin, but someone with direct links into NDB would certainly be useful. Of course, it also helps that she's a nice-looking woman, so I guess it would be more convenient if she moves in with us for a bit. She could bunk in the guest room next to me."

"Good, God," Andy shook his head, "we haven't yet started working with the woman and you're already planning to get her knickers off. Shouldn't you be focusing on setting up a work programme for her?"

"Us ladies can multi-task," Lou replied smugly. "I can plan seduction at the same time that Su and I organise a work station for her. I wonder if there's any chance of her sister coming over sometime, as a threesome with twins has always been a fantasy of mine."

"And if they were into a bit of bondage, I'd be in for that," Su contributed, clearly to wind Andy up. "What do you think, Hyo-jin?"

"I had good fuck with twins in fucking school," she nodded with a smile.

"And there's something about those formal suits that they wear," Lou licked her lips. "I bet they have stockings and minute thongs underneath."

"Well, I bet that they go commando, no knickers at all." Su raised her eyebrows. "We just need an opportunity to find out."

"Okay, ladies, you can discuss your erotic fantasies while Jay and I get some work done."

"What's the rush," Jay smiled, "I'm just waiting to see if buggering features in any of these fantasies. The girls looked to have very fine, tight bums. Almost boyish, I'd say."

Andy headed off to the sound of giggles and suggestions of how anal sex with the twins would best be organised.

Chapter 3 - The slippery Kims

During the Geneva raid, the Chinese had seized all hard drives from the computers in the basement, so a priority for Jay and Andy was to search through the files that they had hacked to check if there was likely to be anything that could possibly lead them to Hyo-jin, one of the few on their hit list who had not yet been captured. It was clear that their number one priority was getting a hold of the Kims and their assistants, but Park would be targeted eventually, along with the other escapee that the North Koreans knew was in Florida.

After an hour of work, it was clear that the files that had been ripped out by the final brute force hack contained nothing on this topic, but there certainly would be something on the hard drives if the Chinese searched them in detail. Jay thus initiated the very sensitive job of breaking through the Chinese Embassy firewalls, which was a much greater challenge than the North Korean villas.

Andy searched through the hacked files for any other material of interest and was surprised to find video logs from monitors secreted in the Zurich villa. These hadn't been picked up during Jay's initial hack and included coverage of a basement computer setup, within a Faraday cage as for Geneva, and also the main rooms in the house, including bedrooms and bathrooms. As the basement had not been covered in Jay's hack of the Zurich property, Andy ran a search to pick up trends and anomalies for the entire time period covered.

Apart from routine servicing activities by juniors, the basement computers were used exclusively by the Kims and their assistants. The highest-ranking anomaly was when one of the assistants sprinted into the room and yanked out the computer power supply. Andy checked the time display. This had occurred only minutes after the power surge Jay had caused in Geneva. The action itself would have been picked up by Jay's tool, even if the man had not been buck-naked. *Strange. Did someone in Geneva immediately warn the Kims? They all seemed a bit busy at the time, trying to extinguish the fire. It could be an autonomous warning system, but, in that case, how was the source of the Geneva fire identified so quickly? There's something important I'm missing.*

Andy switched over the video search engine to the material they had hacked directly from the Zurich villa. He started a semantic search through all video feeds at the time of the Geneva power surge, so the anomaly detector immediately came up with a flashing light in the bedroom in which the Kims were sleeping together. Ignoring their nudity, each ran to the room where her own assistants slept and shouted instructions to their underlings while they struggled awake and then, in turn, raced off without pausing to dress. *Clearly one of these guys pulled the plug in the basement and I'm sure that the others will be checking the house security. The thing is their reaction time: how the hell did these women manage to respond so incredibly efficiently?*

Andy went back to the record of the alarm waking the women and added translated audio. Now it was clear that the flashing light was accompanied by a computer-generated analysis that was playing though the video system. Unlike the video porn that the ladies had previously viewed, the alarm was not being picked up by Jay's hack, but Andy guessed that a view of the Geneva basement was being shown. The Kims clearly had software equivalent to the image analyser that Andy was using and this AI was smart enough not only to notice the anomaly and decide that it justified the alarm, but also propose a response to protect their own computer. *Seems to be as good as anything we have, but maybe not surprising due to their links to the Lazarus group. With the Geneva crowd having bugs in Zurich bedrooms and bogs, looks like this is spying rather than simple video surveillance. I wonder if that's also the case with the video analysers that the Kims have in place.*

"Bollocks!" Andy saw Jay start at this exclamation. "I think we have a problem that you need to look at," he said while he ran the Zurich video searches through to the time of the Chinese raid in Geneva. "Fuck!"

"What the hell's up? I thought you were just going through the old material from Geneva. Have they found out about our role here?"

"Not as bad as that, but the Kim women had the Geneva villa bugged with an AI image analyser set to spot anomalies."

"Shit, so they know about the Chinese raid…"

"I'm just going through the video now. Come over here and have a look." Andy moved to the side, allowing Jay to slide a chair in beside him.

Hacked video from eight different cameras was presented on the huge monitor screen that curved 180° around them. Translated audio from the bedroom used by the Kims was also playing. The alarm first warned of the attack in progress and then identified the invaders as Chinese. A response involving dispersal of all villa occupants was also recommended. Within fifteen minutes the staff were assembled in the main lounge, all dressed in outdoor clothes and each carrying a rucksack, which must have been prepared in advance for such an evacuation. Dam-bi was in charge and issued orders, reminding them that they were to drive in groups of four to different stations and abandon the cars in the nearest car park. They would then each board a different train and make their way to the hotels already booked for them. They each had a fake EU passport or ID and enough cash to keep them in comfort for a couple of months. She emphasised that they were to make no attempt to contact anyone and respond to no attempted contact unless it came directly from her on the secure smart phones that they had each been issued with.

After the general staff left, the assistants set about scrubbing the computer systems, removing hard drives and then reducing them to slag in an industrial oven. When they left, in addition to the ubiquitous backpacks, the assistants each carried two large suitcases and the Kims' smaller bags, which would fit as cabin luggage. "Apart from some computing kit, I guess they're loaded up with cash and valuables such as gems," Jay suggested.

"I bet you're right. Anyway, I'm off to G's lair to see if Ursi has arrived yet. This's now something that we can use NDB input on."

Ursi was, indeed, huddled with the other women in front of a holographic display showing progress with gutting crypto-wallets around the world, results colour-coded onto a slowly-spinning virtual globe. G was first to spot Andy's entrance, as the others were clearly transfixed by the value of the total amount already converted into cash that was spread around hundreds of thousands of accounts in hundreds of banks. The digits of the grand total, expressed as euros, blurred as they counted up, being readable only for numbers above millions. *Reminds me of the US national debt clock, but with the number increasing more rapidly.*

"Hi Andy," G smiled. "I think we're getting to the point of diminishing returns here, as now more than 50% of the wallets we crack have already been emptied."

"Oh, hi Andy," Ursi now spotted him. "I'm not quite sure why Georgie... sorry, G... wants to stop as there must be hundreds of millions still out there."

"Probably tens of billions, but that's just a rounding error on the trillions we already have. But I can keep going if you want, there doesn't seem to be anything else requiring hyper-speed computation at present," G shrugged. "Anyway, what can we do you for?"

"Hi, Ursi. It's actually you I'm looking for, as we need some help upstairs. However, now you mention it, there's probably something that the others can work on instead of salivating over Tera-bucks. If G can provide the decryption needed, do you think you could hack the Chinese Embassy in Bern and grab all in- and out-going communication, making sure that the intrusion isn't noticed?"

"Mmm, I don't see there being any great problem there," Su responded. "It'll take a couple of hours to get the required code together as we certainly don't want anything traceable back to us, so I suppose G can keep stealing until then. Or do you need to reconfigure the hyper-computer."

"Nope, crypto-wallets and decryption for communication hacks are fundamentally the same and that's what I'm set up for now."

"Okay then, G and ladies, have fun while I take Ursi from you."

"And just what are you going to do with her?" Lou licked her lips salaciously, aware that Ursi was turned away from her.

"The Kims have scarpered and I need NDB resources to find them again."

Lou smiled smugly. "I told you so. It's clear that the NDB complements us in some areas."

"Okay, you win," Andy acknowledged as he led Ursi through the door.

"And I bet tanga," Lou shouted after him.

"No, definitely commando," Su contributed.

Andy rapidly closed the door before comments got more suggestive and he ended up having to try and explain them to this pretty young woman.

***

Andy overviewed the situation, showing key video clips from inside the Zurich villa to make his points clear. Ursi quickly picked up on the sophistication of the hacks and associated AIs that both NetSec and the Kims were using. She interrupted with a number of technical questions relating to these, which were answered by Jay.

It was only after Andy had finished that Ursi realised one aspect of the presentation that was notable by its absence. "Wait a minute, you did all of this off your own bat, without even informing Petra?"

"Well, we did let her know about the Korean safe houses," Andy reminded her.

"But NDB were never in the loop as far as the leaks to the Chinese were concerned, were we?"

"This gives you plausible deniability, as we've pointed out before. This was the cleanest way to handle the Koreans from a Swiss perspective."

"A pitched gun battle in the middle of Geneva?"

"This was a battle between a Chinese embassy security team and criminal Koreans, occurring at night and inside a house. No risk at all to Swiss special police groups or of any harm coming to innocent bystanders."

"Petra will be spitting blood," she grinned to defuse this statement. "Anyway, what do you need me for?"

Jay was standing behind the young agent, silently mouthing *anal sex*, causing Andy to glare at him. This was misinterpreted by Ursi. "Am I in some kind or trouble?"

"Not at all," he reassured her while trying to ignore Jay who was now mouthing *not yet*. "It's just that we screwed up a bit with the Kims and need your help to locate them, together with all the other occupants of that villa."

"The Kims I can understand, but why worry about the others? They're not on the Chinese list, are they?"

"They're not on the list, but they'll certainly be chased by the Chinese when they find out that their targets have bolted. If found, they'll be tortured for any information that they may have on the whereabouts of the Kims. I greatly doubt that they'll have anything of value, but that won't stop the Chinks."

"Why do you say that? The last clip that you showed had the sister mentioning secure phones that could be used for contact to be established in the future. Wouldn't these be useful?"

Andy scratched his head, while Jay replayed the video. "I know what she says, but I'm slowly building a feeling for what the Kim ladies are really like. They're completely ruthless and would throw any of their staff under a bus if it'd help them in even the smallest way. I think the staff are chaff: intended to be pursued and even caught, just to divert attention away from the escape route taken by the Kims."

"So, if this is the case, what's our interest in them?"

"For a start, I just don't like people being tortured, especially when nothing will be gained from it. Additionally, the rapid apprehension of these folk could worry the Kims, which has got to be a good thing. We've previously totally underestimated how clever this pair are and I'm now fairly sure that they're actually the ones responsible for the Lazarus hack. It's quite possible that the Geneva guys thought that they were running things, but I suspect we'll find that the Kims were the puppeteers who were holding their strings."

"Well, what exactly would you like me to do?"

"NDB will have records of every Korean who has flown into Switzerland and, through Interpol, can add this to records of all entries to the EU. I guess you can probably focus on entries over the last few years. You then combine this with feed from every CCTV or accessible webcam in Switzerland to find out where everyone went after leaving the villa. I suspect most will have left Switzerland by now, but your partners in our neighbouring lands can follow the trail of video breadcrumbs until you locate them. It'll be easy to create a reason to arrest them. Even a hint of links to the crypto heists would suffice. They should then be taken to somewhere very secure, so maybe the Interpol headquarters in Lyon."

"That seems easily doable, but I imagine Interpol will want more on how we managed to identify these individuals."

"That's the nice thing about the crypto bust, it's so high profile that sensitivity about giving too much information out before all the culprits are caught would be understandable. The NDB has gained so much kudos over the last couple of days that you'll be able to wrap even Interpol around your little finger."

"Well, let's see how that plays out. But you seem to be excluding the Kims and their closest cronies from this search. Why's that?"

"It's far too sensitive. If they're captured, the Chinese will move heaven and earth to get them, regardless if the means are legal or not. Depending on where they're arrested, extradition might not be an option and so, as we previously discussed for the Swiss case, it's better if we keep this under our own control."

"Ah, I think I see where this is going," Ursi frowned in concentration. "I let NDB and Interpol loose on the underlings, but you want me, personally, to chase the Kims."

"Got it in one! I'm sure you're going to fit in well to the team here. You nail down where the Kims are and we'll work out what to do then."

"Right, your ladies have given me an office with a work station, so I'll get started on it immediately. I'll be back as soon as I've got anything for you."

After she left, Andy glared at Jay. "You can be a right tit at times!"

"Confess, man, you're panting to get into her tight little arse."

"Well, it's actually you that's the self-confessed bum-bandit."

"That's true," Jay grinned. "We can share the fun, so you take the front and I'll handle the back."

"Don't you think she should have a say in this matter?"

"Think of seducing her as your good deed for the day, saving the poor lass from Su's nipple clamps

184

and then being tied up and licked to within an inch of her life by that pack of sex-crazed lesbians."

"Well, I'll let the girl make up her own mind about that."

"So does that mean you're go for setting up the double penetration option if that's her choice?"

"Jesus Christ, you're just about as bad as Lou! Can't you just get on with your work?"

"Don't worry, gay guys are like girls, we can also multi-task. It's just sad gits like you who can't dream about shagging while doing their job."

"I give up," Andy shook his head, sadly. "Just try and have a think about how we could seize all the booty that they carry about with them while you're dreaming of buggering our new colleague."

"Why ripping them off? Wouldn't we be as well just chucking them to the Chinks as we did before?"

"I have no idea what goodies the women have, but I'd rather that we had them than allowing the Chinese to get their hands on anything of unknown value. Also, I really don't like these evil bitches and want them to suffer. Relieving them of their financial parachute would be a good start. I also suspect that this loss might turn them on each other, which would be amusing to watch. After that the Chinese can have them."

"All righty! Let's see what I can do to support your nefarious plan."

And I need to ensure that it can't possibly backfire on us. It's easy to think of them as a couple of women on the run, but they're actually mass murderers who'll happily kill anyone who gets in their way.

185

Ursi was back in just under an hour, surprising the men while they were going through some of the recorded pillow talk between the Kims. "Great, I work my arse off to catch the Koreans and you guys just watch porn!"

"Ursi, perfect timing, could you come over and have a look at this."

"I think I'll pass. Unlike you two, I'm really not into girl-on-girl action."

Andy tried not to react to Jay's wink and pelvic thrusts in response to this statement. "This is showing the two Kims in bed together. The translation of their chat is completely anodyne, but I think there's something important that we're missing."

Ursi was now fascinated and moved forward to get a good view of the action. The women were naked, lying together on top of the bedcovers while they casually masturbated each other. The porn movie that they were watching was also displayed on a side screen. It was hard-core lezdom kinbaku featuring two huge black dommes and four, skinny, blond subs. Although always difficult to tell, the subs appeared to really suffer from the tight ropes and other abuse that they were being forced to endure.

"What do you think is strange here, apart from the fact of two rich, late-middle-aged Koreans being into such perverse stuff?"

"I'm sure that there's something important that I'm missing," Andy confessed. "Actually, from my experience of living with my weird partners, the kinky sex is the only part of the Kim's profile that seems genuine."

Ursi gave Andy a strange look, which made him wish that he hadn't added this last point. She then bent forward to look at the women while the machine translation ran. Suddenly she smiled. "Is the translation free or set to Korean?"

"Korean, I think, what else would they be speaking?" Jay replied.

"Shit, you're right," Andy startled the young blonde by giving her a hug. "They're speaking two languages, aren't they? It's the disconnect between the translation and the way in which their mouths move as they're speaking. That's what's been bothering me."

Jay's fingers flew over the keyboard. "I'll just leave the Korean translation on audio and add any other translated words in subtitles".

The video clip played again and text started to scroll past: *clitoris... vagina... rectum... labia...* "The women are simply noting which part of their partner's genitals that they're touching, changing in response to what is being done to the blondes in the video," Ursi observed. "That's quite weird."

"And what language is that?" Andy asked.

Jay checked a side monitor. "Greek, it seems. Modern Greek"

"Now that's beyond weird!" Andy sat back and closed his eyes, trying to make some sense of what the women could possibly be up to.

"Actually, that's not weird at all and helps to sort out one remaining uncertainty that I had."

"Wow, you've taken the wind out of one of Andy's attacks of lateral thinking. I'm sure he'd have come up with something, but I want to hear it from you." Jay was smiling from ear to ear, ignoring yet another glare from his colleague.

"The Kims travelled in a stretched limo to the Belp airfield, just by Bern. Here they met four other women from the DPRK Embassy and three pairs of women set off in three different private jets. In each case, these were specified as diplomatic flights and destinations were simply logged as *within Schengen*. We've already been able to determine that the planes appear to have landed in Corfu, Eire and northern Finland. We'd have been able to sort out which was which eventually, but I am willing to bet there'll be some kind of switcheroo after they land that'll complicate things. It really is amazing that something like this can be carried out even when half the countries in the EU are on the edge of breakdown."

"But Corfu! Why the fuck would Koreans on the run go there? If you wanted to go somewhere remote with just a touch of civilisation, Ireland would work. If remoteness without civilisation, then Finland. I don't even know what's in Corfu, except possibly hordes of Brit and German package holiday tourists."

"Calm down, Andy. Just think about what you're saying." Jay gave him a patronising tap on the head.

Andy stared into space for a moment, then smiled. "Thanks Jay – and Ursi – you've cracked it! It's the defining feature of these women, they plan ahead for all eventualities and always do the unexpected if there are choices to be made. The fact that I can't imagine why the hell they'd go to Corfu is an indicator that it's exactly the kind of place that they'd head for. But now I know where they are, we need to get our arses in gear before arrests of their sacrificial underlings begin to get reported. Ursi, did the girls talk you into staying here overnight?"

"Well, I'm thinking over the option…"

"Great, get anything that you might need for a work trip couriered over here, as we'll be leaving early tomorrow."

"What? Going where?"

"Corfu, of course! You're the one who spotted this link and I might need NDB support when we get there."

"Am I coming too?" asked Jay hopefully.

"Nope. You've got to use the resources here to find out where the Kims are. I've no idea how big the island is, but when you've got a location, you can then set up digs for me and the team as close by as possible."

"What team?" Ursi and Jay said simultaneously, then grinned idiotically at each other.

"The team of me, the illustrious leader; Ursi, the smart kid with the NDB contacts; Su…"

"Not Su, for God's sake," Jay spluttered. "She's the most in-house of the lot of us. She does not, will not, do any field work. She just won't."

"Let me finish… and Hyo-jin. Su's the only one that can control that nutter, so she's got to be in."

"Hyo-jin, are you serious? That woman hates you like poison. She'd cut off her left tit before she'd help you with anything."

"Hence Su! Su can get her to come with us and, when it's clear that our main goal is fucking-up the Kims, I'm sure that we can count on her full support."

"Do we really need her?" Ursi looked confused.

In his usual annoying manner, Andy stretched his arms above his head before replying. "What I've learned over the last few days is that Hyo-jin is inherently more like our targets than anyone I've previously encountered. The differences in their backgrounds couldn't be more extreme. They're mega-rich and well-connected while she's dirt-poor brought up in a government institution. But they share incredible intelligence coupled to a ruthlessness that must be close to clinical psychopathy."

"So, do we definitely need a woman that you've just classified as a psychopath?" Ursi was struggling with the concept."

"Of course, I don't know for certain now," Andy confessed, "but better to have her when you don't need her, than not have her if she turns out to be critical."

"So, you're going to tell Su about this?" Jay introduced the key question.

"Of course not, I'm not that stupid. I'll talk Lou into doing it."

Jay grinned. "Well, that might work. You know, you're not as daft as you used to be!"

"Fuck off, Jay. Just get me the info on a location in Corfu."

"You know that I can multi-task, don't you?" This clearly a rhetorical question as he mimed bum-grabbing behind Ursi's back.

"Whatever, just play nicely you guys." Andy refused to rise to the bait while he focused on how he was going to get Lou to help him out.

Chapter 4 - Close-by in Corfu

Andy was somewhat surprised to find that direct commercial flights from Zurich to Corfu were still operating despite the disruptions of the past couple of days. He guessed that the majority of passengers were being repatriated. Going out would be Greek workers returning home, particularly from Germany, and the way back would be filled with Swiss holidaymakers caught out by developments. Nevertheless, when they boarded the Edelweiss plane the next day, the hostesses did not seem at all surprised to find Swiss flying out. *Maybe a long-awaited holiday takes priority over global chaos for some of those who haven't been directly impacted.*

The small business-class section contained only two passengers in addition to the NetSec team, so they were spoiled by quickly-served drinks and a snack during the short flight. Andy and Ursi sat together, with Su and Hyo-jin in the seats behind them. Although Su had been very unhappy about the thought of being involved in one of Andy's operations, she was slightly mollified when she saw that the villa that had been rented was directly on the beach and that the bedroom that she would share with the Korean looked directly over the Ionian Sea. Hyo-jin was violently against the idea of the trip, due both to being in close proximity to the *rapist cunt* and also her inevitable exposure during travel. The latter was a significant concern, given that the Chinese had identified her as one of their missing targets and had placed a large bounty on her head.

NDB had organised a Swiss passport for her which should be enough to fox most automated tracking systems, but recognition, especially by another Korean, could never be precluded. Nevertheless, the one thing that finally convinced her to come was the thought of being able to trap the Kims and, eventually, hand them over to the Chinese.

After the snack was cleared away, Andy and Ursi talked over the details of the coming action, while the other pair drowned their sorrows with Champagne. Although a private flight could have easily been justified, Jay pointed out that a commercial arrival would be much less likely to trip any warnings that the Kims might have in place. After collecting their checked-in baggage, the team would pick up a cheap hire car and drive north to Almyros beach, near the small tourist town of Acharavi. Although the distance from the airport was only about 20 km as the crow flies, it would take about an hour to drive the winding road through the mountains. Villa Athanasia was selected for their stay because of its close proximity to the Kims' hideout: identified as the Almyros Beach Hotel and Spa. This had been traced via a complex series of shell companies, but it was finally clear that the hotel was owned by the Kims and had been for several years. From this starting point, Jay's AI discovered a previously unspotted network of interlinked properties scattered around Europe. As soon as the action in Corfu was completed, this list would be released to Interpol by NDB, allowing them to be seized as partial compensation for impacts of the Lazarus attack.

Ursi had worked with Jay to identify the Korean safe house, with Jay left behind to attempt to hack into it. This was proving to be very tricky, as the hotel used mains power only to back up solar and this was disconnected just before the Kims flew out of Switzerland, providing more circumstantial evidence that this was their destination.

The only open link to the hotel was through a reception webpage, allowing available rooms to be booked. This showed that the few free rooms had been filled with long-term stays a little after mains power was disconnected. While they were looking through these records, Ursi spoke up – evidently raising an issue that had been bothering her for some time. "The hotel there is now effectively locked down, so how on earth are we going to even confirm that the Kims are actually there? There's hardly a CCTV along the entire north coast."

"That only makes things trickier, not impossible. CCTVs may be few and far between, but webcams, dashboard cams, reversing cams and the like are ubiquitous. All we need to do is hack everything north of the airport and we'll eventually confirm their presence."

"Good God, that's a huge job! You might only need one hack to get into CCTVs, but every individual webcam needs to be hacked separately. That's just not... Oh, I see now, the hypercomputer!"

"Yes, of course. I've taken Lou and Georgie off the Chinese Embassy and they're now setting up the webcam hack. It's just another indication that conventional cyber-security is dead, killed by cutting-edge quantum computing."

"Right, I kind of see how that would work. But there'll be a truly gigantic volume of video to be analysed."

"Even for Jay's best search engines, it'll take a while. But it's completely doable, especially as the time window is quite narrow and the semantic analyser can eliminate most of the cameras as being of no interest to us. Anyway, I'm certain that the Kims are in that hotel, so we can focus our efforts on hacking into it."

"I'm not sure how that's possible."

"Well, I have an idea or two, but it'll be useful to have a look at the local setting before trying to work out details."

"Lou had previously said that you tend to keep your cards close to your chest, and I'm beginning to see what she means."

"That's just a polite way of saying that he likes to be an annoying bastard," Su contributed from the seat behind, where she had evidently been following the conversation. "However, he's not totally useless and seems particularly good with problems that initially look completely impossible."

Andy grinned ruefully. *Good to know, as that's a good description of the problem that we're currently facing.*

***

Villa Athanasia had three rather small bedrooms and a tiny kitchen / living room, but a huge terrace which boasted a good-sized swimming pool, a large, covered dining table and a huge barbeque. Clearly it was planned for living outside rather than indoors. A raised area on the beach side of the terrace presented a stunning view over the Ionian Sea, looking towards the hazy mountains of Albania. Being only a few metres above sea level, the wall facing the sea was substantial and a gate to the beach more like a bulkhead door. Nevertheless, it was unlikely that this building would survive for more than a decade or so given current global warming rates.

As agreed, Su and Hyo-jin took the bedroom facing the beach and immediately set to unpacking their luggage. Ursi and Andy each dropped a case in one of the other bedrooms and went directly onto the terrace, picking up beers from the well-stocked fridge en-route. As he had been designated driver, Andy had avoided alcohol during their flight and downed half the bottle of beer in his first long swallow. "Ah," he sighed, gratefully, "that's not bad at all." He peered at the label. "It's a local Corfu beer called Ionian Pilsner and definitely very tasty." He settled down on a cabin chair by a shaded circular table.

Ursi joined him and then poured half of her bottle into a small glass and took a sip. "Yes, it's really nice. I can see us drinking a lot of this, as it's pretty hot here."

"Seems to be about 30 and looks to be much the same for the coming fortnight. But there's a storm front that'll hit tomorrow, so it could get quite blustery then."

"It's certainly too hot for the clothes I've been travelling in. I think I'll pop in and change into a bikini."

"Dead right, but rehydration is my number one priority." Andy casually stripped off his shoes, socks, trousers and shirt, casually throwing them to the ground before slumping back into his chair with a happy sigh.

"Well, of course that's the other option, but I definitely can't match those lurid Pink Panther boxers of yours," Ursi smiled. Then, in a slow fashion that was clearly intended to tease, began to unbutton her blouse. After slowly peeling it off, the blouse was carefully folded before being placed on a nearby chair. For a moment it looked like she was going to remove the sheer, white bra that supported her large breasts. "Maybe that's a bit premature," she grinned provocatively before moving down to slowly unzip and then step out of her skirt. She was, as Lou predicted, wearing stockings. These were the self-supporting kind, which she then slowly rolled down and removed after stepping out of the black pumps that she had been wearing.

Lou was right again, a small white tanga, although Andy had found himself hoping that Su had been correct this time. "Don't stop for me," he said, hopefully. "I think we can consider this terrace *swimsuit optional*."

"Well, I think I'll opt to stop here," she grinned annoyingly.

Andy finished his beer and rose to fetch another. *Could she be teasing me to get revenge for my reluctance to get drawn on my plan? There seems to be an interesting dynamic building up here, which I just need to ensure doesn't interfere with our work.*

***

Andy took his clothes with him and went into his room to chuck them onto the bed. *Ursi's right, these boxers are hellish. Typical birthday present from Lou. Probably meant more as a joke, without expecting me to actually wear them.* He quickly stripped them off and threw them on top of his other clothes, rummaging through his case until he found a small posing pouch. *Now is this better, or do I just look sad? Or gay? Fuck it, who cares?*

When he returned to the terrace with a fresh beer, Ursi was swimming in the pool. *Unfortunately, still in her underwear.* Su and Hyo-jin were now also on the upper patio, lying naked on sun loungers.

As always, Su's tattoos and piercings drew his eye, leading him to openly admire her trim body. "Well, ladies, can I interest either of you in a beer?"

Su was well aware of his attention and slowly opened her legs far enough for him to see the glint of a gold ring. "Beer? I don't think so. But a glass of Champagne would be good, soon as you like."

Andy grinned. "So, this's me demoted to pool boy?"

"Demoted? You should consider the opportunity to serve me as a promotion. Let's face it, there's not much that men are of use for. Now get your arse in gear before I decide to give it a good tanning."

"Yes, mistress, sure thing," Andy recognised that Su was hamming up for Hyo-jin's sake and it certainly seemed to work as the normally taciturn

Korean was smiling, something rarely seen. "Hoy, rapist cunt, me too for Champagne!"

"As you wish, love. And how about you, Ursi?" He saw she was now emerging from the pool. "Any commands I should add to my list?" Andy thought that she was looking at him strangely, then saw she was being diverted by the sight of Su's tattooed body.

"No, I'm okay with the beer," she mumbled while she blatantly stared at Su, who was now moving to ensure that the blonde had a good view of her assorted genital jewellery.

Jesus, don't tell me that Lou was also right about her sexual proclivities. I head off with three women and end up wanking on my own while they have a Sapphic orgy in the next bedroom.

Andy served the naked sunbathers their fizz, trying hard to ignore the hardware being shown off. He had to peer a bit, but this did include what he now knew were Princess Albertina piercings. As he turned to head back to his seat in the shade, Su slapped him hard on the bum, almost causing him to drop his beer. "Shit, Su that's..." he started, then ground to a halt when faced by the laughing woman. Just when he became aware of how little cover the minimal pouch gave his growing erection, Su grabbed the side string and pulled the garment to his knees.

His tug-of-war with Su while he tried to regain some dignity was quickly abandoned when she grabbed his testicles and squeezed hard. He grunted in pain, but conceded defeat and let her pull the tanga completely down and stepped free of the garment. *Two of them are already naked and...* just at that point he noticed that Ursi's wet underwear was completely transparent ...*and the other might just as well be, so what am I bothered about?*

Just before he settled into his seat, he noticed that Ursi's attention was now focused on his completely erect penis. *Mmm, maybe she's not a committed rug-muncher after all.*

***

Ursi joined Andy in the shade about five minutes later, taking a mouthful of her beer and grimacing.

"Doesn't take long to warm up here, does it?" Andy topped her up from his condensation-frosted bottle.

The blonde leaned forward to look him in the eye. "Just what is all this *rapist cunt* stuff about? Surely you didn't rape Hyo-jin?"

"Well, if you're being technical about it, she may have a point." Andy stopped when Ursi looked like she was going to hit him. "Anyway, the main point was to save her life and reduce the risk of blowbacks to us. Rather ineffectually as it eventually turned out." He then recounted the story of Park's kidnapping, not holding back on any of the details.

Ursi was visibly shocked. "You executed... no, murdered... three men during the kidnap of Hyo-jin."

"It was the kind thing to do, as they would have been tortured to death in a most horrible way because of losing their Golden Goose."

"But you can't be sure of that."

200

"I can be sure that they tried to kill me when I tried only to overhear what was going on in the house. These Russian fuckwits live and die by madcap over-reaction to every threat against them. And one of the things that they punish in the harshest way is failure, especially when it leads to a huge financial loss. They have torturers who can skin a man – or woman – and keep them alive during the entire process. Have you any comprehension what the pain involved must be like? In the old days, there was at least some relief when the pain receptors in the brain overloaded or the victim lapsed into unconsciousness. With use of smart drugs, this doesn't happen. So, it's like the worst pain of a dentist drilling into a nerve, continuously, for hour after hour."

"Okay, shit, I'll take your word for it." Ursi grimaced and took a deep breath. "And Hyo-jin, you were forced to sexually violate her?"

"You can play with legal definitions that'd define my actions as sexual violation, but it was nothing of the kind. For there to be something sexual about it would require that I was getting perverse enjoyment from extracting a ring from a piss-soaked orifice..."

"There're some that certainly would..."

"I know that, I work with them." This admission set Ursi back on her heels. "But I was aiming to capture a known criminal while risking being blown to shit by her bratva minders. For this to work, I had to ensure that she wasn't wearing a tracer, so I stripped her and removed every piece of body jewellery. I thought that I'd done a good job, but her surgical implant fooled me. If I'd known about that, I'd maybe have cut off her arm."

"Christ on a bike, Andy! I thought that NDB exposed you to the hard side of life, but this is an entirely different ballgame."

Andy leaned forward and held her shoulders. "This is important for you to realise. NDB generally deal with normal criminals: spies, hackers and the like. They're usually a world away from the very bad end of organised crime, which can get close to the levels of the war-criminals who end up in The Hague. These are lunatic psychopaths, for whom gut-wrenching atrocities are all in a day's work. The Kims are actually a step further up the ladder of evil. There's no lunacy here to be considered as a mitigating factor: they're coldly calculating every move and will initiate genocide knowing fully what's involved, but not giving a damn."

"And you think we can go up against them?"

"Someone needs to. I'll just continue to do what I think is needed. Whether it's removing rings from Hyo-jin's naughty bits or assassinating some rather dim hitmen. This is because we're amongst the few who're capable of doing it."

"When you put it like that, are you really sure there isn't there anyone else who could do this job?"

Andy looked surprised at the question and thought for a moment before answering. "If you here include this entire team, then no, there's nobody else that I can think of. At least at the present moment, I should add."

"That's what I thought. I don't know whether to be thrilled or scared shitless."

Andy grinned. "Go for scared shitless, because that'll make two of us."

***

By seven pm local time, discussion had turned to dinner. Andy proposed a walk along the beach towards Acharavi, which would take them past the Kims' hotel. This would lead up onto a road that would allow them to circumnavigate it, before walking back past the other side of their villa and ending up in Taverna George. Casual dress would suffice for this, so all were clad in shorts, t-shirts and sandals. Although the beach was a hard-going mix of sand and small pebbles, the total distance involved was only about a kilometre.

The view into the hotel was limited, both from the beach and from the road that ran around the other three sides of the property. Nevertheless, as shown on satellite images, it was possible to make out the main buildings, which sat back from the beach and were separated from it by lawns, a swimming pool and a large bar cum restaurant. Walls and fences around it looked predominantly decorative, but Andy spotted a range of miniature cameras and motion detectors that would make undetected intrusion tricky.

When they arrived at the Taverna, it was already busy. Nevertheless, the owner, who cheerfully greeted them on their arrival, was able to squeeze them onto a table at the edge of the main outdoor dining area. Although there were a few Greeks, who seemed to be well-known to the staff, most of the guests were German- or English-speaking, predominantly late-middle-aged couples with a scattering of young families. The menu was extensive, with a number of local specialities. After some discussion, the team opted for a mixed Meze platter followed by fish-of-the-day, accompanied by the most expensive white wine available. This was local and suitably crisp and dry, while being extremely cheap by Swiss standards.

Andy paid the meal cash, although he noted that direct chip transfers also seemed to be operating here. A large sign declared that crypto payments were no longer accepted, although it was unlikely that anyone had anything left in a virtual wallet by now.

Back in the villa, only a couple of minutes' walk away, the team moved to the seats on the upper patio and settled to watch the sun slowly sink towards the horizon. Due to reflections off the sea, as sunset approached this became too bright to look at directly.

Andy was once again designated as pool-boy and sent to fetch glasses and a bottle of Metaxa from the house while the women stripped off to take full advantage of a cool breeze. By the time he returned, having shed his clothes in his bedroom, Su and Hyo-jin were again naked and Ursi wore only a white tanga. Without her bra, Andy noted that the blonde's breasts were pendulous, swaying free whenever she leaned forward. Somehow, he found the swaying movements of these tits, with their large brown nipples, more erotic than the two hairless pudenda on show. *Maybe the posing pouch would've been a good idea, as the flesh on display's beginning to have a visible impact.*

Despite a stunning climax to sunset as the distorted scarlet sun slowly disappeared, there was no sign of anyone else watching it, either on the beach or the terraces of neighbouring villas. The hotel where the Kims were staying was at the extreme end of the main tourist area and, to the east of it, everything was very much quieter. Andy mentioned that he thought this could be a contributing factor for purchasing this hotel, but Su was convinced that it was more likely to be associated with its clientele. Its main selling points were the extensive spa, a wide programme of yoga activities and top-end vegetarian / vegan cuisine. "There's a clear demographic here," she pointed out. "It doesn't actually say women only, but I guess male guests are few and far between."

"And that's an advantage how?" Ursi wondered.

"I'd guess 90% or more of the hit squads likely to be targeting the Kims will be male, so would stand out if they booked into that hotel."

"That's a bit simplistic," Andy objected. "Look at our team, 75% female."

"But you're the only one of us likely to be killing anyone," she retorted.

"Ah, there you're wrong. I think if it was either me or Hyo-jin put into a cage with the two Kims, there would be more chance of them surviving the encounter if they were facing me."

"Try it," Hyo-jin grinned in a truly feral manner. "Me and the Kims and the rapist cunt all in a cage and I will totally fuck them up."

Su smiled. "Okay, for the first and only time, I may admit I was wrong."

"What about Ursi's underwear," Andy reminded her.

"My underwear, what's that to do with anything?" Ursi looked at Su in confusion.

"Nothing, just one of Andy's puerile fantasies. Anyway, it really doesn't matter why the Kims bought that place, the key thing is that the guests will be predominantly female, with a lot of them middle aged. This means that, if you're thinking about swanning in for a recce and bugging the place, you're likely to set off alarm bells." Su observed her colleague's discomfort. "That's what you were thinking of doing, wasn't it?"

"Well, I had noticed that massages at the spa were available for non-residents..."

"I knew it! Well, that's not going to work."

"Wrong again, I think it'll work fine."

"That's just daft! There's too much chance of you being spotted."

"Ah, but that's the clever part, it's not me going for the massage. It's Ursi."

Su spotted the blonde's shocked look and grabbed Hyo-jin's hand. "Well, we're off for an early night as we've got a lot of shagging to do." Before they left, she smiled and grabbed their glasses and the brandy bottle. "May need some fuel, as it could get pretty wild."

After the couple had entered the villa, Ursi turned to face Andy. "What's all this about? You've said nothing to me about this."

"Well, it was spur-of-the-moment stuff. Su's actually correct. I had intended to book a massage for myself. But I hadn't noticed the female dominated situation that she picked up on. I could hardly confess that I'd missed such an important point, so I ad-libbed."

"So, I'm not actually going to plant a bug in the hotel?"

"In fact, I hope that you'll be able to plant several, but I haven't quite worked out how this will work. We'll pop by tomorrow to book a massage for you. I can be your partner or husband, who's just keeping you company while you get it sorted out."

"Well, I'm still not sure about bugging the place, but we can certainly go by tomorrow for a look. Maybe there won't be any free sessions in the next couple of days."

Sounds like wishful thinking, but better not to rock the boat here. "Fine, we'll just play it by ear. Anyway, I think I'll also hit the sack."

"Okay, I'll just have a swim to cool down before I follow you." She stood and turned her back while stepping out of her tanga. As she slowly walked down the steps into the pool, little gasps indicated that it was colder than she had expected.

Fuck, I wish I could stay to watch this. But if I stand here salivating, I'll just look like a sad git. With a sigh, Andy picked up the two empty glasses and took them into the kitchen. He loaded these into the dishwasher, picking up the groans and squeals coming from Su's bedroom. As promised, she and Hyo-jin were going at it hammer and tongs and, typically, the bedroom door was half open. In addition to her BDSM kink, Su was a blatant exhibitionist. Despite an initial resolution not to, he couldn't resist peeking in on the way to his own room. The naked Korean was tied to the bed, arms above her head and legs akimbo. Su, now sporting a chain that pulled her nipple rings together, sat on her victim's face and wriggled lasciviously. Hearing his footsteps, she winked as she pulled down on the chain. "Have a good wank," she whispered before the pain of her tortured nipples caused her to groan.

"God, just don't let Ursi end up in with them," he muttered under his breath before he headed off for a cold shower.

***

Even through his closed door, the sounds of lesbian hi-jinks were clearly audible. Despite this, Andy dozed off almost as soon as his head hit the pillow. However, before he had fallen deeply asleep, he was roused by someone entering his room. In his dazed state he had worked out that it was the increased sound of wild sex when the door opened that had actually wakened him before he realised who had opened it. "Ursi?" he whispered, spotting the faint silhouette in the doorway.

"Yes, sorry, did I wake you? The sound of those two going at it like bunnies is doing my head in. I don't know how anyone can sleep through it."

"Umm, I thought you might have been in with them," he muttered before regretting these words.

"Not for lack of Su's coaxing," Andy could detect a smile in her voice. "That woman is totally without shame."

"A good way of putting it," he grinned. "She doesn't even understand the concept. But I did

208

notice you getting a good look at some of the goods on offer."

"Well, if you're awake and up for a chat, move over."

He complied and an obviously nude body slid in beside him and reorganised his posture until he was on his back with her head on his shoulder. This reminded him of his last night with G, but as his hand moved down to graze her breast it was clear that this was a very much better endowed woman. "So, you wanted to discuss Su's body?"

"It's not really my thing, but you can't help the tattoos catching your attention. They're obviously top-end and very artistic, but it's the thought of making such an irreversible, or poorly reversible, change to your appearance. There are other options now, I know, but I get the impression that it must have been very painful. Even her bum is tattooed."

"I know exactly what you mean. It's the fascination of the perverse, even if it isn't your kink. I'm sure the pain is actually part of the attraction for Su and a lot of the BDSM community. But there's also the exhibitionism involved, when the more intimate tattoos are revealed during play. Her arsehole, for example, has been well used and the tattoo somehow advertises the fact."

"So, have you tried this well-used anus?"

"Su's presently straight lesbian with a thing for BDSM, although she has a fair bit of bi in her past." Andy carefully avoided a direct answer, well aware that her distinction between lesbian and group BDSM tended to get somewhat vague after she had a lot to drink. "She'd certainly welcome you to try, any time you wanted."

"She already made that completely clear," she giggled. "I think her expression was *no holes barred*!"

"Yes, the woman is completely WYSIWYG. I love her to bits."

"But you always seem to be squabbling. Whenever she's not bossing you about, that is."

"That's just another form of role play. We've worked together, living in the same house, for almost two decades now, so we're like an old couple. We bicker, but it's all completely light hearted."

"Actually, your entire team is very strange. You're all so different, but also very close, including in a sexual way. Do you all shag each other?"

"That's a very personal question," he squeezed a notable erect nipple and was rewarded by a loud squeak of protest. "So, are you thinking of joining us. Worrying that there may be a casting couch big enough for six?"

"Six?"

"You, me, Jay, Lou, Su and Georgie."

"What about Miss Park?"

"Hyo-jin's just in for this job, although I suppose she could hang about longer as Su's love interest."

"So, she's not being offered a job? Could that be because she considers you a rapist cunt?" she giggled.

"It could be a factor," he smiled, "but it's never come up. We've agreed to let her escape with her ill-gotten gains if she helps us. Anyway, I don't get the feeling that she'd fit in well with our team. Or, thinking about it, that she'd even want to."

"Do you think I would?" Andy felt her hand brush against his penis, almost as if by accident. However, it did not withdraw after the contact, instead this led to gentle strokes by the tips of her nails, extending from glans to testicles.

"I think you've a nature more compatible with us than most folk I've met. Should I set up the casting couch?"

"It must be pretty big, if we'd all fit on it."

"Actually, thinking about it, we could probably fit your twin on as well." His scream of pain when she bit his chest actually drowned out those of the climaxing lesbians.

"Jesus Christ, that hurt!" He rubbed his left breast, checking if the nipple was bleeding.

"Yes, well I was warned about you and sisters."

"What? You don't mean Petra? Surely, she doesn't discuss her ex-partners with underlings?"

"Not really a discussion, just a warning. Apparently, you're not only a rapist cunt but also a sister-shagging bastard." Her giggle took the sting out of her words.

"Good God, women! So, I assume that you're going to stay well away from me..." he squeezed her nipple gently, noting that it was now the tips of her fingers running along his growing erection.

"Umm, I don't know. It's funny how your boss telling you not to do something immediately raises your interest in something you hadn't considered before. Also, Petra did let slip that you were very

211

good with your mouth, while she was telling me what a total cad and bounder you were."

"So, I don't need to give up hope then?"

"I'd say your chances might be better than 50:50."

"Petra didn't happen to have this talk also with your twin…" Andy's scream this time was even louder, which even seemed to pause the action in the other bedroom.

Chapter 5 - Quantum spyware

Next morning Andy slipped off the edge of the bed that he had been pushed to during the night, managing to avoid disturbing the woman sprawled over the rest of the mattress. The single sheet had been thrown back and he paused to admire her well-toned body. She was lying on her stomach, facing away from him. Her light golden tan was notably even, with only the smallest trace of a lighter colour around her waist that could result from wearing a string tanga.

With a shrug of regret, Andy forced himself towards the kitchen, where he made a cup of strong filter coffee. He found his posing pouch mysteriously draped over the toaster and pulled it on before extracting his laptop from its charging station. Thus, fully kitted-up, he headed out to the patio to establish a secure satellite link back to base while he listened to the soporific sound of waves washing over pebbles on the beach. Just as he was about to check updates on the project files, he caught a movement out of the corner of his eye and spotted a woman with long silvery-blonde hair emerging from the neighbouring villa. Half-way down the beach she casually dropped the towel she had wrapped around herself and strode into the waves for an early morning skinny-dip.

Twenty minutes later, Andy looked more closely when the woman emerged, trying to work out what age she might be. Suddenly he received a painful nip on the shoulder. "What, you've spent the night with me and you're already ogling another woman?"

"Not ogling, admiring. And trying to work out what age she might be."

"So, you're not salivating over her big boobs?"

"Not salivating, although large breasts certainly have their attractions."

"She's even older than you are," again another nip.

"Matters not a jot. She's evidently fit, healthy and very self-confident. Look at the way she strides up the beach, well aware that we're watching her." Andy waved at his neighbour and got a wave and a cheery grin in response. "Of course, she may be so relaxed because you're also in your birthday suit."

"Shit, so I am," Ursi giggled in a delightful manner, before helping herself to a sip of his coffee. "I'd totally forgotten. Shows what hanging about with you bunch of nutters does for me. I'm being corrupted."

"Who's being corrupted?" Andy and Ursi twisted round to see Su emerge with Hyo-jin in tow. Naturally, both women were also naked."

"See what I mean," Ursi grinned, before sitting down on Andy's knee, which helped hide the bulge in the front of his pouch.

"This woman here thinks you're a bad influence," Andy reported, surreptitiously caressing a buttock that was out of Su's line of view.

"What us? Who was shouting the fucking place down last night? What were you doing to the poor girl, you beast? We could hardly hear ourselves scream," Su finished with a grin.

"Rapist cunt," agreed her lover.

"I'll have you know that it was me doing the screaming," Andy squeezed the buttock tightly, causing Ursi to squirm in a most distracting manner. "This bloody girl bites," he offered his bruised chest for inspection.

"Oh, those are nice ones," Sue licked her lips while she got close enough to offer her own tits for inspection. "I think I've probably got more bruising, but it's hard to tell because of the ink."

Ursi carefully inspected Su's tits. "Yes, I can see what you mean. But Andy was screaming an awful lot louder."

"That's just men," responded Su dismissively. "They simply can't handle pain. Now have a look at Hyo-jin." The Korean allowed Su to pull her forward and then lift her leg to show clear lines of bite-marks on her thighs and buttocks. "Now those are real bites and my girl didn't scream at all. Or, at least, not very much."

"That's not what it sounded like to us," Andy whispered in Ursi's ear.

"Anyway, lass, you've certainly got potential and we can always find a place for a domme. Unless, of course, you are into a bit of M as well as the S, which is okay also."

"Why don't we let Ursi take a rain check on that and grab some breakfast before we start working on how to make life really miserable for the Kims?"

"Does this mean that you've got a plan now?"

"Well, sort of… maybe. Anyway, let's have breakfast first." *This gives me about an hour to*

215

dream up something, as my mind was on other things both last night and this morning.

***

The planning meeting was held al fresco, sitting around the large dining table, which was shaded by a roof and situated on the lower part of the terrace, on the other side of the swimming pool. Although Andy considered the chances of them being targeted to be negligible, they were surrounded by a dome of anti-sound that was complemented by an AI dialogue generator, which used the words spoken therein to synthesise a discussion of holiday options that would roughly match their mouth movements. Not very sophisticated, but an extra layer of protection that required no effort to set up.

Andy started with his and Ursi's planned visit to the hotel which, all being well, would provide an opportunity to plant some bugs. Andy would wear clothes hiding a number of minute multi-spectral scanners, which Su could monitor in real time and provide guidance for anything that might be of special interest. Ursi was concerned about these being picked up, but he assured her they were organic/ceramic composites that were effectively undetectable. The weakest point was the two-way communication, which utilised a frequency-hopping satellite link running over bands assigned to GPS and television. If it was known in advance that this was being used, it would be detectable, even if not hackable in real time. *Although this assumes, as Jay always points out, that there's been no leaps in technology that we don't know about.*

"Fuck-all for me?" Hyo-jin was clearly pissed-off.

"Actually, the most important job of all." Everyone looked in surprise at Andy, wondering what rabbit he would pull out of his hat now. "Our big problem is that we just don't understand these women. Every time we think we've got them nailed down, they come up with a strategy that we'd never even considered. It's not just that they're incredibly smart, there's a cultural difference that always seems to catch us out. Your job is thus to follow everything that we're doing, everything we're planning, and let us know when we're going to screw up. I know you've got a vested interest here and want them taken down even more than we do. Now you can help us do that."

"Okay, but I go in when you're going to fuck them up." Hyo-jin's clearer English indicated that she was very serious here.

"Well, I've not yet decided if we go in."

"You will go in, as it is the only sure way to fuck them. And I go too."

"I thought more of you providing backup support, like Su. But if you think it's important, you can tag along if we decide to go in."

"You will go in and I will fuck them up really good."

"I can live with that," Andy decided, although he noted both Su and Ursi looked unsure. "Okay, let's get kitted up and make this happen. We can then discuss first results over lunch." *As long as we don't get any other nasty surprises.*

***

The spa hotel sat in extensive grounds, with a large swimming pool between the residential block and the fence along the beach. Reception was in the middle of the block, facing a large car park. Although it looked to have originally had guest rooms on either side of reception, those on the left-hand side, as seen from the parking lot, appeared to have been converted into a single large residence with access limited by numerous *private* signs. This impression was confirmed by a map of the hotel in reception. There was nobody present, but the desk held a notice in three languages stating that anyone with questions should come to the bar. While appearing to look through some brochures, Andy placed a micro bug facing the reception desk. He then walked with Ursi to the bar, which was in a separate building lying to the side of the pool, where the receptionist was found making up a couple of lurid cocktails. Unfortunately, the spa was no longer offering massages to non-residents, but the girl offered contact details for the off-site masseuse that they used for their guests. Although disappointed with this dead end, Andy surreptitiously placed a couple more bugs in the façade of the bar.

After the short walk back to the villa, Andy checked the scanning information obtained by Su. Following extensive image enhancement, it was confirmed that no Koreans were amongst the guests lounging around the pool, although an indistinct figure on an upper terrace that was part of the private wing was a possible match to one of Dam-Bi's assistants.

"Well, with no massage available, that's your bugging plan out the window." Ursi was plainly relieved by the failure of Andy's ploy, but trying to hide it. "So, what do we do now?"

"There are two options that I see. We can either try to image the upper parts of the private wing from the sea or go for bugging with a micro-drone."

"Given the risk of spooking our targets, I go for the least invasive option," Su said while Hyo-jin nodded.

"The last time I tried this it didn't go too well," Andy grinned wryly, "but I can mount high resolution monitors on the front of a paddleboard, which I can rent in Acharavi. I guess I could paddle the entire length of the beach and back in a couple of hours."

"How good are you on one of those stand-up things," Ursi enquired.

"Last time was on Lake Maggiore, which was okay as far as the paddling was concerned."

Su quickly grasped Ursi's point. "Well, we've strong onshore winds this afternoon, calm conditions tomorrow and a storm coming in the following day, which may get pretty wild by the evening, as there are already severe weather warnings issued."

"Tomorrow's maybe not so bad, as I need to set up and test the scanners. There's also a crazy option that Georgie suggested once that I'd like to try out. Luckily, we can combine that with another walk past the hotel on the way to the Petra beach bar, which'll be ideal for lunch."

"Are you going to tell us what that crazy option is?" Su asked.

"Let's see first if we get anything at all from it."

"Well, at least give us a hint," Ursi emphasised her request with a painful nip to the back of his neck.

"Ouch! Bugger, that was sore. Okay a hint, let's see. So, it's a bit like muon tomography, but less mainstream."

"That's a hint?" Su shook her head then winked at Ursi. "You've definitely got to hurt him more, next time. Your bites seem to work well, so maybe stick to them. However, if you want, I've got a selection of nipple clamps that might help do the job."

"Good grief, can't you get your mind off BDSM for a bit. How about thinking about what we'll have for lunch."

"Multi-tasking on it at this very moment," she smiled smugly. "Lunch is the easy bit. It's sorting out your punishment should your hint be a red herring that's going to be tricky."

Well, to me it's a good hint, but maybe in retrospect an easier clue would've been sensible. Anyway, got to get some kit put together.

***

Fundamentally, the equipment was set up for synthetic-aperture, multi-spectral scanning. This used an array of modified, room-temperature squids to monitor emissions from all electronic equipment in the hotel. This was complemented by detection of interferences within, or perturbations of, the background electro-smog of TV, radio, navigation

220

and communication signals. While he walked around the target, this produced a vast volume of data, captured in millisecond time steps and linked to precise differential GPS locations. Actually, most of the hardware that he packed into a large rucksack handled data storage as, even with the best broadband available, transmission back to Switzerland would take many hours for data that he would capture in less than twenty minutes.

Andy was a bit vague about what happened thereafter, but Georgie's supercomputer would structure the flow from this database so that the walk around the hotel was represented by electromagnetic fields at differing frequencies defined in four dimensions.

"Then it's just a straightforward waveform inversion process. Although, of course, it's data-heavy enough to require the full power of my hypercomputer," she had grinned following this statement, confirming his suspicion that this was complex beyond belief and probably beyond the wildest imagination of almost anyone else on the planet.

***

Although it was too hot to get really hungry, early lunch at the Petra beach bar was a drawn-out affair, based on slowly grazing through a selection of local meze, washed down by several carafes of extremely cheap, but eminently drinkable, local white wine. Over lunch, Andy was persuaded to describe Georgie's monitoring tool and explain what this had to do with muon tomography. This persuasion was mainly in the form of Su's tightening grip on his scrotum and Ursi's nails pressing deeper into his foreskin, all of this happening under the table in a busy restaurant. Given the need to maintain a low profile, Andy's capitulation was inevitable.

As he explained it, muons are highly-penetrating particles that are constantly generated by cosmic rays. As is the case for artificial x-rays, mapping muons after they have passed through an object allows its internal structure to be analysed. Georgie had used this principle for the more complex case of measuring a large part of the electromagnetic spectrum, allowing a time series of collimated measurements of this background to be used to map the structures that had interacted with it.

"And you think that you can produce a tomograph of the hotel from the kit in your backpack?" Su was clearly sceptical.

"If Georgie thinks it's doable, I'm up for giving it a try."

"What kind of resolution would it have?"

"That's one of the things we want to test. This involves a synthesis of radiation with wavelengths from metres to millimetres, so Georgie guesses about a centimetre or so. This depends on conductivity of materials and extent to which they're actively emitting anything or are close to an emitter. Potentially enough to identify someone using a cell-phone."

Su frowned in concentration. "I can sort of... maybe... see the basic principles involved. But the computational requirements must be mind-blowing. Then again, this was the case also for the last couple of miracles that our quantum guru's pulled off. Anyway, let's see how it goes."

"Fucking hypercomputer magic shit," Hyo-jin seemed uninterested in such details.

Andy noticed that Ursi was looking worried and tapped her shoulder. "Anything up? Don't you think this'll work?"

The blonde frowned before answering. "Actually, I'm much more worried that it will work. Have you thought through the consequences of this?"

Andy suddenly felt as if he had missed something major. "Actually, beyond finding a bit more about whatever the hell the Kims are up to, I haven't really considered there being any special consequences." The worried look that Su gave him confirmed that she had now also seen what was bothering Ursi. "What, specifically, were you thinking about?"

"How about the total end of privacy as a concept? It could actually have a long-term global impact far beyond crashed banks and defunct crypto-currency."

Su was nodding in agreement, while even Hyo-jin was beginning to look worried.

"Actually, Georgie did say something about opening a technological Pandora's Box, but I just wrote that off as geek hyperbole."

Ursi stood up, clearly intending to leave. "I've got to contact Petra, so that she can switch in NDB. This is far too big for us alone. It must be Cabinet level or higher. UN, maybe."

Andy grabbed her arm and pulled her back onto her chair. "Wait a minute now, this is just exactly what you can't do. We're undercover here and can't risk spooking our victims."

"What the fuck?" Ursi struggled against his grip. "You don't have the competence to make decisions at this level."

"Actually, we do and have been doing so over the last week." This reminder was enough to quell the girl's struggles. "First of all, this tool is purely theoretical and the approach could turn out to be fundamentally impossible. So why cause a fuss before we know more? Secondly, even if it is possible, at present only Georgie has a machine with anything like the capability to carry out the required calculations. Our work here is urgent, while any widespread use of this technology is years, possibly decades, in the future."

"So, we just sit on our thumbs and hope that it goes away?"

"That's not what I'm saying. You did a very good job on picking up on an aspect that I'd missed, although I'm sure Georgie hasn't and would have brought it to our attention at some point. It just makes it more urgent to clear the decks and ensure that the Kims don't get up to any further mischief. After that we can then focus on wider aspects of Peta-scale quantum."

"Wider aspects? Isn't total loss of privacy and associated freedom enough?"

"Now you've got to sit back and look at this from a wider perspective. Georgie's incredible work has saved us from two global attacks by using

224

quantum technology that wasn't available even months ago. Within days, this has resulted in another development with associated potential to cause global-level impacts. You don't think that we've now caught everything, do you? This technology is itself EOTWAWKI: much of what we used to know of the world has already been altered. We just don't know how and what to do about it."

***

Back in the villa, before getting down to work, Su and Andy decided to cool down in the sea while Ursi and Hyo-jin were happy to merely splash in the pool.

The NetSec colleagues both had goggles and small training fins but, while Andy wore his minute trunks, Su preferred to swim in the nude. After fighting their way through prickly dune plants and then mixed sand and pebbles, they entered the water to find a smooth sandy bottom, which made fitting fins and goggles easier. Andy set off in a relaxed crawl, curving to parallel the beach and heading east, choosing one of the distant Albanian mountain peaks as an orientation point. He was aware of Su paralleling him on his left side and, just as a check, increased his pace slightly. As expected, Su speeded up to match him. *Now it's going to be tricky, as Su'll certainly race me back. She's definitely a lot fitter than me, but can she swim faster? If we're closely matched, would I be better on a longer or a shorter stretch?*

He swam on for another fifteen minutes, estimating that he had covered about a kilometre or so, then turned back and increased his speed. Su was matching him, but he realised that there had been a following current and now he was swimming against both this and wind-driven waves. The return swim was going to be significantly longer than he expected. Now Su was beginning to pull ahead and all attempts to think through a plan to counter this were abandoned to the effort of simply keeping up. As the gap between them widened, he could feel his stroke getting scrappier while his breathing became heavier. He was still several hundred metres from his goal when he was forced to change to breast stroke in order to get his breathing under control. Spotting this, Su added insult to injury by finishing using a beautiful butterfly technique.

Su was waiting on the beach while Andy stripped off his fins in the shallows and then started to struggle up the steep slope below the waterline. It was possibly due to his focus on the taunts of the tattooed nymphet that he missed the warning of retreating swash and hence was unprepared for the large wave that broke over him, pushing him forwards onto his knees before the back-flow dragged him under in a flush of course sand. Spluttering, he struggled to his feet, just in time to be bowled over by another wave. He finally managed to stagger out of the water on his third attempt, only to trip over his posing pouch, which was now around his ankles. Kicking the offending garment loose, he climbed to his feet and was then aware that Su had been joined by the others, who had clearly been drawn by her screams of laughter.

"Well, I hope you hyenas are all happy, enjoying my misfortunes," Andy tried to sound upset, but could not hide a grin as he saw the funny side of his antics. "I've got gritty sand in places that I don't even want to think about."

"Oh, you poor old sod," Ursi struggled to stop giggling. "I'll come into the shower with you and help you get rid of that stuff."

"Right, and I've a speculum in my kit that'll help ensure that you don't miss any," Su laughed.

"Use wire brush on rapist cunt," Hyo-jin contributed, causing the other ladies to hoot with laughter.

"Okay, I'm off for a shower," Andy retrieved his dropped fins and pouch before setting off back to the villa, closely followed by the hyenas.

"Do you think he'd really benefit from the speculum?" Ursi asked Su in a stage whisper.

"No doubt about it. He's actually well into getting things stuck up his bum," she replied, loudly.

"Except, perhaps, gritty sand..." again the stage whisper.

"Even I'd draw the line there," Su laughed, "and you wouldn't believe the things I've had up my arse at one time or another."

Andy tried to ignore the continuous banter while he rinsed goggles, fins and swimwear in the pool shower and then commenced the trickier job of washing embedded sand from his body. As promised, Ursi joined him in the shower and started with the job of removing sand trapped under his foreskin. This was facilitated by his growing erection as her hands caressed his penis and testicles, egged on by Su who was closely watching the action.

Initially Ursi found Su's voyeurism disconcerting but, slowly, she discovered that it provided some strange kind of erotic stimulus to her increasingly blatant masturbation of her partner. Andy was clearly beyond caring, not that he would have been bothered much in the first place. Nevertheless, it was a shock when Su joined them in the shower.

"I thought you were straight gay these days," Ursi mumbled when she saw that the tattooed woman was spreading Andy's buttocks.

"I am," she grinned. "Only helping you clean up my colleague here. I have to admit that watching a beautiful woman fist a man has its attractions also, and would be happy to help you get in the mood for that," she lowered her head to let her nose rub against a prominently erect nipple.

"I'm not going to fist him, for God's sake. Just clearing sand from his willy."

"So, you're going to leave him with an arsehole full of grit?"

"Well, I guess he can manage that bit for himself."

"Needs fucking wire brush," commented Hyo-jin, who was following the action while unashamedly masturbating.

"Seems a shame not to help, after he provided such a comedy show," Su grinned lasciviously and moved her hands so that her finger could slowly slip into the proffered orifice. "See, just like that," she withdrew her finger and wiped sand onto her thigh.

Ursi passively let Su rearrange her hands and direct her index finger into a noticeably gritty anus. "Hell's bells, Andy, you weren't joking. How on earth did you manage to get so much sand up your bum?"

"Weak sphincter," Su answered before he had a chance to respond. "Here, let me show you..." Ursi's finger was replaced by three of her own, causing Andy to groan, despite the distraction provided by his continuing penile manipulation.

"Not the right fucking way," Hyo-jin muttered before she joined the others in the shower, making body contact with both women while keeping her distance from Andy. "You have this rain shower thing, but also this other thing," she detached the small, wall-mounted shower head. "All girls know about this nice other thing from porn, though we don't have these in fucking school," she expertly unscrewed the sprinkler head and moved the lever to transfer flow to the bare hose. "This you stick up rapist cunt's arse!"

"She's completely right, you know," Su removed her fingers and gave the Korean a quick kiss. She took the gushing hose from Hyo-jin and passed it to Ursi. "Go for it, lass. Consider it a bit of water-sports floorshow while my lover and I watch."

Ursi was so bemused by this turn of events that she had complied before thinking it through. Andy was braced against the wall, grunting, before she realised what she was doing and removed the implement, unconsciously retreating from the flow of expelled water."

"Okay, that's the first rinse. I'd say three or four more," Su moaned. Ursi turned to see that the lesbians were energetically masturbating each other.

"Not as good as wire brush but…" Hyo-jin screamed as her body went rigid under the force of her orgasm.

"Well, I suppose it's doing the job," Ursi muttered before following Su's instructions. However, she managed only two flushes before Andy came and sagged against her, evidently completely spent.

"Buggeration!" she groaned, aware of how excited she had become during this process.

"No, he's not going to be much good to you now," Su observed, clearly recognising Ursi's plight. "We women, on the other hand, have much more stamina."

"No, that's not what I do. You're very nice, but I'm not interested in sex with women. I've never had the slightest inclination in that direction."

"Proves only that you haven't met the right woman – or women in this case." Su moved over and crouched in front of the tall blonde, rubbing her face against the golden pubic hairs.

"No, no, stop that…" Ursi then felt a thin body squeeze between Andy and herself, while hands caressed her breasts and painfully squeezed her engorged nipples. Her first orgasm came soon afterwards, but it hardly seemed to remove the sexual tension that blotted out any conscious thought.

When Andy finally recovered from his post-coital disorientation, he could not work out if he was disappointed or incredibly turned-on by Ursi's enthusiastic participation in the lesbian ménage-a-trois with Su and Hyo-jin. *So much for straight hetero! Then again, it's hard for any woman to stand up to Su when she's in predator mode. A lot of similarity with Heidi and Beat in her commitment to encouraging partners to widen their perspectives and explore their sexuality in ways that they'd never considered previously.*

Despite the obvious temptation, he forced himself to refrain from any attempt to join the group. He noticed that Su had already spotted that he was watching and knew this would only spice-up the action for her. But direct involvement would not be appreciated, and could tip Hyo-jin over the edge into her barely-controlled psycho persona.

Okay, some technical work to take my mind off writhing female flesh. Let's see if I can quickly work through first input from Georgie's miraculous monitoring machine.

Chapter 6 - The death of digital privacy

The link to Wettingen was set up and tested by the time that the women finally returned from their antics on the terrace. Andy was amused by the differing looks he received: a smug grin of triumph from Su, a mixture of confusion, embarrassment and post-coital exhaustion from Ursi and a glare from Hyo-jin. Andy grinned: *probably annoyed about her earlier lack of a wire brush.*

"Okay, gals, I guess you must have worked up a thirst out there. Ready for an Apero?

"We just need a quick shower first," Su pushed her partner in the direct of their bedroom. "And maybe some mouthwash, as I seem to have a tongue covered with blonde pubes," she laughed delightedly, while Ursi blushed.

"Fine, whatever, I'm just happy to be sand-free, even in the most inaccessible places," Andy replied, causing Su to laugh and Ursi's blush to deepen.

As she was about to enter her bedroom, Ursi turned to Andy with a glare. "What the fuck's going on here? Am I just fresh meat for you group of pervs?"

"Group of pervs, no doubt about that." This admission seemed to take the wind from her sails and her look of confusion returned. "But we'd never force anyone to do anything that they didn't want to. Did you feel pressured to do anything last night? As I remember it, you came into my bed and

232

initiated all of the action. Okay, just now Su may have taken advantage of you to some extent, as I bet you were really hot from everything that she encouraged you to do to me. The key thing is, do you regret what you did, either with me or the other women? Or is it more that you're confused because you got pleasure from actions that you had already a preconceived idea of being perverse or kinky or just downright dirty?

"Bugger! When you put it like that, I'm really not sure. Is this a reflection of my prudish nature?"

"Well, from my perspective, you didn't look prudish at all in your role of meat in a Su - Hyo-jin sandwich." Andy's laugh turned into a yelp when the blonde bit his chest.

"And there certainly is a sadistic side to you that I hadn't expected," he added, rubbing the bite mark. "Anyway, I need to get some clothes on sharpish as I feel a bit vulnerable when you're in man-eating mode."

Ursi suddenly brightened and grinned. "Okay, I'm off for a shower and will be ready in a trice."

"Yes, you can skip the mouthwash. There's not the slightest trace of a pubic hair on either of your well-shaven partners." Although a quick turn caused the slap to miss his groin, the crack of its impact on his buttock was a reminder of the danger of toying with his volatile colleague.

***

Su and her lover drank champagne, while Ursi and Andy had beers, occasionally dipping into a bowl of peanuts. Once the ladies seemed settled, Andy broke the news that Georgie's first analysis of the tomographic scan indicated that it seemed certain that internal structure within the hotel could be distinguished and the only question was how good the spatial resolution would be. This should be established within a few hours, at a planned video meeting.

Ursi was clearly disturbed by the invasion of privacy now facilitated by this new technology but, as Su pointed out, hacks of wired households, as illustrated by the cases in Geneva and Zurich, allowed much more invasive monitoring of even the most intimate goings on behind closed curtains. However, this served only as a reminder to Ursi, who pointed out that such hacking was carried out completely at NetSec's discretion, without the constraints imposed on government-controlled organisations. This was something that she felt was fundamentally wrong, although conceded that, it some cases, the ends may justify the means.

Andy shook his head in dismay. "I don't know what the big deal is about assured privacy. It's something that the man in the street has never been guaranteed, but was usually a result of nobody having enough interest in them to carry out the work required to invade it. Sure, digital privacy has largely vanished, but mainly due to the general public taking advantage of all the *free* services available on the internet. I think it was in an old Heinlein novel that I first saw the term TANSTAAFL: *there ain't no such thing as a free lunch.* You only get such services when you open up your digital life to the service provider. It initially appears that it's used only for marketing but, with advances in machine learning, your entire life can be analysed in fine detail – as is done by Jay's tools. It couldn't be done if the muppets involved hadn't signed this Faustian contract in the first place."

"That's a bit of an oversimplification," Ursi objected. "But, whatever, they're not invading the privacy of your home."

"Come on," Su jumped in, "what about all these voice-accessed apps? With any of these, Google, Meta, Apple, whatever have an open microphone – and probably a camera – that you have installed and let them do what they want with it. Indeed, with most mobile phones, you are allowing yourself to be tracked 24/7, constantly leaking not only your position but also biometric data, communication records and all the other nice information that your cheap or free apps provide."

"Okay, that's one thing – the naivety, or stupidity of the general public. But there are those who deliberately avoid such traps exactly with the aim of ensuring their privacy. But now that option is gone."

Su frowned. "Well, they'd probably need to stay indoors, to avoid the cams that are almost everywhere nowadays. Remember, that how we traced the Kims here."

"It's more fundamental," Andy objected. "Those who require secrecy will always be able to assure it, but they must recognise that this is a technological rat race with the hiders constantly competing with the seekers. For our own safety, NetSec and, in particular the WhiteHatz operation, needs top-level security and you can be sure that we'll introduce anything more needed to defend against this new scanning option."

Ursi shook her head. "That's okay for rich geeks like you, but it's not an option for the general public."

Su rolled her eyes, but left it to Andy to respond. "Why would anyone use such technology to focus on any of the great unwashed? The secrets that are heavily guarded are generally military, commercial or crime-related, so my previous arguments apply."

"But what about repressive regimes, who spy on their citizens in order to enforce draconian restrictions on political, religious or lifestyle choices?" Ursi ground to a halt when she realised that Andy, Su and even Hyo-jin were shaking their heads. "Okay, I see now that this is your point: such regimes already have technology for population-scale monitoring and don't actually need anything as sophisticated as your new toy. Nevertheless, I worry that the tools that we're developing will make analysing such monitoring data easier."

"Ah, there you're correct," Su smiled. "There's no doubt about that."

"And, I suspect, we're going to get more evidence of the power of Georgie's knowledge mining in the near future," Andy added.

Not surprisingly, this did not cheer Ursi in the slightest.

***

After the drink, it was a rather subdued group that went for a pre-prandial stroll along the beach, each considering the wider impacts of the surveillance technology that they were testing. Possibly because of this distraction, Ursi stumbled over uneven paving of what had once been a beach access road and fell heavily, badly scraping both her left knee and forearm. Su quickly helped her to her feet and, despite her protestations of being fine, kept an arm around her as they walked the last thirty metres to the back gate of the villa.

To make things easier, the ladies stripped off and helped wash grit from Ursi's superficial but bloody wounds in the garden shower. They were drying her off when Andy returned with a first aid kit. After settling her down on a chair in the shade, he applied antiseptic cream before covering the scrapes with gauze held in place by elastic bandages. "These scratches will be painful, but just need to scab over, so I don't think stitches are required. How do you feel otherwise?"

"I'm okay," she protested. "There's no point in making a fuss about this. I simply wasn't watching where I was going and tripped. I'll be fine."

Ursi was clearly in pain, so Andy offered her a painkiller while Su fetched a glass of water to wash it down with. "Actually, you're limping a bit. How's your left ankle?"

"It felt sore when I was walking back, but is fine now that I'm sitting."

"Could just be twisted, but there is some swelling already," Su observed. "Probably best to get it x-rayed to be on the safe side."

"I'm sure that's not necessary. You've got this monitoring system output to analyse now," Ursi protested yet again.

"Although the waveform inversion on the hyper machine will be effectively instantaneous, pre- and post-processing on the supercomputer will take several hours, assuming that this works at all. Anyway, we've plenty of time to get you checked out." Andy was flicking through his palmtop. "The nearest clinic is just a couple of kilometres away, so I'll just call to see if they can see you now."

Ursi shrugged. "In that case, I'll need some clothes that aren't spattered with blood." She made to stand up.

"Just sit there and tell me what you need," Su commanded in her best domme voice. "Just in case there's something buggered up, best that you keep weight off that foot to the extent possible."

Ursi forced a grin. "What a strange concept, a caring dungeon-mistress."

Su raised the blonde's chin and kissed her on the lips. "You've got some serious misunderstandings about the fundamentals of BDSM, I see. Don't worry, nothing I can't sort out in the comfort – or otherwise – of my own dungeon."

"Something for my bucket list, I suppose," Ursi replied with obvious insincerity, causing both women to grin.

"Okay, stop tempting our NDB colleague with promises of torture and let's get her to a Doc," Andy interrupted. "They can look at Ursi immediately, so I'll drive her over now. You ladies can start on the analysis if and when we get something from Georgie."

"Which won't be for a few hours," Su pointed out, "so plenty of time for topping up our tans."

238

"You're covered with tattoos and Hyo-jin's white as a sheet and also covered in sun-block. So how does that work?"

"With the tools of my trade, there're many ways to organise a bit of al fresco tanning of a hide," she turned Hyo-jin to point out the whip marks on her buttocks and leered lasciviously. "I generally save these for my beautiful girls, but I'd make an exception in your case."

"Tempting though that is, I'll pass for now. Got to get our invalid seen to." Andy smiled at Ursi, helped her to her feet and supported her as she hobbled to the car.

***

Although clearly suffering a bit from shock, Ursi was also bemused by Su's open and unapologetic proselytisation of a BDSM lifestyle. During the drive, she voiced her own misgivings about this culture and Andy couldn't help nodding as they matched well with his own in many cases. Her questions about why you would want to be punished, or have someone hurt or humiliate you, had no real answers. As he pointed out, "*de gustibus non est desperandum*: there really is no way at all to rationally discuss the tastes of others. Georgie's got an interesting perspective on this though…"

"Well Su told me that Georgie in some of his or her personas is well into the M side of things."

Andy grinned. "She puts it down to a lack of interest in sport."

"Sport, what's that to do with anything?"

"She reckons that sport is masochism for the masses, providing them with regular doses of pain

239

and the resulting endorphins. I can't really argue that she's wrong there."

"That's a bit simplistic, most sports don't involve pain."

"Then, according to Georgie's definition, they're not real sports."

"What about golf, or snooker for that matter?"

"Games those are. Just because they are covered on sports channels, doesn't actually make them fit the definition."

"Okay, I can give you that. But swimming, running, cycling, whatever – they don't need to involve pain."

"Yes, if they don't then it's just exercise. It's pain that's the essence of any sport."

"Fine, that's pain. But what about this big BDSM thing about humiliation? You don't get that from sport, do you?"

"Ah, so you've forgotten my sporty swim this afternoon already. For me there was enough humiliation there to last me for the rest of the year, at the very least."

Ursi smiled, this banter evidently taking her mind off her injuries. "I guess I have to give you that also. I'll just need to remember to be very careful about taking you up on any possible joint sporting activities."

***

At the clinic, a pretty young doctor, looking more like a schoolgirl than a medical professional, removed the bandages and checked Ursi's cuts. She confirming that these could be left to heal naturally and that the new coverings that she provided should

240

be kept in place for a week or so. She also provided a prescription for analgesic and antibiotic pills to cover this period.

This helpful and cheery medic contrasted markedly with the large, surly woman who x-rayed Ursi's foot. After a quick scan of the radiograph, she identified a hairline fracture and prescribed a cast and crutches for at least a fortnight. She was clearly extremely unhappy when Andy requested a copy of the scan but, after much argument, finally transferred it to him after he threatened not to pay for the work otherwise. A fast assessment by the expert system back at base confirmed the fracture, but noted that it was so minor that a support bandage and minimising the amount of weight put on the leg for a couple of weeks would be sufficient. Although the hefty doctor protested vehemently, there was nothing she could do to prevent her instructions being ignored. The pretty doctor stayed well clear of this argument but, when it was decided, volunteered to bandage Ursi's foot, much to her colleague's evident displeasure.

After a quick stop at a pharmacy to collect the prescribed medicine and purchase an adjustable walking stick, Andy drove Ursi back to the villa. She was now much more relaxed and cheerily contrasted the two doctors: one the dream that you would like to have to take care of you and the other a complete nightmare. At the villa, Ursi was able to easily walk with the stick, which was a much more comfortable option than the primitive crutches on offer at the clinic.

Sitting together around the terrace dining table, Su activated the security shield before presenting the preliminary results from Georgie. "Our in-house genius split the job into two parts, so that she could do some checks on applicability of this approach. Firstly, she did the simpler job of synthesis of all active emissions from the target in any of the measured EM frequencies. This also has the benefit of already giving us something to look at now," she passed round what looked like very dark sunglasses. This option allowed the ghostly holographic image of the residential block of the hotel to be viewed despite the brightness of the day – and also without any risk of being spied upon.

The presentation included a voice-over by Georgie. "We here have the overall structure of the rooms as delineated by emissions from power cables, wireless devices and electrical or electronic equipment." Arrows identified some of these. "The completely dark area in the basement is clearly a shielded server room. We can distinguish between fixed source locations and those varying with time, with most of the latter being communication devices carried by anybody present in our targeted part of the building. Currently, there seems to be eight of them." This showed up clearly in an animated sequence.

"The Kims and their six lackeys," whispered Su.

"This is, of course, very low resolution, a decimetre or so, but acts as proof of concept," Georgie continued. "The next iteration will build on this by analysing passive interferences with the electro-smog background, which should give us a

242

lot more. I'm now fairly sure that identification of individuals will be possible. But we'll know for definite in a couple of hours."

The holo-sequence stopped there and the team slowly removed their glasses. "Well, we now have pretty good confirmation that our targets are present, so we can go ahead with planning an attack," Andy concluded.

Ursi frowned. "Yes, and the intrusive surveillance cat is well out of the bag," she pointed out. "I'm still struggling to get my head around what the consequences of this will be, but it's such a paradigm shift in the field that the full range of impacts is mindboggling."

"Probably best to just put that on the back-burner and focus on the attack of our immediate target," Su suggested. "In particular, are the benefits to us worth the risks of letting Andy loose here, or would we be better cutting our losses and just leaking our findings to the Chinese and letting them do the dirty work?"

"I will kill the Kim cunts," Hyo-jin offered with an evil grin. "If they escape, they will try to fuck me up, so best I fuck them first."

"There's certainly an argument for that," Andy conceded. "These women are so slippery that I wouldn't be surprised if they have moles in the Chinese high command."

"Rapist cunt is probably correct," the Korean admitted with evident reluctance. "All top Chinese are corrupt bastards, so there are always leaks to Kims, Yanks and Ruskies. To whoever pays most money."

"Okay, so I start planning intrusion," Andy announced. "This'll be based on small attack drones that I'm having delivered, so there shouldn't be any direct risk to us until we go in to check the aftermath. The critical factor will be having a detailed map of the residence and everyone in it prior to the attack. Hopefully we'll have this map soon and after that, according to Georgie, further refining it will be a very much faster job. I think we'll be go for tomorrow night."

"There's a big storm approaching then," Su reminded him.

"So much the better. This'll just give us additional cover and, if there's any lightning, further EM illumination of the target."

"And you really think that's doable?" Ursi frowned.

"Let's just see what Georgie's detailed analysis looks like and then we can make a go – no-go decision. Basically, it's just a quick drone attack, then in and out to extract the Kims. We can leave the others to the Chinks. The thing is that this place has the cover of an operating hotel, so options for intrusion counter-measures are inherently limited." Andy hoped that he showed complete confidence, but couldn't help having reservations given the way that these cunning women had managed to surprise him in the past.

**

To spare Ursi's foot, the team dined on food delivered from a nearby restaurant, complemented by a couple of bottles of cheap, local wine. The second analysis from Georgie had been received

244

shortly beforehand, but they decided to postpone discussing it until after eating.

With the usual security in place and wearing incongruous virtual reality glasses, Andy set up the link to Switzerland while Su distributed coffees and large glasses of Metaxa. Lou started by wishing Ursi a rapid recovery and then passed directly to the currently androgynous punk Georgie, sporting red hair and wearing black trousers with braces, a filmy black blouse and a black crop-top with a bizarre Mondrian-like logo. The distraction caused by this apparition vanished when, from a first glance, it was clear that the polished tomograph had very much higher resolution. Not only were individual pieces of electrical equipment identified but, in most cases, their functional specifications could be determined.

The Corfu team were dumbstruck by amazement before Su eventually spoke up. "This's absolutely incredible. Even with the forewarnings from Andy, I'd no idea that it'd be possible to obtain so much information by simply walking around the hotel wearing a backpack."

"But that's just the start," Georgie grinned. "Just see what Jay can do with this."

Jay took over the presentation and then showed the results of his image enhancement and synthesis for the eight individuals present in the residence. In all cases he could identify them with over 90% confidence. "I focussed on the Kims and went through a final iteration of polishing with Georgie's refined input and got a confidence level for them over 99%," he concluded.

"Jesus!"

"Christ!"

Ursi and Andy responded simultaneously, breaking the tension and causing everyone to smile.

"Well put," Lou nodded. "This is a miracle of technology worthy of religious awe."

"Or supernatural dread," Ursi added.

"Yes, Ursi, your concerns here are completely valid and will be a main focus for us as soon as this operation is finished. I really hope NDB will extend your attachment so that we can work together on this. It has large potential impacts for both Swiss national security and commercial interests – I guess especially in the finance and pharmaceutical sectors." It appeared that Lou had come to similar conclusions to Andy and Su in terms of applicability of this new tool.

"I though Andy wanted to ensure that nobody was informed about this new threat before you'd analysed it further."

"That's definitely still the case, but I think we can dream up a credible reason for you to continue to work with us without going into details of this new development. Of course, this is assuming that you want to."

Ursi frowned but then nodded her head. "Your team includes some of the weirdest folk that I've ever encountered, but I think I'd like to be a part of it. For a bit, at least, to see how it works out."

"Excellent, I'll make up a story for Petra to get her warmed up to the idea," Lou smiled, clearly looking forward to further baiting Ursi's boss. "Anyway, Andy, Jay, Su. How does it look for the planned operation?"

"I think we could go now, based on what we've already seen," Andy responded. "Nevertheless, better belt and braces in this case," he smiled at Georgie, "so I'd propose waiting until tomorrow night."

"Yes, we could have an additional monitoring run tomorrow morning to check the speed of real-time updates," Jay added.

"And we need to switch in Hyo-jin, to check exactly what the Kims could be up to at present and minimise the risk of surprises tomorrow evening," Su contributed while the Korean nodded.

"Okay, I guess we're done for now, so have a good night's sleep," Lou winked and cut the connection.

"Yes, good point," Su grinned lasciviously. "We're off to bed, even though there may not be much sleep for a while. Fancy joining us, Ursi."

The blonde smiled wanly. "My foot is throbbing a bit, so I'll take a rain check there. I could go another brandy though, just to kill the pain."

"Your wish is my command," Andy topped up both their glasses before Su annexed the bottle and headed off, hand in hand with her lover.

"So, tell me now, just exactly what are you planning to do tomorrow?"

Andy grimaced. How was he going to dream up something that hid the fact that he still really did not have a clue?

Chapter 7 - Moving on

Andy was up early next morning, drinking a coffee and watching the huge waves that presaged the incoming storm hammer against the beach. Much to his disappointment, he had slept undisturbed for a solid eight hours. The gratuitously loud lesbian lovemaking had quickly died away and, despite his hopes, Ursi had failed to appear again in his bedroom. The question for him was: did this reflect the pain in her foot or a reconsideration of the relationship they seemed to have built up during the previous night?

His brooding was diverted when his naturist neighbour appeared. After dropping her towel, she stood on the surf line, obviously pondering whether or not it would be sensible to enter the water under such stormy conditions. Clearly deciding that discretion was the better part of valour, she turned back and despondently trudged back towards her towel. *Time for my good deed of the day.* Andy stood and waved at her, only then realising that he was also in his birthday suit at the present time.

The statuesque woman spotted him and waved cheerily, throwing the towel over her shoulder before heading up towards the wall that separated his villa from the beach. As he had guessed, she was German and was clearly disappointed at missing her early morning dip. Her accommodation was clearly much more modest, so Andy invited her to use their pool – an offer that she gratefully accepted. She was doing laps when Ursi emerged with her coffee.

"There's a naked matron in our pool," she commented in a whisper while she settled beside him on the upper terrace.

Andy feigned surprise, tapping an index finger against his chin. "O my God, so there is! I just hope they don't charge us extra for her!"

"It's the woman from yesterday, isn't it?"

"It is indeed. I invited her in when it was clear that the sea was too rough to swim in. It seemed like the neighbourly thing to do."

"And you like ogling her big boobs."

"Not ogling, just admiring. Not that yours are too terrible."

Ursi then seemed to realise that she was clad in only a selection of bandages. She first automatically moved to cover herself, then realised how pointless that was. "See, a couple of days with you lot and I'm totally corrupted."

"There's nothing corrupt about it. It's just rejection of religiously-inflicted morals that're well passed their sell-by date. Our neighbour, whose name is also Ursula by an odd coincidence, clearly doesn't give a shit about whether anyone sees her in the buff. And why should she. Enjoying the freedom of swimming naked does no harm to anyone."

"So, there's nothing at all sexual about it?" She raised her eyebrows to emphasise her scepticism.

"Nope, definitely not. If you want to see sexual provocation, visit our friends Heidi and Beat. They can be dressed from head to toe, but with a rigout and demeanour that has *time for sex* written all over it."

"Did someone say it's time for sex?" Su interrupted. "Has this anything to do with the naked woman in our pool?"

"Well, actually, you're also naked," Ursi pointed out.

"Yes, but I live here. And, in any case, anywhere that I live I can wear clothes if and when I want."

At that point, their naturist neighbour slowly emerged from the pool and shook her head to provide a shower of spray from her hair. "Mmm, that's really good," she sighed. "Our place is fine when I can swim in the sea, but this pool is great when the weather is trickier. Oh, Andy, are these your friends?"

Andy was glad that Hyo-jin had not yet emerged, so he didn't need to translate Ursula's Hochdeutsch for anyone. "It's great that you enjoyed it. We hardly ever use the pool so you're welcome any time that you fancy, whether we're here or not. Anyway, this is my friend, another Ursula although we all call her Ursi."

"Oh, no, Ursi, that looks painful." Ursula peered at Ursi's bandages. Clearly the fact that Andy's friend was also nude was considered unremarkable. "What happened to you?"

"Just a trip on an uneven bit of road. Really, it's not as bad as it looks. Anyway, I'm glad that you had a nice swim." Ursi was trying not to stare at Ursula's large breasts, which jiggled wildly while she towelled her hair."

"And this is Su…" Andy put his arm around his colleague's shoulder.

Ursula stared at Su's body. "Hi, Su. I must say that those are wonderful tattoos! I was often tempted, but my husband always managed to talk me out of it. Maybe just as well, as I'd be a rather wrinkly canvas by now," she laughed.

"I think you look great," Su responded with a twinkle in her eyes and a tone that was clearly suggestive. "I'm a bit of an exhibitionist, so you can have a closer look if you want."

Ursula's cheery smile widened. "I better get back for breakfast now, but I'd be happy to take you up on that offer later." With a wave she headed back to her own villa, still vigorously drying her hair.

"Ah, yet another matron beguiled by my Sapphic charms," Su grinned.

"I think she only want to look at your tattoos," Andy pointed out.

"That's how it always starts," Su responded confidently. "I predict that she'll be in bed with Hyo-jin and me in no time."

"Good grief," Ursi shook her head in disbelief. "Do you try to seduce every woman that you meet?"

"No, of course not. Just the interesting ones. And you look pretty interesting to me," she drew Ursi into a kind of group hug, which gave her the opportunity to caress the NDB agent's shapely bottom.

Andy noticed that Ursi seemed somewhat perturbed by this obvious groping, but didn't attempt to pull away. *Please don't let it be a lesbian foursome tonight – I'm not sure my self-confidence could handle that.*

***

The wind was building up while black clouds moved in from the west, a harbinger of the incoming storm. As heavy rain could not be far away, Andy elected to quickly walk round the hotel again to check on the improved monitoring option. As he left, Ursi was swimming in the pool for the gentle exercise that the good doctor had recommended while the others lay basking in the last rays of the watery sun.

Both data capture and subsequent transmission had been considerably speeded up by a differential filter that Lou and Jay had cobbled together. This involved removal of background that was unchanged since the previous scan and hence allowed focusing on things that had changed and, in particular, the persons present. After returning to the villa, Andy had to wait less than an hour before the first results were available. Despite the wind and threat of immanent rain, the team assembled at the outside table for Georgie's presentation. The quantum guru was back in Hello Kitty mode and, after Lou had checked on Ursi's condition, launched immediately into her presentation. "Well, there's good and bad news. Which would you like first?"

"Good, definitely the good," Su quickly answered.

"Well, the kit works even better than I had hoped. We're now able to both identify those present and actually monitor their movements during the scan. If we build further on this for a third scan, I'm fairly sure that Lou, Jay and I can refine the analyses sufficiently that we'll be able to give you results in real time."

"Bloody hell, that's truly amazing," Andy commented.

"And bloody frightening," Ursi added. "There're many regimes that'd kill for this technology."

"Not to mention dodgy industries, politicians and criminal groups," Lou acknowledged. "Yes, we're painfully aware what a double-edged sword this is."

"So, was that also the bad news?" Su enquired.

Jay took over the presentation. "No, the bad news is specific to this case. The six underlings are clearly present, but there's not a trace of the Kims."

"Fuck me," Andy groaned. "How's that even possible?"

"The CCTV and webcam hack has been running in the background ever since the Koreans arrived in Corfu, so I focussed on any anomalies in the case of vehicles leaving the hotel since the scan yesterday. From this, I picked up a drinks-delivery van, which seems to unload at a back door of the residence that has no cam coverage of any kind. The strange thing is that it then drove directly to the commercial entrance of the international airport and, after ten minutes, drove back to Acharavi. At present it's still sitting in a public car park."

"I guess you've pulled logs for all aircraft leaving after that time," Andy frowned.

"Yes, we're working on that now. The commercial flights are easy, but there are at least three private jets that could be possibilities. Their common characteristics are logged destinations that are very small airfields in different EU countries and an absence of independent confirmation of their arrival."

"Shit! This is the Kims' shell-game approach once again. Right, finding them is now our top priority. I also want to find out how the hell they were possibly tipped off."

Ursi looked sheepish. "I think I may have an idea about that. What time did our targets do their disappearing act?"

"Just after five, yesterday afternoon."

Andy slapped his forehead. "That would be about an hour after we went to the clinic."

"Yes, and on the admission form, I had to specify my accident insurance, even though we were paying cash."

"Which, of course, runs through NDB. Bugger! If the Kims have a background hack running that picks up any local anomalies, that could have rung alarm bells."

Jay nodded to agree with Andy's interpretation. "It'd need to be rather sophisticated, but it's certainly doable. Especially if this was an AI set up when the property here was purchased, it could iteratively evolve to be very sensitive and, after their escape from Zurich, would have a special focus on any potential links to Switzerland."

Andy shook his head in dismay. "Okay, I guess that's all our planning here up the spout. We may as well head home."

"Not in the next twenty-four hours, you're not. Corfu airport is already closed due to the approaching storm, which looks pretty bad," Lou reported.

"Bollocks! I suppose we can first focus on finding out where the Kims are heading and how we can chase after them. We'll need to be extra careful after spooking them this time. In any case, we can inform the Chinese so that they can pick up the sacrificial lambs that were abandoned here. This might, at least, divert some attention from the Swiss link that we've now exposed."

Lou nodded. "Jay and I will set up a leak to the Chinese embassy in Athens, informing Petra only afterwards, so that she has complete deniability." Ursi rolled her eyes at this, but said nothing.

"I guess we all know what to do," Andy summarised. "Su and Hyo-jin should work with Jay on tracing the Kims, as we need any hints on the likely behaviour of these women that we can get."

"And what are you going to do?" Su asked.

"I'm going to have a little brainstorming with Ursi and Georgie to think about what other miracles Peta-qubit computers can pull out of the hat for us."

"Do you think that'll actually help us at present?" Lou did not sound convinced.

"Not the slightest clue, that's why we're doing the brainstorming." Andy smiled in his usual annoying way, causing both Su and Lou to groan aloud. He was happy to tease his colleagues, but was beginning to suspect that something special was going to be needed to prevent the Kims from continually eluding him.

***

To Andy's amazement, his prepared introduction to the brainstorming was completely superfluous. Immediately after Georgie had checked that Ursi was indeed recovering well from her injuries, she launched into her concept of how to go forward on their project. "It's relatively straightforward, as Jay has already set up the tools for sophisticated data mining, the traditional semantic web stuff."

Andy and Ursi looked at each other with raised eyebrows, but Georgie was clearly oblivious to this and continued. "This runs well on a conventional supercomputer and a bit quicker on a quantum machine, a few orders of magnitude or so. But we could do so much more on a hypercomputer. Instead of starting with the constraints of search parameters and dredging through appropriate parts of the global knowledge base, we just provide a few hints about how to solve the problem and stand back."

"How does it actually find the solution we want?" Ursi asked with a frown.

"Ah, that's an extremely difficult question that I haven't even started to look into. I've never liked the term artificial intelligence, especially when we're just identifying correlations using a generative, semantic, neural network. A quantum neural network is quite another beast, however, and the AI label might really be justified here. Anyway, maybe best just to accept this as a black box that does stuff."

"I guess I can accept that, so what do we need?" Andy scratched his head in evident confusion.

"Well, I've actually specified the problem: *where are the Kims most likely to be and how did they get there?* So, I just need a few hints to get the system moving as effectively as possible. Can we link in Hyo-jin for a minute?"

"No problem…" Andy dropped out and a couple of minutes later the Korean was included in the link, together with Su to act as an interface, if needed.

"Okay, Hyo-jin, I just want you to answer a couple of question to start a search for our elusive enemies. I want you to imagine that you are one of the Kims and are deciding what to do after they spot a Swiss security operative on their doorstep."

"Seems fucking stupid," Hyo-jin scowled.

"Just have a go, love," Su put her arm around the Korean's shoulder.

"So, anyway, if you were a Kim and suspect you may've been traced from Switzerland, what'd be your first reaction?" Georgie continued.

"Fuck off quickly, far away, out of Europe."

"Excellent. And how would you do this?"

"Stupid question. They have to fly to fuck off fast."

"Yes, but you've been traced to Corfu. Maybe this isn't a good option?"

"Change plan completely. Fly a different way and break the trip."

"Why would you leave your underlings behind?"

"Too easy to trace and maybe not possible to take along on some escape routes. Fuck them anyway."

"Where would you not go?"

"Fucking States. Far too many mad bastards there. Not anywhere with lots of Koreans or Chinese, who might recognise the world number-one evil cunts."

"What would you need to have in your safe house?"

"Must be a place with everything under control and other escape routes already in place. Needs good transport links, but not too many people."

"Okay, that should do it," Georgie smiled. "Thanks a lot Hyo-jin, that's been very helpful."

"What the fuck was that all about?" Su frowned. "How's this little Q and A session going to help find the Kims?"

"Well, we'll find out in a couple of minutes."

"What?" Andy and Ursi asked simultaneously, causing Georgie to laugh.

"Yes, well, Hyo-jin's input was feeding directly to the super machine, which is now building the semantic algorithm to frame the enquiry and organise related fast feeds from the global internet knowledge base. That's the slow bit. This then drops into the hyper-computer and we immediately have the answer."

"And that answer will be?" Ursi enquired.

"Where the Kims are and how they got there."

"And you're sure it'll work?" Ursi continued.

"Well, not one hundred percent, of course, as this's a novel application. But the basic principles are effectively the same as the decryption and waveform inversion applications."

"I'll take your word for it," Andy shrugged.

Ursi shook her head. "You realise, of course, that this is yet another paradigm change in search engine fundamentals, which could have huge socio-economic and security impacts?"

"Yes, the hyper-computer is certainly a game changer, as I've said many times," Georgie nodded. "Okay, here's the answer. The Kims are in the

Maldives, somewhere called the Reethi Faru resort. They own a couple of villas there. The travel plan is complex, so I'll transfer the file to you."

"Christ almighty," Andy gasped. "How on earth did it do that?"

Georgie grinned. "I've told you before, that's a very difficult question that I haven't been able to nail down yet."

"Hyper-quantum fucking black magic," Hyo-jin commented.

Andy, Ursi and Su could only nod in agreement.

***

The hyper analysis indicated that the entire delivery van and associated departing private flights were an elaborate ruse. Biometric and gait analysis of hacked images from all kinds of cameras indicated that the Kims, both sporting blonde wigs and wide-brimmed hats, walked to the Petra restaurant, took a taxi from there to a nearby shopping centre and then drove a rental car to the airport. They boarded a scheduled flight to Athens using Maltese passports and then transferred, now with lurid red and blue wigs, to an Etihad flight bound for Abu Dhabi and thence onto another flight to Male. They entered the Maldives using Swiss passports and were immediately shuttled to a chartered seaplane flight to Reethi Faru.

Due to rising sea levels, the exclusive holiday resorts on the Maldivian atolls were being gradually abandoned as the costs of flood defences became prohibitive. Reethi Faru had gained a reprieve by selling some of the luxury villas in the resort to foreign investors. The two largest *water villas* appeared to be owned by an Australian businessman, who was a non-executive director of one of the Kims' network of shell companies. The Kims were now entrenched in one of these villas, while local staff lived in the other.

Andy was flabbergasted. "This's nothing like I would have expected, but I suppose it makes a lot of sense. Unlike Corfu, there's no way that we could sneak onto a small atoll like that without being picked up by smart monitors. As the resort is still open for business, I guess we could subcontract intrusion to some private group with no direct connections to us. What do you think?"

"And do what?" Su was scanning through aerial images of the island and, in particular, the villas extending along a long causeway on its west end. "The villa can't possibly be approached by stealth along that boardwalk, which is the only access. So the only way to apply Georgie's miracle monitoring would require a drone, which is explicitly forbidden in that resort. The water immediately around the villas is shallow and isolated from deeper water by a manmade reef, with only a few open access points. Again, undetected intrusion will be impossible if the Kims have prepared this place like they have the others."

"Fucking sure thing," Hyo-jin scowled. "This is not a place for Kims to live, just to hide out until it is safe to move back to the real world."

"So, what do we do now? Leak this information to the Chinese and let them sort it out?" Ursi asked.

"Fucking cunts will know Chinks' movements for sure, because those bastards only use their own people. Any Chinese operation will likely have Kim clan's moles and for definite they will be watching for this, as they will know it was the Chinks who hit the Geneva house."

"So, I guess it's up to us then," Andy shrugged. "The first tricky bit will be getting from Corfu to the Maldives without hitting a tripwire somewhere."

"Actually, I ran an inverse of Jay's tracking algorithm to look at this," Georgie said shyly. "It can easily run on the supercomputer and there was one nice option that had a very low risk of being picked up, especially as you don't fly to Male, which is a bit of a bottleneck as far as Maldives access is concerned."

Andy frowned. "So, how does that work?"

"Fly back to Switzerland and change identities. Set off immediately as two pairs, one via Vienna and Mumbai and the other via Dubai, but both ending up in Colombo. There you pick up a liveaboard dive charter, which will appear to have been booked six months ago. A couple of days cruising and you'll be in the best diving areas of the northern Maldives."

"Nice one, Georgie," Andy grinned. "Not only an access concept that's very unlikely to be picked up, but one that gets us a bit of gratuitous diving. Just to ensure that we look the part, of course."

"No underwater shit for me," Hyo-jin stated categorically.

"Well, let's just play it by ear," Su smiled. "What about you, Ursi, do you dive?"

"I've qualified as an open water diver, but haven't dived in the last couple of years."

"Oh, well, we'll get you back in form pretty quickly. Then we can look at novel experiences for you. For example, have you ever had sex underwater?"

Andy groaned theatrically and rolled his eyes. Su was completely incorrigible and, regardless of what dodgy situation they were in, could also find time to fit in a quick bit of seduction. Not, of course, that he had anything against underwater sex, per se, but preferably one-on-one with the shapely blonde rather than as an observer to one of Su's Sapphic scenarios. And even better if it was after the Kims had been sorted out. He was sure that, despite the incredible feats that Georgie could pull off with her new technology, it wasn't going to be easy to beard the Kims in their new lair.

Chapter 8 - Quantum AI attack mode

Four days later, their charter boat was approaching *The Labyrinth,* a dive site close to the Reethi Faru resort. Ursi, Su and Andy had now dived together with the guide who was part of the crew and become familiar with their kit and the way in which scuba was organised on board. This would be their first dive without the guide and Su, who had most diving experience and thus would act as leader, was double-checking the dive plan on her computer.

The water was a warm 28°C, so both Andy and Ursi were wearing only swimming briefs and reef shirts. Su was even more sparsely clad, wearing only a skimpy tanga bottom. The boat catered predominantly for rich clients from northern Europe, so the Sri Lankan crew were unbothered by this, despite the much stricter constraints on naked flesh in the Muslim countries of this region.

All three were diving with nitrox, despite Su being the only one specifically trained to use this option. The smart dive computers worn by Andy and Ursi, which were linked to both their own regulators and slaved to Su's, made this as easy as diving with conventional compressed air.

From the boat, they gradually dropped to a depth of 30 metres, then slowly threaded their way towards the top of the reef through a maze of narrow gullies. The labyrinth was well-named and filled with an amazing diversity of fish of every colour, shape and size imaginable, set against a backdrop of amazing coral formations. For Andy, it was close to a complete sensory overload. There was just too much to take in, especially as this piscatorial wallpaper was in constant 3D movement. Although the dive was so fascinating that time seemed to fly by, when he climbed back on board after 70 minutes underwater, Andy had the first inkling of a plan for the attack on the Kims' seemingly impregnable redoubt.

**

Early next morning, waking up beside a rather sweaty Ursi, Andy's concept for a raid on the Kims was beginning to crystallise in detail. A virtual meeting with the entire team provided him with a chance to check that this was not totally off the wall. However, the situation in the Maldives actually came last in the agenda, which initially focused on an update of the global status of the finance industry and then went on to the specific case of Switzerland and the boundary conditions for NetSec as a company. The bottom line here was that a global recession was inevitable and, as usual, would hit the poorest communities most. The one silver lining was that Swiss support of many of the worst hit would effectively be funded by the cash ripped off from the billionaires who were predominantly responsible for this inequality. This was especially pleasing given that it was the last thing that such plutocrats would have considered, had they any say in the matter.

Lou finished with some numbers on suicides amongst the great and the good, many of whom had been gutted by the crypto-crash. Ursi looked guilty, but Andy and Su laughed aloud. Jay was also smiling. "Whenever shit hits the fan, it's generally the poor that suffer. Nice to see that the boot is now on the other foot."

"All very Robin Hood," Lou frowned, "but these hara-kiri types are the runts of the pack. The big boys aren't going to accept loss of wealth and power without a fight."

"Well, they'll be going toe-to-toe with the NDB, who've already got the funds secreted away in inaccessible accounts," Jay pointed out.

"Not true, actually," Georgie contributed, today a boy dressed in a sombre black tracksuit. "I could extract all of that in no time."

"Okay," Jay conceded, "inaccessible to anyone who is not a genius with the most powerful computer in the world in their basement."

"Yup, that's more like it," Georgie grinned.

"Anyway," Andy broke in, "can we come back to us here, twiddling our thumbs in paradise? We've got to draw a line under the initial Korean attack in order to start moving forward cleanly. This means that we need to take out the Kims."

"Doesn't look easy," Lou scowled. "In fact, I'd say almost impossible without bringing in outside support and risking a lot of collateral damage."

"Well, I do have an idea here." Andy paused and allowed the wave of annoyance from the others to pass over him. "I'll need a bit of help from Georgie and it won't be easy, but I think it's doable."

Georgie's grin widened. "With the tools I've got now, if it's doable, then it's easy."

There was no reply to that.

***

As Andy later explained to the Maldives team, the tricky bits were, firstly, confirming that the Kims were indeed in the villa and, secondly, getting a team to the villa with the kit required to counter any defences that might be in place. The former was Georgie's task, as he had an idea for drastically enhancing the images that could be obtained by combining images from an on-board telescope at the limits of line-of-sight to the villa and a couple of spy satellites that occasionally looked on to it from a low angle. This would allow the Kims to be identified if they went out onto the covered deck during the observation period, even if light levels were very low.

"Basically, it's just the same as any other synthetic aperture analysis. Here we increase the data input by including all reflections from waves and then it's just another standard inversion problem." Georgie's explanation elicited a grin from Andy and a frown from Ursi.

"Wasted time," Hyo-jin concluded. "The evil cunts are there and will have top-level defences and a good escape plan. You need a lot of idiots with big guns, so you can move in quickly. Assault from the front is the only way."

"If the defences are good, how would a heavy team like that work?" Su wondered out loud.

266

"That is why idiots with big guns. These are cannon food, to keep the evil bitches busy while we come in from the back."

"But you also mentioned their good escape plan," Ursi reminded her.

Hyo-jin grimaced. "Needs luck, so hit in the middle of night and use gas like rapist fucker did in Locarno. Maybe it will work."

"I don't like maybes," Andy's grin widened, "and we don't need cannon fodder, which would be the weakest part of this approach in any case. We know how good the Kims' surveillance systems are and I don't think we'd be able to get an assault team anywhere near the island before they hit an alarm. Shit, I don't want to even take this dive boat over the horizon in case we're spotted."

"Rapist is not completely stupid," Hyo-jin reluctantly conceded.

"Okay, smart guy," Su glared, increasingly Andy's evident amusement. "What's your cunning plan this time?"

"I think we're safe in assuming that the villa will be surrounded by sensors covering land, sea and air approaches. Any comms therein will certainly be in a Faraday cage, with power isolated from the mains. I'd guess all external data flow would be through optical cables and then via a line-of-sight laser link to a commercial satellite somewhere. However, cable links and repeaters mean that the satellite link could be tens or hundreds of kilometres away."

"Well, that sounds fairly invulnerable," Ursi looked relieved.

"Not really, you see the Faraday cage is predominantly aimed at avoiding either leakage of, or access by, radio waves and other low-frequency, long-wavelength radiation. If all their communication is based on the hardware inside that cage, then this is the vulnerability that we can exploit."

"Blow it to fuck," Hyo-jin nodded. "But we only kill the Kims that way, not the torture that we agreed."

"Yes, well that's why we don't use explosives on the villa, just a collated EMP generator."

"An EMP pulse won't impact anything inside the cage," Su interrupted.

"But we'll use a pulse with a particularly high x-ray component. That'll go straight through the Faraday cage. We can be sure that the Kims will have ultra-high-performance computers, which are particularly vulnerable to high x-ray doses. We're lucky that they're in a thin-walled, wooden villa on stilts over the water. It wouldn't work against a Faraday cage in a deep underground basement."

Su still looked unconvinced. "I know that there're optically-pumped x-ray lasers, but these produce very short pulses and take time to recharge. How'll that work?"

"Well, being a boy scout, I have a bank of super-capacitors and an x-ray laser in our kit. These weren't actually selected with this application in mind, so there's some cobbling to be done. If I go for the shortest pulses, which're about a picosecond on this kit, I could get something like microsecond recharge times. It'll take a while to fully charge the capacitors before we start. But, after that, if I go full out, we could probably fire for about ten seconds."

"And you think that'll be enough?" Su frowned. We'll need to be far enough away that we don't cause an alarm in advance and we don't know where the Faraday cage is located."

"Ah, that's the cunning bit. We initially have a beam wide enough to illuminate the entire villa and use Georgie's collimated squids to detect the resulting EM emissions from the first hit in order to map the entire contents of the house. The Faraday cage will stand out and hence we immediately focus the beam on any solid objects within it."

"But your first hit will probably set off all kinds of alarms."

"Might do, but certainly external monitors will pick up the irradiation at some point. I'm betting that these would not be in the villa, but scattered around the perimeter. Somewhere far enough away to give a reasonable advance warning of something strange happening. But these can't be linked directly to the villa with optical cables without a lot of work that would have given the game away. They'll be optically linked to a satellite repeater and maybe further repeaters to ensure that the dataflow can't be traced."

"And this helps us how?" Ursi was still confused, but Su had started to nod.

"Speed of light!" Su got in before Andy. "I guess we'll be reasonably close…"

"I was already planning on setting up on the uninhabited island of Ufulandhoo. This's only about a couple of kilometres from the villa and has dive sites around it, so we shouldn't hit any trip-wires getting there. Anchor the boat in plain view and set up a barbeque on the beach. We then send the crew off in the Zodiac for a couple of days R and R, giving us freedom to get our kit in place."

Ursi was still frowning, so Andy continued. "After our first x-ray hit, we get the return signal in about point one microsecond. This allows us to focus in on the target and hammer away at it with a Megahertz frequency. Depending on how convoluted the Korean communication network is, their monitoring signal may cover thousands or even tens of thousands of kilometres. Even without processing times, this'll take tens or hundreds of microseconds, which means the first hundreds or thousands of hits can't be avoided. Even if they have an offensive system capable of targeting us here, it'll take seconds for it to be aimed and fired, as something like a laser powerful enough to hit us here would have to be charged up. During this time, the entire processing unit will be frying and should be slag well before a significant response could be implemented."

Now Su frowned. "Yes, that's all fine, but you're forgetting about the time needed for Georgie to deconvolute the first signal and do the focusing. Here we're up against speed of light for our communication, even if all hypercomputer calculations are effectively instant."

"Georgie pointed this out to me, which is why she modelled in advance the signatures of a credible range of cage distributions within the villa. We now have these locally to allow automatic focusing as soon as we get the first return. Georgie will use this to refine the focus as required within the first millisecond or so."

"And you're willing to bet your life… actually all our lives… on you being correct?"

"Not at all, love," Su put her arm around the slim blonde's waist, "Andy's too much of a coward to go for an option with that kind of risk."

Andy winked at his nemesis. "You've got me to a tee. This'll all be running under expert-system control. We'll be on jet skis, ready to head for the villa from a completely different angle as soon as the attack commences."

"Even then, you're sure that we won't get picked up by their monitors?

"It'll be tens of seconds before we're underway from the anchored dive boat, so the entire control system will be well fried by then."

"And you'll know that how?"

"We'll be preceded by a swarm of drones that'll explode in the event of any active counter-measures. If they're untouched, then we're go for intrusion. Any colourful explosion overhead and we turn tail and run."

Su and Ursi looked at each other and shrugged, clearly out of arguments against Andy's plan.

With perfect timing, Georgie broke in. "Okay, I've now got visual confirmation of the Kims. They're on the covered terrace having a sundowner at the present moment. So, I guess we're go for tonight."

"We need to get a move on with our beach barbeque to cover installation of the x-ray attack system," Andy frowned as he scratched his head. "We should get that all done while there's still light. We can relax after the meal when we're cruising towards our jet ski dispatch point. We'll aim to start at 2 am, so there's even time for a snooze before we gird up our loins for action."

"A snooze, you've got to be joking," Ursi shook her head.

"Of course he's joking," Su laughed. "If we're risking life and limb, the most obvious thing to do beforehand is to have a good shag! So, Ursi, are you in for a quick bit of girl-on-girl action?"

"Jesus, Su, you're completely incorrigible," Ursi shook her head again, but seemed marginally less terrified than before.

***

The team kitted up in black, skin-tight suits that were both waterproof and included an inner bullet-proof, fullerene-carbon-fibre mesh. These were complemented by combat gloves, boots and helmets with inbuilt communications. The heads-up display on their visors defaulted to enhanced light amplification, allowing them to see clearly despite a night when the new moon appeared only rarely through heavy cloud cover. Their utility belts contained weapons and other tools in waterproof pouches.

While the jet skis raced towards the villa, Georgie provided a first report on progress with the attack over their helmet comms. "EM bounce-back synthesis confirms that the women are in the right-hand bedroom as you approach the villa. The Faraday cage is in the centre of the left-side bedroom. I guess we can take it that all computers are well fried, given the lack of any counter attack. I cut back the pulse rate of the x-ray laser to ten hertz after eight seconds, so this is providing only an illumination source for the squids."

"And what about our targets?" Ursi asked.

"They're up and moving about in their bedroom. I guess there was some kind of alarm linked to an electro-mechanical dead-man's switch, so they know that they're under attack. They haven't attempted to leave the bedroom, so are probably waiting for reinforcements. I've no idea if wiping out their central server will have prevented a call for help going out but, in the worst case, we could expect a heavy team getting mobilised somewhere in the vicinity, probably the neighbouring villa."

"Bugger, this could get messy." Andy crouched lower on the stand-up ski to help maximise his approach speed. "Anyway, launch the gas attack on both villas and then use the drones to set up a perimeter around the one where the Kims are lurking so that we can detect any unexpected guests to our party."

"Already done," Georgie responded smugly. "However, our targets are still moving, so either there's something blocking the gas rounds or these ladies have some form of protection against the gas."

"Well, keep an eye on them and see if there's any specific threat that we'll need to take into account," Andy quickly checked their progress in the ghostly display projected onto his visor. "We'll be through the entry channel and into the inner lagoon in three minutes and it'll then be only a minute to the villa. Thank God it's calm tonight. I don't want to think about what that pair could get up to if we gave them more time."

"Calm, what's fucking calm about it?" Ursi muttered over the comms link. Andy then realised that the sit-down skis carrying her and Hyo-jin were gradually falling behind. On the other hand, Su was right on his tail. He grinned. Despite her known distaste of field work, it was clear that Su's competitive spirit was taking over for the moment.

Time seemed to slowly drag until they reached the inner lagoon and then go super-fast as the villa approached. Andy almost fell into the water when he jerked the ski into a right-angled turn that brought him sliding broadsides in a plume of spray towards the steps leading up to the villa terrace. More by luck than judgement, just as he was losing balance, he managed to jump off the craft and land sprawling on the bottom of the stairs. Scrambling up rapidly, his left foot was snagged at the top of the stairs and he fell heavily forward.

Automatically twisting to see what had caused his fall, Andy froze. The front of his boot was still caught there and showed a razor-sharp cut. "Fuck! Su, watch out when you come up. It looks like a molecular-fibre trip-wire. It would've cut my fucking foot off, if not for the armour in my boot. We've taken down all their electronic defences, but the bitches also have purely mechanical traps."

Aware that the protective layer in his gloves was much thinner than that in the rest of his suit, Andy extracted small shears from a pocket and cut though where he expected the wire to be on the outside of his boots as, even with his enhanced vision visor, it was impossible to see the ultra-fine fibre. Once cut free and without tension, the wire was effectively harmless, but Andy made a mental note to be especially careful when later taking off his boots.

Su was now standing at the bottom of the steps, looking up at him. "You okay now?"

"Yup, all fine now. Just follow behind me so that I hit any traps first. But not too close, just in case."

"Fine, but this carry-on reminds me just how much I hate field operations."

"Okay, I'm at the door to the main lounge now. Probably better to go in though here rather than directly into the bedroom. This is sliding glass, but opaque, probably one-way, so I'm just going to give it a quick multi-spectral scan before I try opening it."

Jay provided the interpretation of the scan. "There're some serious bolts holding the door in place, probably deployed automatically as soon as the alarm sounded or power was lost. Looks like you're going to have to go through the glass."

"I'll bet it's seriously bullet-proof, but a shaped charge should do the job."

Andy slapped the charge onto the middle of the door but, just before he detonated it, picked up Hyo-jin's muttering. "Rapist bastard is going to fuck-up. That is just what evil cunts will expect him to do."

"Wait a minute, Su. Move down the steps until you're below the level of the deck. I'm just going to move along to the far corner here, just in case your Korean pal is right on this."

"What's the problem? It's a shaped charge and the blast will go inwards…" Su gasped as the door exploded into a hail of razor-sharp shrapnel that passed over her head. "Fucking hell, how's that even possible?"

Andy breathed a sigh of relief. "I'd guess that was anisotropic, hyper-stressed glass. Incredibly strong, but when it fails it does so catastrophically with the blast direction set by its stress field. Again, a defence that's inherent to the design, works even in case of total black out and fails safe as far as the occupants of the villa are concerned. Despite our suits, we'd have been seriously hurt if we were standing in the way of that."

"Okay, that's me out of this. Do your fucking Rambo stuff and leave me here to wet myself in peace."

"That's fine, just stay back, Su," Ursi broke in. "I'm just about to climb up the right-hand steps onto the terrace, with Hyo-jin close behind. We'll provide the backup for Andy."

"All of you stay back until I've cleared the entrance, as other booby-traps are likely." Andy struggled to hide the waver in his voice caused by his close escape. "I'm just entering the lounge, so the room with the Faraday cage is to my left and the Kims' den to my right. Their bedroom door looks solid, so I'm going to use another shaped charge – but placed on the door-frame rather than the door itself."

"Just stay well clear when you set it off," Jay instructed. "I can't imagine what kind of defences they could have built in here, but there's likely to be something deadly on the other side of that door."

Andy retreated onto the terrace before he blew the door, noting that it flew away from the bedroom not into it, just before a hail of bullets fanned through the open doorway. More seriously, he saw a line of holes appear in the wall, stepping towards where he was sheltering. "Armour-piercing rounds!" he screamed while throwing himself onto his stomach. He squirmed around to locate a couple of flash-bang grenades, which he threw into the lounge at an angle that would bounce them into the bedroom. He was cautiously climbing to his feet when a form flashed past him and hurled itself into the villa.

His recognition of what was happening coincided with Ursi's shout. "Hyo-jin, get down. Don't go in there before Andy's cleared the place."

Georgie's map of the villa ghosted onto Andy's visor. The three Korean women were clearly blasting hell out of each other and wild shots were going everywhere.

"Andy, can you get to Hyo-jin?" Su shouted desperately.

"I don't know how anyone is still alive with the amount of shooting going on, either bad marksmanship or very good armour. Anyway, I'll chance it." He jumped up, ran at a crouch into the lounge and then took a running dive though the bedroom door in the direction of a hallway that should lead to a baggage storage area and the en-suite bathroom. Rolling onto his knees he could see Hyo-jin crouching at one side of a huge bed, raising her Uzi to fire blindly towards the other side of the room. Just after he worked out that the Kims were at the other side of the bed, a bullet nicked Hyo-jin's arm and she rolled onto the floor, dropping her weapon and screaming in pain.

Georgie's map was detailed enough to show figures cautiously standing up to improve their angle of fire onto Hyo-jin's position. *They don't even know I'm here.* Andy grinned as he stood and moved around the corner into the room, blasting at his two targets with his assault rifle on full-automatic.

As his bullets hit them, his targets flew through the air, slamming into the wall behind them and slumping to the ground. Even in the heat of battle, Andy was shocked by the realisation that he had just shot two women. This provided Hyo-jin with the opportunity to push past him and start wildly stabbing his nearest victim with a huge hunting knife. Time seemed to slow as he took in the ongoing action. It looked like the Kims, despite being clad only in heavy-duty armoured vests, had survived his fusillade. Hyo-jin clearly intended to remedy this and was concentrating entirely on what looked like Gaeun, slashing every bit of exposed flesh on her arms and legs while using her other hand to pummel her face.

This display of psychopathic rage distracted Andy for long enough that Dam-Bi had already started to swing her rifle in his direction before he was aware of the threat. A bladder-loosening shock of fear registered just before a bullet hit his visor and everything went black.

***

Andy slowly regained consciousness, much amazed to be alive. His helmet had been removed and he lay hauled halfway onto a bullet-ripped bed, looking up into the concerned faces of Ursi and Su. Even Hyo-jin's scowl looked less fierce than usual. "Jeez, I'm not dead," he sighed.

Su immediately smiled. "Of course you're not, you daft bugger, but not for lack of trying." She bent forward and kissed him gently on the forehead. "Thanks for going after my mad girlfriend, I really appreciate that," she whispered in his ear. Immediately afterwards, she punched him on the shoulder. "So, get your undead flabby arse in gear, you big wuss. It's time to blow this joint before the Chinks appear on the scene."

Andy pushed himself to his feet and gently shook his head before he looked towards their targets. Amazingly, Gaeun was still alive, although looking like she had been through a meat grinder.

He looked at Su, who grimaced. "After my girl, the ripper, finally cooled down a bit, we managed to get her to back off and stopped that bitch's bleeding to the extent possible."

"Hyo-jin let you do this?"

"Her idea," another grimace. "She hopes that Gaeun will be alive when the Chinese get here and do a proper torture job on her".

"Bollocks! Probably kinder to put a bullet though her brain."

"I thought about that also, but doubt that it'd end well," she glanced meaningfully in the direction of her blood-soaked partner.

Andy bent over to look at the body of Dam-Bi, sporting a neat hole in the middle of her forehead and lying in a pool of blood and brains.

"You've Ursi to thank for that," Su grimaced again. "Your helmet protected you from the first round, but a second hit would have been end-game for you. Luckily, blondie here shoots at competition-level, so she was your guardian angel here."

The NDB woman looked unhappy and had a suspicious stain on the front of her suit which seemed to fit with a subtle smell of vomit. "I didn't have any choice, it was her or you," she muttered.

"Completely fine with me," Andy stood and put an arm around her shoulder. "You can think of it as a kindness, anyway. If you hadn't killed her, she'd be looking at the same years of torture facing her compatriot here. Anyway, Su's right, time to clear out of this place. Back to our dive boat and away from here as quickly as possible. With a bit of luck, the Chinese will cause such chaos when they rock up that we'll be able to quietly vanish."

"But, before you go, remember to destroy the Faraday cage and pick up those cases that the Kims had with them," Lou added over the audio link. "I'm sure we'll find rich pickings there that'll add to our international relief fund."

"Minus one permil, of course," Andy added, which brought a smile even to Hyo-Jin's face.

Part 5: Technological singularity

Chapter 1 - Do not meddle with the Swiss

Despite the success of their mission, when the Maldives team returned to Wettingen it was to face increasing numbers of questions about how NetSec had actually managed to pull so many rabbits out of hats in such a short period of time. Their actions seemed little short of miraculous, with the only saving grace being that very few people actually knew of their role in this tectonic shift of the global socio-political landscape. Nevertheless, those who did know were getting extremely worried, which was very much in line with the concerns that Ursi had been bringing up throughout her attachment.

After releasing Hyo-Jin to her bolthole in Luzern, the rest of the team were now assembled in the main meeting room, which had AI syntheses of progress so far ghosting on the main screens. As usual, Lou kicked things off. "Hard though it is to believe, our actions over the last couple of weeks are putting serious pressure on us."

"We've saved two global meltdowns and also helped to take out two of the most wanted people on the planet and the pressure's on us?" Su was clearly on the edge of exploding.

"Yes, love, that's exactly the case. The saves came from Switzerland and it wasn't too hard for the big boys, the US in particular, to work out how this was done. Obviously, they don't have details, but they're smart enough to know that we've got quantum-computing supremacy in some shape or form."

A rather cryptic Georgie in jeans and a football top scowled in confusion. "So what? From the very beginning, this had to be obvious. It's just a fact and there's nothing they can do about it."

"Ah, there's the rub. The messages from Washington request, in the strongest possible terms, that we turn control of our computers over to them. The only other alternative is to show that our computing facility is permanently decommissioned."

Georgie exploded. "Fuck them and their claims to be the only super-power! If not for us, they'd now be part of the third word. Arrogant bastards! If they want to mess with Switzerland, then upon their own heads be it."

Andy grabbed the irate geek and crushed her to his chest. "It's a pisser, I know that, but we're just little Switzerland. We can't go head-to-head with the big boys, and especially not the US of A."

"Why not? If we're ever going to do it, this is the time."

"Seriously? You're proposing that we stand against the States here?" Lou was clearly having difficulties getting her head around this bizarre concept.

"Why not?" Georgie grinned. "There's never been a time when we have so much international credibility and the US has so little."

"Come on, this's just arm-waving. The US is a nuclear super-power and we're very good at banking," Lou looked into his eyes. "This asymmetry is just something that we have to live with."

"Or not," the quantum guru grinned. "What if the nuclear card is simply removed from the gameboard?"

In the subsequent hubbub, Andy simply sat back with a grin. *Sharing a bed with a truly weird person who might be one of the smartest humans on the planet ensures that life will never be anything but interesting.*

Ursi looked shocked. "You're talking about hacking the US military, aren't you?"

"That would be daft and would cause global destabilisation, which is just what we don't need at present." Ursi looked relieved until Georgie continued. "No, I'll hack the military of all nations with any weapons of mass destruction and insert kill switches that'll allow their entire WMD programmes to be emasculated. That'll cover nuclear, biological, chemical and also cyber weapons."

Lou scowled. "Really, don't you think that's a bit ambitious, even for you?"

This question resulted in only an enigmatic smile. "Yes, it takes a bit of getting used to. But I'm that it's the power of our computing tools that's making the Yanks shit themselves. It's a technological singularity, you see. Or maybe you don't see," she scanned the quizzical looks on his colleagues' faces.

"Okay, let's put it this way," she frowned in concentration. "It's a bit like invention of the wheel. This was developed to do one thing, like moving a heavy load. But, as soon as it is available, thousands of other applications emerge. Things like pulleys, steering wheels, clocks, whatever. It's just the same here. We've now got effectively limitless computing power, which was specifically developed to hack into operating systems. But, as soon as we have it, we can rip into blockchains, develop novel tomography tools, use AI pattern recognition on the entire internet. Basically, these applications need only minor modifications of our initial set of quantum computing algorithms. Indeed, we can use our new AI tools to improve these algorithms and the associated hypercomputer hardware, effectively lifting ourselves by our bootstraps, so the sky's the limit here."

"Jesus," Ursi's face was wan. "I saw the risks of some of these developments, but I hadn't considered them all together in this way."

"Right enough," Lou nodded. "It's rather scary, isn't it?"

"On the other hand, there's a silver lining here," Andy winked at Georgie, who was still grinning like the proverbial Cheshire Cat.

"And that is?" Ursi managed to beat Lou to this question.

"We are, for the moment, the only ones with a functional system…" Andy answered.

"And we can keep it that way for as long as we want," Georgie added.

***

Georgie and Andy sat together silently while the others struggled to understand the full implications of this technological singularity and what it meant for the group. After almost an hour of heated discussion, Lou clapped her hands for silence. "I think we all now recognise that we'd greatly underestimated the implications of the work Georgie's been doing to support our recent successes. Nevertheless, the cat is now out of the bag. Even if all the potential applications might not be fully recognised, the fact that the Americans are seeking to control it shows that Pandora's Box is fully open, if I can mix my metaphors. Anyway, to me at least, Georgie was spot on when she stated that this must not be handed over to the Yanks. We've all seen the damage that they were responsible for as the dominant super-power and I shudder to think what could result if this kind of cyber-technology was in the hands of one of their nutty presidents."

"I share your concerns, of course," Ursi interrupted, "but this isn't a decision that we can make. Finally, this is something that has to go to Petra and then up the tree to the Bundesrat and maybe even the UN."

"Not an option," Lou stated in an uncompromising manner. "This technology's far too dangerous for us to bring it into the global political arena. Think about it. The US is currently trying to strong-arm the Swiss government. We've already acknowledged that our facility being placed under US control would be a global catastrophe. Even if it was simply decommissioned or mothballed, we can be certain that the Yanks are pushing forward at full speed to develop something equivalent, so the net effect would be the same. So, as Georgie put it, we have to tell them, in no uncertain terms, to *fuck off*. But, can you really see any politicians doing this?"

"Can anyone do it, to the fucking Yanks?" Jay interjected.

"I've got a feeling that we can," Lou answered. "Look at that smug grin on Andy's face. It's another cunning plan, isn't it?"

"Funny that you should ask," he paused with an index finger tapping his chin. Although clearly intending to wind Lou up, he continued quickly in response to her killer stare. "Well, singularities are transitions, times for changing paradigms, getting rid of outdated ideas. I think we've now got the ability to guide how things evolve. So how about starting with elimination of the entire concept of a super-power?"

Apart from Georgie, who merely smiled happily, the others looked shocked by this hubris.

Ursi was the first to recover enough to respond. "Even if we really had the ability to do this, we don't have the right to make such decisions."

Andy glanced at Lou, who shook her head and slowly formulated her disagreement. "No, love, it's not a case of whether we've got the right, it's more us having the responsibility to do this. Like it or not, we're in the driving seat here and there are some decisions that we alone must make."

"Very well put," Andy winked again at Georgie. "So now we know what to do in general terms and just have to sort out the details. And, in particular, list the miracles that we require from the quantum team."

"There'll be a list will there?" Jay laughed. "I thought wiping out the super-powers would be enough to keep us going for a while."

"Well, first we need a response to make the Yankees back down, taking pressure off the Bundesrat. We can then wipe out the threat of WMDs, which'll be the first step to wiping out many of the major powers. What next?"

Su grinned. "That'll be assuring world peace, wiping out poverty and saving the environment."

"Okay, I'll put those on the list," Georgie responded, looking confused when the others burst into laughter.

***

"Okay, quieten down," Lou called the meeting to order in a schoolmarmish tone, which was particularly incongruous given her diaphanous clothing. "Let's just get this US nonsense out of the way first, so that we can focus on real problems. Andy, what's your plan here?"

"Mmm, it's a bit rough at present, but our immediate response should be to leak this communique from the US, along with our response."

"And the response will be what?" Lou frowned, suspiciously.

"We are certainly prepared to put our cyber-defence work on hold, but the latest threat that we've identified is to the nuclear powers, not

287

Switzerland. Thus, they should confirm that they are capable of defending against it."

"Oh, what threat is this? Ursi enquired.

"That's the hack that Georgie previously mentioned, opening back doors and putting kill codes into military WMD control systems."

"So, we're going to hack the US military and then tell them about it?"

Andy smiled at the blonde agent. "We're going to quietly hack them – and the other major powers – before telling them there's a threat. We can imply that it's probably coming from China. This we leak to a few hundred news sites, putting the US under huge pressure."

"But surely the Chinese will deny this," Su mused aloud.

"Actually, I'm sure that they won't. They've suffered such a loss of face recently that this suggestion of the ability to hack American security will be seen as a positive message from their perspective, even though they know that they have nothing to do with it. This will be evident to them, as we'll also have hacked their arsenal."

Lou looked unconvinced. "Maybe this'll buy us a little time, but the US will eventually decide that either this is a bluff or that it must be the Swiss cyberwar group behind the hack."

"Yes, that's the cunning bit of the plan. An anonymous group, again appearing to be based in China, will provide details of the backdoors and kill codes for all military systems to the Secretary General of the UN. They will suggest that she uses these to pressure the major powers to finally implement their long-promised WMD elimination plans. This, of course, will also be announced to the world press."

"Christ on a bike," Su gazed at Andy, clearly bemused by the audacity of this plan. "The upper echelons of the US will not be happy bunnies when this is dropped on their plates."

"And that's just for starters. The hacker group will offer a demonstration of their abilities if the US, or any other power, attempts direct action against them. This will involve shutting down the entire country involved for 10 minutes."

"Shutting down, what'd that involve?" Lou asked with a worried look on her face.

"After 1 hour's warning, all power, communications, air-traffic control, road and rail operations, military infrastructure will be shut down. Basically everything except for safety-critical and emergency services."

"For God's sake, Andy, that's a bit over the top, "Lou objected. "After the chaos of recent days, it'll be carnage."

"Serves the US bloody right for daring to threaten us," Su gave a wicked grin. "Especially if there's prior warning and yet nothing is done to stop it, the US government will take most of the blame and could well fall."

"Yes, well, in any case, they won't consider fucking about with us again," Georgie noted.

They thought over this apocalyptic scenario in silence, but nobody could find any reason to disagree with his conclusion.

***

While Su, Jan and Georgie went off to plan the practical details of hacks of military communication networks, Lou settled down with Andy and Ursi to work out how their actions were going to be communicated to Petra and, through her, to the Swiss government. Before they started, Lou fetched a bottle of chilled Chablis and three glasses – *to lubricate the brain cells*, as she put it.

To the surprise of the others, Ursi gulped down a large mouthful of wine and kicked off. "I know I've continually voiced my reservations with the way that you operate and your constant avoidance of required government oversight. However, in this case, I'm beginning to realise that you might be right. I can't escape from the thought of a fuckwit like Trump or Biden controlling the tools that you have, which gives me the screaming heebie-jeebies. It'd certainly be at least as bad if the control lay with the US intelligence services, who we know are riddled with corruption and self-interest, especially at the upper levels. Andy, you may be mad as a brush, but your lunacy is well-meant and kept within bounds by the common sense of your colleagues. As I've mentioned, this stuff scares me shitless, but I'd rather be helping you than anything else," she finished, looking down in a rather sheepish manner.

"Well said, lass," Lou enveloped her in a hug, squeezing the blond head against her massive bosom. "So, what kind of story are we going to concoct for your mistress in the NDB?"

"I don't suppose that the truth would be an option," Andy suggested, hopefully.

Lou slapped him on the side of the head in a distinctly matronly manner. "Have you even seen that work for a career civil servant?"

The question was obviously rhetorical, so Andy waited patiently for the punchline.

"Of course not," she continued. "Petra, nice lady that she is, doesn't want to know the truth. She wants to have a credible story line that she can pass on to her own masters and mistresses. This will be our warning about an attack on the US and other major powers, probably by a group based in China. Given how strongly the States feel about our cyber-defences, we tell her that we'll hold all active operations until a consensus position is reached."

"Should we tell her that we'll be leaking all of this externally?" Ursi wondered out loud.

Lou sighed. "The key thing here is to cover our arses, which inevitably means that Petra has got to be able to cover hers. We need to warn her about what's going to happen, but careful wordsmithing can convey a message that's false even if the component sentences are strictly true."

Andy grinned. "I know what you mean. We tell Petra that we have received the message from the US and, while not prepared to transfer our tools to their control, can discontinue operations until this issue is fully resolved by bilateral dialogue."

Lou nodded her head, clearly glad that her point had been picked up. "Yes, the word *can* is critical there. It implies that we are going to stop our work – and we could – it's just that, in actual fact, we're not going to."

"Right, we then need to present a threat that makes the Yanks think again about pressurising us," he scratched his head, frowning in concentration. "Maybe we can state that we've good evidence that a serious hack of military computers is underway, but we assume that the US cyber-defence is sufficient to handle this."

"That's strictly true, although it's us that are doing the hacking," Lou agreed. "But isn't there a risk that they'll guess that?"

"Mmm, well we could state that we have already identified the backdoor that has been used to access the Swiss national control centre and give them enough details to allow them to check if they have suffered similar infiltration. That could put them off the scent."

Ursi looked uncomfortable. "So, we're going to hack our own military computers and then provide details of how it was done to the Americans?"

"Sounds rather improbable, doesn't it. Anyway, we won't actually hack anything. We just open up a backdoor into our national system and provide details of where this was installed and how it was blocked. The Americans can use this only to identify similar vulnerabilities in their own systems and attempt to close them."

Ursi was only slightly mollified. "Okay, if you say so. But doesn't this defeat the entire point of allowing the US WMD control system to be compromised."

"Not at all. By the time the backdoor is closed in the US, we'll have already loaded the Trojan and passed the kill key to the UN, along with those for the weapons of the other major powers. This will, of course, be leaked to the press by the unknown hackers."

Ursi shook her head. "But this comes back to my original question. Do we let Petra know that we're leaking highly sensitive information to the press?"

Lou smiled. "I see how Andy's thoughts are going here. We tell Petra to be aware that anyone with appropriate tools, of the type that we know China has, can break the blockchain currently used to encrypt sensitive communication. She should make sure that the Americans are also aware of this. Of course, this'll be too late and we can use the leaks as evidence that our warnings were justified."

"Took the words right out of my mouth," Andy gave his statuesque colleague a hug. "Anyway, I've been producing a draft while we talked, so let's give it a polish and then you can send it off."

"Maybe not, I think it'd be best if it came from Ursi."

The blonde looked like she was going to object, but finally shrugged her shoulders. "Fine, although the messages will be misinterpreted, there isn't anything here that is an actual lie. I'll do it."

"Wonderful," Lou smiled. "Now we've got that out of the way, we've got time to squeeze in a quick ménage-a-trois before lunch."

Andy and Ursi looked at each other and both rolled their eyes, then burst into laughter, to Lou's evident confusion.

***

Georgie was already setting up the hacks into all military systems worthy of the name, which would then require only a single command to initiate. "Do we really need to do them all in parallel?" Su inquired. "Isn't that a bit of a give-away that it must be us doing it?"

"I don't think so. How would they be able to find out that it was actually a simultaneous attack?" Georgie frowned as she thought through the process. "Anyway, I can stagger implementation on the super-machine, if you prefer. It's just neater to do the blockchain cracks in parallel on the hyper-computer."

Lou looked confused. "As you've already demonstrated, conventional passwords are dead and you can now hack into any network that's accessible via the internet, but surely the military have hard intranets without any external access. I'd have thought these would be invulnerable?"

"You'd be surprised how many links I've found to military intranets," she grinned. "It's true, however, that the big boys with nukes are a bit more careful. I'm sure that most of those involved think that their systems are fully isolated, but, in real life, there's not much you can do with a fully-decoupled net. In order for a system to be used for either offence or defence, it needs to access an external monitoring and communication network. Of course, if such a system utilised only optical cables, I'd be scuppered." Georgie looked at the ceiling in an unfocussed manner before continuing. "Or maybe not, but it'd certainly be a lot trickier. However, most, if not all, advanced military systems include dedicated satellite links and these I can certainly crack." A holographic image showed the cloud of satellites in Earth orbit, with military ones identified as a host of glowing red dots.

"You sound very confident about that," Lou noted, suspiciously. "You wouldn't, by any chance, already have something running here."

Georgie shuffled her feet, looking rather uncomfortable. "Well, it was just a look-and-see project. I haven't actually implemented any hacks yet."

"Come on, lass, out with it," Lou lightly slapped the back of her head. "What mischief have you been up to?"

"Well, after the cash started flowing from our cyber-currency hacks, I diverted a minute amount of our cut into hiring time on commercial satellites and setting up multi-spectral scans of military communication systems. It was only a few hundreds of millions of dollars, so lost in the noise of the cash flows at that time."

"Shit!" Andy broke in. "If that can be traced back to us, we could be exposed as players in this action."

"Yes, of course, that's clear." Georgie shook his head as if this was completely self-evident. "All of this ran through one of the remaining operational banks in Hong Kong. The hires themselves were spread over a number of shell-companies, so it'd be tricky to spot this as a concerted action. Anyway, the original source of the funds is inherently untraceable but, if there are any suspicions, they'll certainly end up leading back to China."

"But what about the monitoring data? Can't this be followed back to us?" Lou was clearly very worried about this risk.

"Well, first of all, someone would need to know that this action was ongoing. How would they spot what we're doing, given the huge flux of data resulting from about ten thousand active satellites?"

Andy suddenly grinned. "But there's more to it than that, isn't there, you crafty little sod?"

"Well, I was inspired by some of your cunning plans and set the system up so that all data is automatically posted on an open site on the dark web. It's read-only, but anyone at all can access it without leaving a trace."

"Belt and braces, good job! There's so much shit on the web that it's unlikely that anyone would recognise it for what it was and, even if they did, what could they do with it?" Andy clapped his roommate on the back.

Lou, however, still looked worried. "Okay, this is the passive side. I guess this allows you to identify all the key links to ground stations. But I'd imagine that these are very tight beams: radio, laser or something like that. Even if you could detect them, how do you intercept them?"

"I'm not sure that satellite-to-satellite would be doable without actually breaking into the line of sight, but satellite-to-ground and vice versa is quite straightforward due to atmospheric scattering." Georgie looked around, noting that only Su was nodding. "It's only synthetic aperture stuff, combining the timeline of measurements from a number of different satellites with a bit of waveform inversion of the scattered signals guided by a hyper-AI module. Basically, it's just the same as I did for remote scanning of the Kim hideaways, but in the optical part of the spectrum rather than the lower frequencies for those cases."

Lou was still struggling with the concept. "If you say so. I confess that I don't understand the nuts-and-bolts, but I'll accept that, in principle, this gives you the capability of reading communications. This doesn't allow you to modify signals, so I don't see how this allows you to insert a backdoor into the system."

"Yes, well, of course that's done in the satellite itself." Again, only Su was nodding. "These satellites need to be very accurately positioned and avoid interferences from any other orbiting materials, so it needs functionality in lower EM frequencies such as radio and microwave. I can spoof these and, as complete system isolation is impossible in something as small as a satellite, break into the laser circuits. This then lets me play with interference while monitoring how the laser single responds. It's then just machine learning until we tailor this to allow us to piggy-back whatever we want onto incoming or outgoing signals."

Ursi covered her face with her hands. "That's another cornerstone of cyber-privacy out the window," she mumbled. "Where will this end?"

Georgie simply shrugged. "I told you that all the old ideas on privacy were dead in the water. We simply need to adjust to this new reality."

"And be very glad that it's us that are currently controlling it. In other hands it would be catastrophic."

"Mmm, I've a few ideas about that…" Georgie started before Lou waved for silence.

"Let's sort out the world's problems one at a time. So, for the hack of the military systems, you could emplace backdoors that'd allow us to shut them down at any time." She then noticed that the quantum guru was looking sheepish. "Bugger it, you've already got them in place, haven't you?"

"Well, I needed to test the functionality of the approach, so it seemed to be killing two birds with one stone. But it's only the nuclear powers, so far, and only the backdoors."

"Jesus," Lou sighed, "which ones?"

"All of them. Russia, US, China, France, UK, Pakistan, India and Israel. I even included North Korea, although, after the Chinese went in, I'm not sure that they have any nuclear capability now. For completeness, I also hacked such backdoors in the Swiss military comnet and those of the NATO members, in line with the original plan. I haven't actually inserted the Trojan yet, although it is ready to go."

"So, we are actually set to take out the nukes, are we?" Andy asked. After Georgie nodded, he continued. "Why not just go for this option immediately? I guess that chemical, biological and cyber will be tricky, as these are more dispersed and difficult to distinguish military from other commercial or research applications." Again, he received a nod.

Ursi looked horrified, but the others were evidently considering this proposal as a serious option. Jay was first to speak up. "We need to defuse this Yankee threat ASAP and this seems like the way to do it."

With clear reluctance, Lou nodded. "They've brought it on themselves. Okay, Georgie, load and prime the Trojan on all nuke systems. The NDB should provide a warning of this risk in an open communication to all embassies in Switzerland, with an offer to provide assistance in combatting it."

"There's no chance of any of the bigger countries taking up such an offer. It would be a matter of national pride," Ursi pointed out.

"Well, hell mend them! We'll give them a couple of days and then activate the Trojan in all other military systems." Lou looked at Georgie. "I assume you'll have most of them by then."

"All the national ones, but I'm not sure about militias and rebel groups."

"That'll do for now. We can do mopping up later." Lou looked around to see if anyone wanted to add anything. "Well, if that's all, I could do with a strong drink."

"Good grief, you must be exhausted," Jay contributed in a stage whisper. "Not a proposal for sexual high-jinks?"

"Don't be daft, lad," she smiled while shrugging out of her translucent top. "First a strong drink, then we can just see how it goes from there."

Chapter 2 - Putting the genie back in the bottle

Within three hours of the Americans being warned about the backdoor to their military communications intranet, a massive attack was launched against the NDB servers. Although there had been great efforts made to disguise the source, Georgie's AI had no problems blocking all access attempts, tracing a web of convoluted links back to the CIA headquarters in Langley and organising a devastating counter-attack.

Notification of this was immediately passed to NDB, who were completely oblivious of the shield that NetSec had provided in anticipation of such attacks. Lou summoned the team together and they were just settling down in the conference room when the panicked call came through from Petra.

"Lou, just what the fuck are you doing?" Petra was clearly beyond wasting time on introductory pleasantries. "Tell me that you haven't just attacked the fucking CIA."

"I am not 100% sure what has happened, but it certainly looks like Langley has been creamed. I'm sure Georgina can provide details." Lou waved towards their resident genius, who had transformed into Hello Kitty mode.

"Well, technically, we didn't attack anyone," she smiled. "We were, however, fairly sure that attempts to break into your computers would be made and so I set up a shield for you."

"Without informing us!" Petra shouted.

Kitty was unperturbed. "Why should I? Anyway, it seemed only fair, as BDN was set up to take the heat from our actions. In any case, you got it for free."

"But we don't even know what it does!" Petra was getting literally red in the face.

"It's a shield that blocks conventional hacks. Since we ripped off the crypto wallets, there have been..." she looked at a small hand terminal, "...somewhat more than twenty thousand attempts. Of course, your own firewall would have deflected most of these, but better to be on the safe side, don't you think?"

"Okay, a shield, but what's that to do with attacking the Americans?" Petra spluttered.

"Not an attack from our side, just an automatous response to a major attack on our system. Well, your system, but you know what I mean."

"Automatous! Fucking automatous! You've got a fucking AI making decisions to attack a major ally!"

"Cool it, Petra, you're getting apoplectic here," Lou struggled to hide a grin. "Take a deep breath and start thinking about an attack on your servers by your supposed major ally."

Petra was silent for several seconds with her eyes closed before she continued in a markedly calmer voice. "Okay, let's start from the beginning. What is this shield and how did you manage to take down the CIA?"

"The shield is basically an advanced firewall that checks all external messages and is especially set up to spot attempts to get around the passwords and other protocols that you use to prevent access to your operating system. In most cases these can be easily blocked but, as I've emphasised many times, conventional cryptographic barriers are worthless and the shield is specially set up to identify any attempts to break these using some kind of advanced tool."

"You mean break in the way that you did in your own hacks, with a quantum hypercomputer?" Ursi enquired.

"Well, if you're just doing a single hack without time pressure, a common-or-garden supercomputer would be sufficient. In any case, my shield spots such attacks and automatically blocks them."

"Blocks them how?" Petra interrupted, clearly dreading what Georgie's response would be.

"Our supercomputer runs blocking actions while the hypercomputer is being set up to cut the attack off at source. This is the experimental bit. I'm still working on optimisation…"

"Experimental, fuck me!" Petra then noticed the glare she was getting from Lou. "Okay, sorry, go on."

"Yes, well the easiest way to stop the attack is to simply fry the operating system of the attacker. That's what was done here."

Noting that her boss was about to explode again, Ursi quickly broke in. "Yes, Georgie, so this was completely autonomous, run by your AI?"

"Of course, on the timescales involved, there's no other option."

"But, despite this being run by an algorithm, there is no possibility of a false trace-back that could result in us attacking the wrong target?" Andy added to support his blonde partner.

"There's never anything that's 100% in real life, but…" Georgie waved her finger in Petra's direction while she consulted her palmtop, "…the attack came in parallel via one hundred and twenty-eight different routes. Although these all had nodes in China, this involved a proxy server linked to known US monitoring activities and from there easily traced back to Langley. A very sloppy bit of work on their side. I guess one of the aims of the incursion was to insert a false trace in your servers but, of course, they never got that far."

"Okay, say that we're certain that it was the Yanks who initiated this attack, what was involved in you cutting it off at source?" Petra sighed, bracing herself for bad news.

"As you would expect, my hypercomputer sliced straight through their firewalls, effectively instantaneously. It then inserted very aggressive worms that scrambled all linked databases and then destroyed their hardware."

"Their computer hardware? How did you do that?" Su mused aloud.

"Just the usual stuff, pump-up clock-speed to max, switch out all power limiters, turn off all cooling systems, stuff like that. The neat bit is that it happens in parallel on all processors, turning supercomputers into very expensive ovens. Anything at all that was linked to the attacking system is now slag."

"Fuck!" Petra slumped back in her seat, with her head in her hands. "How in God's name are we going to manage this?"

"Well, actually, thinking about it, I may just have a cunning plan." Andy smiled, aware that he was now the centre of attention.

***

The silence lasted about twenty seconds before Lou finally broke down. "For God's sake, Andy, stop being a complete arsehole and let us know what you're on about."

"Well," he started slowly, in his most annoying manner, "we start by immediately putting a report on the attack on the NDB website, with copies mailed to all partner intelligence agencies."

"We admit that we've just fucked-up the CIA? Are you out of your tiny little mind?"

"Hold on, Petra," Lou commanded. "Andy may be mad, but he's not daft. He's just being his usual irritating self. Come on, out with the rest of this bloody plan."

Andy put a finger to his lips as if deep in thought, before he continued. "Yes, the cunning bit is how we formulate the report. We start by summarising the number of recent attacks on NDB, this being the driver for us to introduce a more powerful deterrent. We then state that we expected a supercomputer attack and that we had already introduced a tool to trace it back to source and neutralise the system responsible. Such an attack has now taken place, although we haven't identified the aggressor."

"But we have," Jay noted.

"Yes, we know who it is, but we've not identified them in public. This is a kind of veiled threat. It also means that the US has to be very careful to hide the fact of their computers being wiped out. They certainly don't want to openly admit that they were the attackers here."

"I suspect there will be many unhappy bunnies in the US intelligence community," Lou smiled. "But surely this will make them much more determined to hack the NDB, even if only as a form of revenge. It may take a while, but they must be able to improve the tools that they're using."

"Certainly, but here's the super-cunning bit of the plan. The announcement also makes it clear that such attacks will not be tolerated in the future and that the kid gloves will come off in future responses."

"Destroying Langley's computer system is us with kid gloves on?" Petra sighed. "What the fuck's your iron fist going to involve?"

"Well, as a start, from now on every hacking attempt, no matter how ham-fisted, will lead to a counter attack that will destroy all the hacker's hardware."

"That's just an extension of what we've already done," Jay observed.

"But also, before we scramble any associated databases, we rip off huge chunks of the most heavily protected material and place them on a read-only database on the dark web."

"If it's on the dark web, who'll be able to find it?" Lou asked.

"Anyone who wants to. The address will be on the NDB website."

"Well, that's certainly going to be a major disincentive for any national intelligence agency," Petra acknowledged. "They'd need to develop a completely independent hacking system, which contains absolutely nothing that would allow its owners to be identified."

"That would take a fair amount of time and require significant resources," Su pointed out.

"Resources that they'd need to be prepared to sacrifice. Their system needs not only to be good, but better than ours. Any time they try it out unsuccessfully, they lose the lot," Ursi smiled and slapped Andy on the back.

"Okay, I reluctantly admit that this seems the best way forward," Petra conceded with a grimace of distaste. "But are you actually able to do this database hacking while destroying an attacking system?"

All eyes turned to Georgie, who merely shrugged. "Sure, just tell me what you want and I'll put it together. It may take a couple of days, though." She seemed surprised at the groans from Petra and Ursi and the laughs from the others.

***

It was clear that, despite their silence, the Americans were unable to completely hide the consequences of their attack on NDB from other major intelligence agencies. This was evident from the fact that, over the next week, even the nuclear powers took up the Swiss offer to support removing the back-doors placed on their military communication systems. Of course, removing access only prevented further intrusion and was too late to save them from the Trojan that was already in place. The only exceptions were the US and China: the former out of hurt pride and the latter as they already had experience with the associated trip wires, which had been copied from those used by the Lazarus group.

The number of attempted hacks of the NDB servers also dropped considerably, especially after their website started showing statistics of the destroyed hardware of attackers and the black site with the counter-hacked databases began to be picked up by the media. National-level attempts stopped after sensitive Mossad documents were released following an attempt by Israel, this causing a public outcry that almost toppled the already-shaky government in that country. Criminal groups and individual hackers still made occasional attempts, but even these were decreasing as the published material was often sufficient to local police or intelligence groups to take action against them.

While Su and Georgie refined their tools to provide a better overview of the ongoing recovery of the global financial markets, Lou spent increasing amounts of her time helping Heidi and Beat plan and implement the distribution of ill-gotten gains from the top of the food chain to support the huge numbers suffering at the bottom. Meanwhile, Jay, Andy and Ursi concentrated on assessing the wider consequences of the technology they had developed.

As was increasingly clear, the technological singularity resulting from combination of quantum hyper-computers with advanced AI would provide previously unimagined capabilities that required a paradigm shift in the way that society was run. In effect, this was equivalent to the introduction of electronic computers and all their associated spin-offs, but with capabilities developed over days rather than decades. This was a characteristic that terrified Ursi, amused Jay and caused Andy to become increasingly remote while he struggled to develop another of his cunning plans.

***

For Andy, his already complicated love-life had taken on a new dimension when Ursi decided to move in to share a bedroom with Georgie and him. Although he had noticed that the NDB secondee had been getting closer to their resident genius, this development came as a complete surprise. The first ménage à trois encounter, with Georgina, seemed like a fluke but the second, with George, gave him the first hint that something significant was developing.

Now, after a week spent together, the transformation of the previously rather staid blonde to someone who adjusted naturally to the transformations of their shared, gender-fluid bedmate seemed nothing less than miraculous. *Or, possibly, an indication of the corrupting influence of NetSec as a group.*

However, despite the distractions of an evening of energetic and rather kinky sex with a strangely ambivalent G, Andy was now beginning to get seriously worried. Just before his cryptic lover drifted into post-coital slumber, Andy whispered the question that had been preying on his mind for some time. "If someone else had an equivalent set up to yours, would they be able to trace the events of the last month back to us?"

Luckily, Ursi was dozing and clearly missed this and the mumbled response. "Of course, if they knew the right questions to ask." This confirmed his worst suspicions, but he resolved to keep this from the others until he had at least some idea of a response. If any of the one-time major powers had the slightest inkling of the role of his team in recent developments they would certainly be marked for assassination – or worse.

**

It was a rather sombre team that assembled to discuss what Andy had described as *some deep shit*, but, typically, had not expanded upon.

Lou looked particularly worried. "Okay, Andy, what's this about? I'm getting exhausted with all this saving the world crap. Tell me we've not got another crisis on our hands."

"Well, it's not as urgent as the past threats. And, although there are global implications, my main concern are the direct threats to us personally."

"Fine, but none of your usually silly-bugger playing around," Su glared at him. "Just get to the point."

"Right, well let's start at a global level. We know that we've developed transformative technology that changes the boundary conditions for our wired civilisation. The constraints set by the abilities of conventional computers have vanished and we've just begun to scrape the surface of what will be possible with the AI tools that we now have. Of course, the chaos caused by recent global disruptions will slow things down, but knowledge of the capabilities that we've demonstrated will certainly make it easier for others to follow in our footsteps."

"Yes, we know all this," Su interrupted. "Georgie has been saying for ages, very openly, that this is an inevitable consequence of quantum computing developments. That genie is already out of the bottle."

"But is it? Presently we're ahead of the field here with a combination of hardware that is at the biting edge and, more importantly, Georgie and a support team that can get the best out of it."

Lou frowned. "This might be the case at present, but how long will we have such superiority? I'll bet that, after infrastructure recovery, advanced quantum computing will be top of the budgets for most advanced nations. They're bound to catch up, it's inevitable."

"Ah, that's the point. You're basing this conclusion on the way the world was before we hit this singularity."

"Come on, Andy," Jay spread his arms in a conciliatory manner. "It's a fact of life. There's never been any technology ever developed that didn't spread."

"That's history, reflecting the fact that re-bottling genies wasn't an option in the past."

The team were shocked into silence, but Lou noticed a small grin that Georgie was trying to hide. "Okay, you pair of buggers. Out with it! What cunning plan have you two been cooking up?"

"Well, it's actually Andy's plan..."

"Depending critically on Georgie..."

Lou punched the table in annoyance. "Stop shifting the blame. What do you have in mind?"

Andy smiled, but moved on quickly in response to a glare from Lou. "As long as there's only one genie loose and we control it, there's no reason why we can't scupper any attempts to repeat the trick."

Su shook her head. "Really? How's that possible?"

Andy waved at Georgie, who pointed at a holo-display, recognisable as a representation of the internet. "As you've seen, we can run the hyper-AI to mine the entire world knowledge base, allowing us to answer any reasonably posed question. Basically, it's a simple neural network with a couple of hundred layers, although time resonance adds additional..."

"We can get into the nitty-gritty later, just cut to the functionality," Lou commanded in her most severe domme voice.

"Right, okay, functionality. This's just like the case of finding the Kims in the Maldives. In that case we gave a few hints and asked relevant questions in natural language: *Where are the Kims? How did they get there? How can we approach them with minimum risk of being spotted?* It's just the same here, we ask appropriate questions like: *Where are the most advanced development programmes for hyper-computers and what are their likely capacities?* And Bingo!" The hologram now displayed a globe with a scatter of red points linked to text blocks of technical specifications."

"That's very impressive," Su conceded, "but that's only identifying the potential genies. It doesn't stop them being unbottled."

Georgie looked imploringly at Andy, who then took over. "Well, we just set a limit on acceptable system capability, based on what we know will allow the most problematic functionality to be established. Our AI then ensures this isn't exceeded."

Lou groaned. "And just how does it do this?"

"Not a clue," Georgie admitted. "Do you want to try out an example?"

"Jesus Christ, no! I'll just trust that you can do it." Lou looked shaken.

"Yes, well almost all of these systems will be linked to the internet or an intranet that we can hack into, as they're not much use otherwise. This gives us an easy way to disrupt coherence time, for example, which builds in an automatic limiter. Our tool will also spot even totally isolated systems, but disrupting these may be more intrusive."

Lou shook her head. "You've just shown again how massive this technological singularity is. I've been following its development, but I still can't get my head around it."

"Yes, it's very tricky," Andy nodded. "But that's the good news…" Lou slapped him on the back of the head, forcing him to shorten his annoying break. "The bad news is, of course, that we can be sure only that this'll delay the emergence of the problematic functions. General technology is developing at such a rate that completely novel approaches to quantum computing could emerge, which might not be spotted by our system. Although it gives the impression of being infallible, it's really only advanced machine learning and can miss unexpected developments. The important thing, though, is that this gives us a lot more time to prepare for the transitions that will be involved."

"How much time?" Ursi managed to beat Lou to this key question.

"Tricky to tell," Georgie shrugged her shoulders. "I think at least a decade, maybe even two or more. But we should certainly start encouraging key players to start thinking about this."

Lou brightened up. "Well, that doesn't seem like such bad news to me..." she ground to a halt when she saw that Andy has raised his eyebrows. "Oh, for fuck's sake, don't tell me there's more bad news waiting for us."

"Well, that's an overview of the global situation, which might not be so bad as long as we can keep our hands on the reins. For us, personally, there're a few other things that we need to get sorted out. This starts with NetSec going bankrupt..."

Andy and Georgie sat back and waited for the chaotic babble to die down.

***

It took five minutes for the hubbub to die down and Lou to regain control of the meeting. "Well, even for you, that was a bit of a bombshell. I assume that you're now going to lay out more details of some nefarious plan."

From the concerns on the faces of his colleagues, Andy decided that he should come to the point more directly than usual. "First of all, we've got to consider that, if we're ever uncovered as the force behind the humiliation of the nuclear powers, we would go immediately to the top of their shit-lists. This is one of the reasons for blocking development of systems like Georgie's which, given the right questions, could certainly lead to us being exposed. But, even without such tools, there'll be a lot of attention focussed on security software teams in Switzerland. We've been careful to give all of the credit for our actions to the NDB and have added other links to concentrate suspicions for hacking activities on South Korea and China. Nevertheless, we're known to be a top-level cyber-security team that works for government departments, and so we'll certainly be looked at, sooner or later. But not, of course, if we've already gone bust, as one of the many victims of the cyber-attacks."

Ursi couldn't hide a nervous giggle. "And here I thought that your biggest problem was hiding the mega-bucks that you've accumulated due entirely to such attacks."

"Yes, that cash can also be seen as a liability, although it's flowing through WhiteHatz, so is decoupled from NetSec" Andy nodded. "Anyway, we'll have less problems here after the company is dissolved following bankruptcy."

"And what exactly is going to cause this bankruptcy," Lou inquired suspiciously.

"That'd be due to a couple of our clients suing us."

"And which clients would these be?" Su broke in.

"A couple of small banks and investment houses that were creamed due to the original Korean attack. We were providing them with assured protection and hence they're suing our arses off."

"But we've no such clients. All our NetSec work is in Switzerland and only covers organisations with some kind of governmental link," Lou pointed out.

"Actually, we do, as of a couple of hours ago. Everything is, however, set up to show that the contracts were set in place a couple of years ago."

Lou was clearly confused. "Even if we were sued like this, I'm sure that we could argue force majeure. I'm sure most other firms like us will be doing that."

"That's a chicken-shit way out and is diverting a lot of dosh towards useless lawyers as they fight out such cases. We are, however, an honourable company that accepts responsibility and hence won't contest the action. We go bankrupt and the claimants share out all available funds. The company is closed and we disperse."

Lou shook her head. "I'm not saying that, under the current situation, it's actually an issue, but the banks involved will be doing well. Even in terms of declared income, we're a very successful company with heavy commercial liability insurance."

"Not to worry," Andy grinned, "these banks actually belong to us via a convoluted mesh of shell companies that we're already using to spread out our one permil rake-offs."

Ursi frowned. "But there's a bit of larceny in there. You will, in effect, be ripping off the insurance company involved."

Andy laughed out loud. "Yes, we would be, if we didn't already own that also."

***

The room was quiet for a couple of minutes while the team thought through this plan. Finally, Lou shrugged her shoulders. "I can't say I'm very happy about the idea, but I can see the threats to us and this seems a way of minimising them. Bugger, I really liked this company and our entire team, including all the support staff. I suppose, however, we can keep WhiteHatz going in some way or another."

"I'm afraid not. The links between it and NDB will be much trickier to trace, but these're known to a number of Petra's staff and a select number of higher-ups, all the way to Bundesrat level. They can't be assumed to stay tight, so that's got to go also."

Su rolled her eyes. "I guess you've got another off-the-wall idea to cover this, haven't you?"

"I haven't worked it out in detail and will need a bit of help from you and Georgie, but I have a general concept."

"Out with it!" Ursi nipped him painfully on the back of the neck.

"Ouch! Well, even though WhiteHatz is hidden in the dark web, its existence is certainly known to many of our clients. We need to show that it's gone, completely wiped out."

"Right, and we do that how?" Ursi emphasised her question with another nip.

"Well, that would be a consequence of our failed attempt to hack the NDB, when our entire computer system was fried and a load of sensitive files uploaded on the web. Our site will just have a notice saying taken down by NDB and that's that."

"But the attack would need to have a credible justification. WhiteHatz had a good reputation amongst the few people who knew that it existed. Would anyone really believe that we, all of a sudden, decided to attack the Swiss government?" Lou frowned.

"Yes, I know, that's the problem. But the approach to find a solution is clear..."

"And the solution is..." Ursi slapped him on the back of his head.

"Not a Scooby," Andy grinned. "But I'm sure that Georgie's quantum AI will come up with something so clever that we couldn't have ever dreamed up. All we need to do is ask the right questions."

"Which are?" Lou looked very close to losing her temper.

"Again, not a clue. But we've got a very clever team here and I'm sure they'll come up with something. My bit's done, coming up with the clever strategy. The rest of you need to start pulling your weight."

Andy chortled from his refuge below the conference table while he dodged a hail of kicks, punches and thrown objects.

***

Andy was correct in that the concept produced by the AI was truly Byzantine. The storyline was that the hack was actually set up by a Russian state-sponsored Bratva gang using North Korean expertise. It had never expected to break through the NDB firewalls, but provided a fabricated link back to the WhiteHatz commercial web page, thus directing the automatic retaliation to that location.

"A nice story, but full of holes," Lou commented after Andy introduced this to another group meeting. "Why should we be selected for such treatment? Surely the Russians have more to do than pick on minnows like us when their entire economy is in shreds."

"That's where the Bratva link comes in. Those in the know will be aware, or at least suspect, that we've taken down a couple of these groups. These criminal bands are closely related to the Russian government or, at least, the top oligarchs in this kleptocracy. Despite all the other problems Russia is facing, many of the past power-brokers will be predominantly interested in trying to recover or replace the ill-gotten gains that were ripped from their crypto wallets. As a combination of revenge for what we've done in the past and defence against our potential role in combatting their future activities, they would certainly like to see us removed from the playing field."

"I'm sure of that," Jay responded, "but these guys would be much more likely to blow us to buggery than attempt a complex hack like this."

"They certainly would, if they had any idea of who we are and where we might be found but, with our current defences, they've no chance of finding this out."

"Of course, they could if they had a computed like Georgie's," Ursi pointed out.

"Exactly the reason for blocking the development of anything like that for as long as possible. The one thing they could find, however, is the web site we use for communication with clients."

"So what?" Su asked. "There is no way that anyone could hack from there our internal net by that route."

"Ah, yes, that's where the North Korean link comes in, which is quite believable, as we know from our own experience. What if the Lazarus group had also installed hidden backdoors in some secure website maintenance apps?"

"But they haven't, at least as far as anything that we have ever used is concerned," Lou objected. "In any case, we code the key bits ourselves. Any other approach would be downright sloppy."

"Yes, but we don't do everything from scratch. We cobble together the routines that we need, but these are often generated outside, usually by coding-wallahs in India."

"Yes, it'd be a waste of our time to do otherwise," Su observed. "But I'm still not sure where this is going."

"Well, if the Lazarus group was behind a couple of the top coding companies, they could certainly hide the backdoor functionality, distributed between several different apps. Surely that'd be possible."

"Possible, yes, but why would the Lazarus group be doing this when they already had the hacks into much more critical finance transfer systems?" Lou still did not seem convinced.

"We don't need a full justification, only a storyline that's credible. Based on the components of this story, we then develop the records of a hack into our system that would result in an attack on NDB and ensure that this can be traced by forensic analysis of the database ripped from our computers, just before they were destroyed by firewall counter-attack."

"Byzantine indeed," Lou sighed, "but it has the advantage of quickly removing us as a likely target for anyone looking for the NDB defence team."

"Yes, I've got to admit that it's more convoluted than anything I would have come up with on my own. Even if WhiteHatz is known to have been a player, it'll be difficult to find anything other than the fact that it has ceased operation. It'll require a lot of digging to find out how it was wiped out and even more to trace back the Bratva and Lazarus links. Of course, as Lazarus has already been ripped apart and the cyber side of Bratva activities is going the same way, these links will simply lead to dead ends. Actually, literally dead ends, as any of the players that could be identified have already been killed over the last month or are on the top of Chinese hit lists."

"Okay, I'm convinced," Lou sighed. "I guess we go ahead with this as long as there're no objections." She looked around at the nodding heads. "I assume Georgie can quickly set this up."

"I already have done," she nodded while flicking through a palmtop, "and that's it now implemented."

"Fuck, that was quick," Su rolled her eyes. "I should have expected it, however. So, we're now formally unemployed, bankrupt and homeless. What do we do with ourselves now?"

"Well, we're rich enough to retire and certainly, after the stress of recent weeks, I'm ready for a long holiday," Lou stretched, straining her blouse almost to bursting point. "I suspect, however, Andy also has ideas about that."

"No, a holiday would certainly do us all good and would help further lower our individual profiles, as this is what might be expected following the demise of NetSec. It's up to the rest of you, of course, but I don't really fancy the idea of retiring as yet. The great thing is that, due to our financial situation, we can just dabble as we want and don't need the formality of a company any more. We're just a bunch of pals, ex-colleagues, who get together every now and then for a bit of work-therapy."

"Well, what kind of work might that be," Lou asked suspiciously.

"No idea, just depends on whatever catastrophe the world next needs saving from."

There was no response to that.

Chapter 3 - Aftermath

A summer Betriebsausflug was quite common for Swiss companies: this being an occasion when the firm organised a day out for all employees. Indeed, when there had been a successful year, it wasn't unusual for a longer trip, staying somewhere nice for a couple of nights. Lou reckoned that saving the world a couple of times and earning billions of Euros into the bargain really justified pushing the boat out, so she had organised a week-long trip to the Tessin for all staff – including cleaners, cooks and gardeners – along with their families. In this particular case, it would be easy to interpret the trip as a last-gasp attempt to spend money before all the company's assets were seized as part of the bankruptcy proceedings.

Lou had booked an entire 1st class carriage on the slow, direct train from Zurich to Locarno and, due to the bottles of Champagne and hampers of lunchtime snacks, the entire trip started off with a distinct holiday air. Midway through the trip, just after the train had exited the old Gotthard rail tunnel, Lou called for silence and presented the concept that had been developed for the future of staff after the closure of NetSec.

The most important news was that, despite generous redundancy packages, all staff would have the option of being re-employed by a new organisation that would take over the office premises. Not surprisingly, given the uncertainties from recent economic perturbations, this option was greeted with great enthusiasm. Lou was touched by the concern shown for the fate of NetSec owners, which brought her close to tears as it reminded her of the family feel of the entire organisation.

Lou then explained that, as NetSec was registered as a GMBH, a limited company, the bankruptcy had no direct impact on the finances of the owners. The company was scheduled to close down all operations within 6 months, the minimum time needed to sort out the complex process of termination of existing contracts and selling off all assets, including the premises in Wettingen. Due to the loss of crypto-currency as an option and lack of confidence in banks, there was a large market for top-end property, especially in stable countries that had weathered the financial collapse, with Switzerland one of the most popular locations. The contract for sale of the building was completed but, for the accommodation units, it had been agreed that the NetSec team would have the option to rent these. Thus, even with the demise of the company, social contacts would be maintained.

She did not mention that the sale was actually to the well-established property management company that WhiteHatz had previously set up to launder income. This had the appearance of being handled as an investment, with income provided by rent of serviced offices / apartments.

During the walk from the station to the nearby Hotel Arcadia, Su put her arm round Lou's waist. "You presented that well. I think we've a lot of happy bunnies here. It was definitely a good idea to get everyone away from the office so that they can think things through before making a future commitment."

Lou smiled and gave her slim colleague a squeeze. "Yes, indeed. I was worried when we first started talking about closing the office, because I really like the staff we've recruited and the resulting relaxed office culture."

Su snorted inelegantly. "Relaxed mainly because you wander about with your tits on display most of the time."

"We're almost halfway through the 20th century, so it's about time that we escaped from Victorian puritanism. The hotel I've booked is less exclusive than I would normally have chosen, but suitable for all the kids and close to the Piazza Grande in the centre of the town. Also, there's a swimsuit-optional spa area, so we'll probably see a lot more of the staff, in a literal sense, than we normally do in the office."

"Lou, you're completely incorrigible! So, despite the kids, you'll still be letting it all hang out?"

"Certainly. Naked flesh isn't something that you can hide from kids any more. A five-year-old can find stuff online that our parents would have had to go to a brothel or an Amsterdam sex shop to get near to. It's much better that they grow up with it naturally and then can explore what they want in a safe and natural way."

"Oh my God, is this your latest fads – sex education?"

"I hadn't thought about it as such, but our reconstruction funding gives us a lot of flexibility in replacing the old colonial, industrial and military legacy of support to the third world with something a lot better. I definitely think sending sex educators rather than missionaries from dysfunctional religions would be a good start."

Su slapped her forehead. "So much for sarcasm, you're taking everything I said seriously. So, it's safe sex for you now, instead of any kink that is on offer?"

Lou laughed. "Sex should be safe, but doesn't mean that it can't be kinky. Talking of which, what have you got planned for tonight? The kids should be off to bed by ten and I've reserved the spa for us until two, with a free bar." She surreptitiously slipped her hand higher underneath her colleague's blouse until she encountered a hard nipple. "Mmm, I guess that you'll be ready for safe kink by then."

"You can bet on it. I just need to see how I can extricate Ursi and Georgie from Andy's clutches."

"Why split them up? I think it might be about time for a celebratory team gang-bang."

"Well, if you put it like that, it sounds like fun. I just hope I've brought enough toys with me."

"There you don't have to worry. I had a chat to Jay and Georgie before we set off and we had some rig-outs and equipment delivered in advance. It won't be Beat and Heidi standard, but I'm sure we'll be able to have a lot of fun." As she observed how Su's nipples were now on prominent display, Lou was confident that this was a sure thing.

"Are you sure about this, though. I know Switzerland is getting more liberal, but we may be pushing it a bit here."

"I guess you haven't been keeping up with Jay's investment diversification strategy. Otherwise, you'd have guess that one of the reasons I selected this hotel is that we're now actually its owners."

***

On return to Wettingen, the practicalities of reorganised the accommodation units were sorted out. Each of these would be transformed into a separate apartment, with the floor containing the pool and the gym set up as a common area for the residents. Basically, the team would live as before, but with more of an appearance of living separately.

The biggest modification was the isolation of the office space, which was rented to a new think tank set up by the ETHZ – the world-class technical university in Zurich. This was focused on establishing global resilience and was funded by the Swiss Science Foundation and supported by the EU and UN. The NDB was represented on the think tank's board of management by Vicky, Ursi's sister, who was the only member of the board aware of the previous role played by NetSec and the fact that the computer hardware used was still operational in an isolated sub-basement.

The think tank was supported by working groups on specific topics and here Georgie participated in the team looking at impacts of advanced AI while Lou and Andy were in the one covering robust global infrastructure.

***

Su travelled with Hyo-jin to Bangkok, helping her organise plastic surgery to modify her facial features and fingerprints. This was complemented by high-tech – and completely illegal – laser modification of her retinas prior to the biometric scan required for Hyo-jin, now renamed Nancy Lee, to obtain a Thai passport. This was facilitated by the fact that the Bangkok Bank was one of the victims of the initial Korean hack and the fabricated records of *Nancy Lee* being employed by them for a decade, with responsibility for Taiwanese operations, would be extremely difficult to check. The collapse of both this major bank and corruption of government financial records resulted in extensive civil protests and failures of key infrastructure, making the city even more chaotic than it had previously been and, as such, an ideal location for Hyo-jin to have her identity laundered.

After the minimum time in Bangkok needed to get this transformation sorted out, the couple moved to a beach resort while they planned how to proceed further. Su booked a suite at the La Vella resort in Khao Lak as a quieter alternative to the chaos of Phuket. The hotel itself was directly on the beach and, as a result of the continuing economic chaos, less than half full. Despite everything, there were reasonable numbers of tourists from Europe and the Antipodes, although the usual hordes of Chinese and Russian nouveau riche were noticeable by their absence.

Although this was primarily aimed as a relaxing holiday, Su was determined that this should contribute to the establishment of a distinctly different Nancy personality. This started with a radical short haircut and followed by extensive tattoos and piercing at a particularly well-recommended body-modification parlour.

Su was gently lying with her partner after a long ink session, involving an octopus covering both buttocks, when the Korean quietly started talking about her background. Her English was greatly improved and, except when angered, her swearing had almost disappeared.

It transpired that her grandmother had been a teenage *comfort woman* during the 2nd World War occupation of Korea. She ended up pregnant after multiple rapes by Japanese soldiers and, due to the scandal associated with this, was unable to find a husband and forced to bring up her daughter alone. Due to this history and her appearance, even her daughter, Hyo-jin's mother, suffered from discrimination, but eventually was employed as army liaison for abducted Japanese in the '80s. She was responsible for encouraging young male abductees to teach Japanese to Korean agents, with the assumption that her half-Japanese parentage would make her more acceptable to them. Although she was in her mid-40s at the time, Hyo-Jin's mother became pregnant after a drunken night with an abductee almost three decades her junior. Now with even more Japanese blood, mother and daughter were scorned and, after her mother's suicide, Hyo-jin was put in an orphanage as she was considered completely unsuitable for adoption. Based on her performance in elementary school exams, she was selected for special schooling at age twelve.

Su stroked the short stubble that was all that remained of Hyo-Jin's previously paged hair. "I've always thought that you were a bit screwed-up but, having lived through all of that, I'm surprised that you're not a hell of a lot worse. The challenge for you will be to forget all your history, to the extent that's possible, and start building up your profile as the successful Nancy Lee. Actually, I need to start calling you Nancy from now on, to help you get used to it."

"I don't know why you chose this stupid name: it's not sensible for a Thai national."

"I know, but this is what Georgie's AI came up with. Typically convoluted, but not inconsistent with your physiognomy and the melting pots that big cities in Asia have become. The key thing is that you don't look particularly Korean and I doubt that even anyone who knew you well in the North Korean or Chinese hacker communities would recognise you now."

"Maybe not, especially if I was naked," she smiled while she twisted round to try to view her bottom.

"That seems a good reason to be naked as much as possible," Su snapped a photo with her phone to allow her partner to view the tattoo properly.

"It's not so good for that here. Maybe we should go somewhere with lots of naked women. Don't you think that would be fun?"

"Well, let's hide out here for a few more weeks until things settle down a bit more and then we can get a lesbo dream tour sorted out. In the interim, there are some top-end escorts that we could hire to make our evenings more interesting."

"Maybe we should get a couple of black girls with big tits," Hyo-jin laughed. "Anyway, where will we go to meet the best lesbians in the West? Maybe Lesbos?"

"I've actually never been there, but it does seem to be a popular destination for girls, with a number of women-only resorts." Su frowned in concentration. "There's somewhere that's the birthplace of Sappho – Eressos, I think it's called – which is supposed to be good. It should actually be something for my bucket list: a roll in the hay with a couple of Lesbian lesbians."

"We should go there first, then we can plan more visits."

"Seems like a plan. But now it's time to take your mind off the pain of your tattoos – a nice blowjob for you, that'll give me a chance to better inspect your inked butt." Just before her mind was taken up with other things, Su couldn't help feeling momentarily dazed by the way in which her life had gone completely topsy-turvy since she first encountered this strange woman.

**

Jay agreed that dispersing the team for a bit was a good idea and decided to spend some time in Japan, a country that he had visited only briefly in the past, without managing to get out of Tokyo and see any of the countryside. His plan was to establish a base in Tokyo and use the Shinkansen to travel around for trips of a week or two. For this, he rented a Mori serviced apartment in the Toranomon area, which was conveniently central and within an easy walk to the Shimbashi JR station.

After a couple of days to get over jet-lag and a rather annoying cold that he managed to pick up en route to Japan, Jay started to explore the night life of the Megalopolis. The gay scene was very much concentrated in and around Shinjuku, which was easily accessed by metro from Toranomon Hills, with only the easy change from the Ginza to Marunouchi lines at Akasaka Mitsuke. After several pleasant evenings, inevitably involving a pick-up and transfer to a gay-friendly love hotel, Jay discovered the extensive contact sites used by many Japanese singles, couples and groups to arrange liaisons. The swinger scene was particularly well established and closely linked to a number of fetish bars and clubs. As recommended on many sites, Jay engaged a Japanese escort to show him around, a young male-model named Akira.

Even for someone as experienced as Jay, the kink scene was an eye-opener. Apart from the usual weirdos found in such places, there were a surprisingly large number of basically hetero couples seeking to link up with single males – in most cases with the woman in the pair being the driver for such experimentation. Akira explained that this was due to the great popularity of yaoi manga and anime amongst young women. Such *boy love* homoerotic stories were quite distinct from gay manga in that they were marketed to girls and usually produced by women.

Always game for something new, Jay was easily talked into joining Akira and a married couple in their late twenties for some fun in a private room. The woman, Shoko, was kitted out in extravagant black femdom wear, featuring a leather bustier with integrated suspenders, stockings and thigh-length boots with ridiculously high stiletto heels. It was clear that she was going to control the action, which involved her husband, Tatsu, being tied to a bondage x-frame and then subjected to oral and anal sex with both men while she masturbated with a huge dildo. Although it seemed like some kind of strange yaoi rape trope, it was clear that Tatsu was a more than willing victim.

After the session, it was apparent that the young couple expected to pay for services rendered, but Jay convinced them that just having a few drinks together would be more than sufficient. This was eased by the fact that Shoko and Tatsu both spoke good English. Over drinks in the main bar, with Shoko still in her domme rigout and the men showered but still naked, Jay learned that the alt sex scene was suffering from recent incursions by organised crime, mainly yakuza. This was making the contact bars and clubs increasingly expensive and requiring care in selecting partners due to an influx of gang-controlled prostitutes. More seriously, many of the common party drugs were now being spiked with fentanyl to make them addictive and build the drug market. One of the reasons for this seemed to be the effective demise of cyber-criminality, previously a major income source for the Japanese mafia. Thus, Jay was confronted with one of the completely unexpected areas of collateral damage resulting from the NetSec counter-attacks, which he realised was made worse by the loss of yakuza funds held in cybercurrencies.

Next morning, Jay established a link to a secure server run by Georgie and used this to call Su, as Thailand was closer to Japan in terms of time zones. After explaining the background, he got to his suggested action. "We've a responsibility to minimise fallout from our past actions, so I think we should help the community here out and remove the threats from criminal gangs."

Su shrugged. "There must be hundreds of thousands of similar cases and we can't sort them all out. I get the distinct feeling that you're getting well into this swinger-fetish bunch, but it isn't as if they're really threatened. It's certainly costing them a bit more to indulge their perversions, but I'm sure that they can afford it."

"But remember they're pushing opioids. It isn't a serious threat so far but, when this peaked in the US, drugs were killing more per year than died total in the Vietnam, Iraq and Afghanistan wars. Anyway, that's not the main point. We've now got the tools to sort out shit like this and, if I'm prepared to do it pro bono, I don't see what the problem is. Fundamentally, it's the same as you helping Hyo-jin establish a new identity."

"Talk of the devil, here she is," Su pulled her partner into view. "Let me introduce you to Nancy Lee. What do you think?"

"Fucking hell, is that really her? I'd have walked past her in the street."

"Good job, ain't it? And look at these tats…" Su pulled Nancy's pants down and turned her towards the camera."

"Wow, inked arse! That octopus looks good enough to eat."

"Tasty indeed, but for girls only."

"Fantastic, but to get back to my question. Can you help me set things up here? This is actually helping our kind of people, those that reject cultural norms and who often get caught out when things go tits-up."

"Okay, sure, when you put it like that, why not. And, on the topic of kink, what's the lesbian scene really like in Tokyo. I've heard lots of good things. It seems almost too good to be true."

"Right up your street, especially on the fetish, lezdom side. I'll set you up whenever you fancy a visit."

"Well, after our R and R in Khao Lak, we're heading for Lesbos," Su grinned. "It's some kind of fantasy of Hyo…, of Nancy's. I suspect, however, it'll mainly be vanilla Sapphism, so a trip to Japan thereafter might be just the job."

"So, what have you got for me?"

"I've got a link to Georgie's general purpose hyper-AI, which can do the detailed planning for you after you decide the approach that you're going to take. Access needs to be authenticated by Georgie, so let her know when you're ready to go. After that, any support you need can be provided by the normal system back in Switzerland."

"Excellent. Do you mind if I bounce my ideas on the action off you?"

"Fucking up the yakuza has got to be fun, even if very dangerous. But you've got to get this right or they'll go all *Kill Bill* on your arse."

"It may not be up to an Andy type of cunning plan, but I aim to let the AI do the heavy lifting. All I need to do is ask it to identify all organised crime groups and then wipe them out. I guess this will probably involve hacking into their computer systems, ripping off all incriminating information and releasing this to both the police and a public website."

"You could end up with a lot of overkill there," Su frowned. "You need to be aware that not all activities that are formally against the law are fundamentally wrong. Remember that there are still countries where prostitution or homosexuality is illegal, so simple brothels or bath-houses could be classified as organised crime. A blanket attack on anything considered criminal in specific countries could also wipe out opposition groups in repressive regimes. This is the very thing that Ursi keeps going on about. The power of this tool is so great that, if used at all, we have to be extremely careful that we don't cause irreversible damage."

"Shit, I clearly hadn't thought this through. What about if we restrict this only to Japan?"

"I don't know enough about the laws there, but do you? I think the safest option is to try to make the goal very specific and have any attack as surgical as possible, focused only on the key organisations and those within them who are known to be dangerous. I'd also get Georgie to run some simulations of any potential actions before you initiate anything for real."

"Bugger! You're right, of course. The big actions that we took in the past were forced upon us. We didn't need to worry about some collateral damage, because the hazards associated with doing nothing were so much greater. Sorting out Hyo-Jin, or Nancy as she now is, was extremely specific and risks of blow-back are minimal."

Su nodded. "I guess it's a Spider-Man kind of thing: with great power comes great responsibility."

"Okay, I'm going to think about this a bit more and then organise a chat with the full team. I should probably also chat to Andy beforehand. He seems to have a knack for this stuff."

"Yes, he can be a complete pain in the arse, but he's good at what he does. I'd still bounce any plan off the full team before initiating any action, though."

"Certainly. So, otherwise, what have you and the transmogrified Nancy been getting up to in Thailand?"

"Mainly keeping fit, eating great food and having lots of decadent sex. Actually, we're just finishing an Apero and considering a pre-prandial bonk. Want to watch?"

"God, you're such an exhibitionist! However, I'm a gay guy, so why should I be interested in your lesbian shenanigans?"

"Well, I'm going to focus on Nancy's latest tattoo..."

"Right, you've talked me into it. Let me grab a beer and settle down for a bit of porn to get me in the mood for the night ahead."

***

Lou had moved in with Beat & Heidi for a few weeks while the modifications to her apartment was being carried out. This was convenient in that she still spent most of her working days supporting the aid distribution project which, despite the technical support tools at their disposal, required a lot of thought in order to find an optimal way of balancing support of those most suffering from the global economic disruption against the risk of demotivating them by removing their drive to stand on their own feet. Some clearly beneficial options, such as making free contraception universally available and supporting education of women, were technically straightforward, but often needed mobilisation of international political pressure to force adoption by some of the more repressive regimes.

Lou's frustration with lack of progress in some areas had reached the point that she was now considering unleashing the power of the hyper-AI to break logjams. After chatting to Su and Jay, she was further reminded of the potential dangers of this course of action, but also determined that, if required, she would push to initiate this option.

The possibility of collateral damage was a special concern when it came to interfering with the leadership of sovereign lands. Here she kept in mind the potential for chaos, such as that unleashed by the CIA's political interference since the middle of

337

the 20th century, when they replaced leftist democratic governments by right-wing dictatorships and fomented unrest that benefited primarily the US military-industrial complex. Indeed, even when replacing dictatorships and fundamentalist religious regimes by democracies seemed to be justified, in practice this often resulted in replacing one group of corrupt autarchs by another that was just as bad, if not worse.

After running some ideas through the AI, Lou decided to bring the others into a video chat before going further. After introductory pleasantries, she got straight to the point. "We're now in the strange position of having more power in our hands than any government. In fact, possibly more than all of them put together. This is a total paradigm change as far as global politics is concerned, so extreme caution is required. In case of uncertainties, we may be better to do nothing at all and just let the normal processes run as before. But, given some of the obvious evil in the world, is sitting on the fence a justifiable option?"

"I think we've all been struggling with this over the last few weeks," Jay contributed, with the view of the brightly lit Tokyo Tower through the window behind him emphasising that mid-morning in Switzerland was early evening in Japan.

"Yes, but I'm sure that Lou has a specific case in mind," Su said, with the backdrop in her case being a bright tropical sunset as seen from the balcony of her room.

"Yes, I have indeed: the Taliban in Afghanistan. I think that in terms of human rights and, in

338

particular, hideous treatment of women, this bunch of bastards should be top of our hit list."

"There's no shortage of repressive regimes that abuse women, but I agree that, if we are going to test a surgical approach to using our powers for good, this would be an ideal example to start with," Andy nodded. He was squeezed between Georgie and Ursi on a settee in a suite with picture windows looking over Gamla Stan, the old town of Stockholm. "However, this will be extremely tricky, given that Afghanistan has been at war for centuries. They don't call that place the *graveyard of empires* for nothing."

"Yes, I suppose the country is so fucked-up that it has the advantage that, even if we screw up, it's difficult to imagine how it could get any worse," Su added. "So, what options had you been thinking of? I could imagine that a tailored virus that targets old men with beards could do the job for you."

Lou smiled while the others laughed. "Actually, tailored viruses were included as an option, aimed to take out predominantly older men. The problem is that this would be difficult to target precisely and the risk of collateral damage both inside and around Afghanistan would be too great."

Su grimaced. "I wasn't actually thinking that you'd take such an option seriously."

"Again, this is one of the scary aspects of the power of the tools we have to hand. The gene-editing technology actually exists, or could be readily developed by our AI, to allow tailoring bioweapons to very specific groups. We can easily target within particular ethnic groups, based on sex, age, medical history and other relevant characteristics."

"But surely you'd need a top-end lab and lots of specialist infrastructure for something like that?" Su mused aloud.

"Everything needed for development is available in medical research labs around the world. As operations within these are largely computer controlled, there's no problem for us to take them over, together with any pharmaceutical manufacturing or distribution facilities that we want. However, as you can imagine, this is a Pandora's box that we don't want to even think about opening. In fact, I suggest that the AI maintains a watching brief on research related to this topic, with the option of nipping it in the bud if it seems to be getting close to application."

"Christ on a bike!" Ursi grimaced. "The more I hear about what we're capable of doing, the more it scares me shitless."

Andy put an arm around the blonde's shoulders. "What really scares me is the thought of anyone else getting a hold of this technology in the foreseeable future. Anyway, Lou, what're the options that came to the top of your list?"

"Well, the first step is fairly straightforward, cutting off all supplies of arms and military supplies to the country. We allow humanitarian aid, but anything with military applications will be precluded."

"That's nothing that hasn't been tried before, with a marked lack of success," Su noted. "Afghanistan's borders are notoriously porous and enforcing a strict embargo has always proven impossible."

Lou nodded to acknowledge this point. "Again, this is where the power of our AI comes in, as we can monitor all communications in the entire region and spot in advance any preparation to supply the Taliban. We simply publish all of this on a website and allow the local security forces to do their jobs."

"That's unlikely to work," Su responded. "A general characteristic of many of such security forces is that they support this brand of Islamic fundamentalism and thus, directly or indirectly, the Taliban.

"Yes, that's why the AI also monitors the reactions of all involved. There are many other players in the region who'll step in if warnings are being ignored; not only NATO and the Israelis, but also many of the other Muslim states in the region."

"Okay, Lou, that might work to some extent," Su conceded, "but it'll be a slow process. Anyway, I don't think any of us would have a problem with giving it a try." All team members nodded in agreement.

"Yes, so that leads on to the second step, which is a bit more controversial. We put a bounty on the heads of the top Taliban leaders. Five million dollars for each of them assassinated, paid on demonstration that this did not involve injury to any others."

"Wow!" Jay commented. "Here's me planning how to wipe out organised crime, while you're suggesting that we move into the assassination business, paying hit-men to murder people that we don't like."

"Well, that would be hit-men and -women," Su pointed out. "I suspect that if this bounty was sufficient to allow them to escape from that hellhole of a country, there'd be plenty of women and girls happy to add a bit of arsenic to the dinner of their husband or father."

"And there'd also be a queue of the old warlords, who'd be happy to build up their funds, while wiping out some of their domestic opposition," Andy added. "While it's true that most of them would be improvements over the Taliban, many are total bastards in their own right."

"Okay, there may be lots of folk who'd kill our targets for the bounty, but I just can't condone this," Ursi interrupted. "I'm completely against both capital punishment and state-sponsored assassinations. There's got to be a line that we don't cross."

Andy twisted around to face her. "I can sympathise here. The risk of collateral damage and the arbitrary way in which targets are selected make it completely unacceptable. If you have captured and clearly identified a culprit, the decision on capital punishment tends to depend on whether you think it might act as a deterrent to prevent further crimes or if there are socio-economic issues. For example, the costs of long-term incarceration of a criminal need to be balanced against the good that could be done otherwise with such resources."

"And there's also the irreversible nature of such an action, in case you have the wrong person in your cross-hairs," Ursi added.

"Yes, but say we have someone who's clearly responsible for crimes against humanity and will continue to commit them unless stopped." Lou was evidently wrestling with her own conscience here. "If we're sure of the target and can do it without harming anyone else, aren't we obliged to take action? If we can stop atrocities and don't, aren't we guilty of tacit acceptance of such actions?"

Su frowned. "Maybe it depends on our degree of confidence in our case against any of our targets. Can we be absolutely sure that we won't ever make a mistake?"

Georgie, strangely incongruous in a sailor suit of the type typically worn by Japanese schoolgirls, then spoke up in a tone displaying more certainty than shown by any of the others up to this point. "This is something that you don't need to bother about. Nothing is ever sure in life, but the AI can give you confidence exceeding 99% level, and probably far above this, if that's what you want. In any case, it'd be very far better than the uncertainty associated with any human-managed court case."

"I guess this's the point. We now have a tool to support decisions with respect to culpability that goes beyond anything that previously existed." Lou summarised. "Do we use it or not?"

Ursi still wasn't convinced. "Even if this process was infallible, would we ever be justified in encouraging, actively sponsoring murder? And, here, humans are involved. Despite any of our planning, mistakes will be made and innocents will be caught in the cross-fire. It's inherent to your plan."

"Yes, I noticed that weakness," Georgie spoke again in the same confident tone. "We can, however, easily get around it if the AI actually takes over the assassination."

"No fucking way!" Su interrupted. "You're suggesting something like Skynet. Will you also have killer Terminator androids?"

Georgie seemed to consider this for a moment before replying. "Well, I might be able to do androids if you really want, but there're actually much easier ways of getting the job done." She seemed confused by the nervous laughter this comment drew from her teammates.

Lou was first to respond to the shock caused by this announcement. "Yes, love, I think we'll pass on the Terminator option. So, what were you actually thinking of doing?"

"Well, everywhere in the world there are accidents just waiting to happen. There are easy options like pacemakers going wonky, medicines being mixed up, brakes of cars failing or their GPS malfunctioning. The relatively primitive state of Afghanistan makes this trickier, but most of the top leaders have access to technology that they deny to those lower down the food-chain. This is much slower than other options, but has the advantage that it's very difficult for the regime to spot that it's under attack. It really looks like a run of bad luck, which we can extend by jinxing military infrastructure.

"I can see that Ursi's still unhappy," Lou said, "but this suggestion by Georgie looks a lot neater than any other option that I've looked at. Why don't we run a few simulations and then, if it looks good, give it a first trial run for a few weeks."

Georgie looked worried. "If Ursi's not happy about assassinations, we could just dial down lethality a little." Looking around at the confused faces she continued. "We can aim to incapacitate victims. Of course, for some of the older ones, we can't preclude lowering their life expectancy, but we won't kill them."

"Actually, this could have a greater impact," Andy mused. "Something that could be interpreted as a martyr's death might be shrugged off in a way that a long debilitating illness wouldn't. This seems like a definite improvement for this option."

"Well, for illness, we could tailor some…" Georgie started before noticing Lou's look of horror.

"No, girl, we really don't want to go there. Let's start with technological accident scenarios, while we initiate the block of armament supply to the country and whatever you can do to bugger-up their military infrastructure. Then we can make a final decision in… Well, what do you think Georgie, how much time will you need."

"Let's say a couple of days. Unless, of course, you're in a rush." Smiles from Andy, Jay and Su contrasted with the looks of horror on the faces of Lou and Ursi.

***

After the telecom, Andy, Ursi and Georgie wandered through the quaint, cobbled streets of Gamla Stan before finally selecting a restaurant for late lunch. The Ardbeg Embassy offered a range of craft beers and snacks with a Nordic flair, in addition to a huge selection of malt whiskies. Andy ordered a draft IPA and a burger with mushrooms while the others went for different Swedish gins with tonic, which came with a shared plate of assorted game.

Although the old town was fairly busy with tourists, the restaurant was quiet and, after initiating an app that would make electronic eavesdropping impossible, Andy felt it was quite safe for them to chat freely, especially if they stayed well clear of topics related to their work.

As Ursi was still not quite au fait with all Georgie's gender variants, she asked Andy about this choice of dress after their colleague headed off to the toilet. "I know Georgie's happy to answer such questions directly, I'm still a bit confused," she confessed. "And, is it Georgie today, or should it be Georgina??"

Andy laughed. "I've been sharing a bed with her for years and I still get mixed up. No matter what she appears to be, Georgie always works. Lou can always spot which name and adjective fits best, but I often guess wrong unless it's Hello Kitty."

Ursi smiled. "Yes, that Georgina rig-out is a bit of a giveaway. She really loves that pink shit, doesn't she?"

"She does indeed and it means she's in little girl mode. Quite how that fits in with the associated BDSM stuff is beyond me, however."

"Beats me too. I must confess that Su and Co. have been leading me gently into some kinky stuff, but it's definitely getting close to the edge of my comfort zone. I notice that you're usually a rather reluctant participant in those games."

"Too much of a wimp," he smiled. "Anyway, back to the clothes that look like Japanese school uniforms. You don't see them often, but it's an indicator of trans-sex mode. Here George and Georgina both work, but I'd just stay with Georgie. If it looks like a schoolboy uniform, she's tranny – chick with a dick sort of thing. The sailor suit is much rarer, indicating full hermaphrodite or futanari. I think she generally finds this frustrating, as she can't use her usual strap-on and still allow for the option of vaginal or anal penetration. I haven't seen that particular rigout for years. Anyway, she's on the way back, so why don't you ask her directly?"

Ursi still looked uncomfortable after Georgie took her place, so Andy spoke up. "I see you're in Japanese jailbait mode today. I thought gakuran was your preferred trans kit."

"Gakuran?" Ursi interjected.

"Japanese schoolboy uniform," supplied Georgie with a wicked grin, "a bishounen favourite. These are beautiful, androgynous, young Japanese men. When I'm feeling that way, just dressing up in that uniform gets me turned on," she leaned towards Ursi and, after checking that there was nobody in

347

sight, gently nibbled her earlobe. "Very often AC/DC, so there's hope also for Andy," she smiled.

"But what about today? You're more cosplay Sailor Moon or something."

"Actually, more cosplay Futanari Schoolgirl," her grin became distinctly wicked.

"I seem to remember that wasn't a great success last time."

"No, a real wet squib. But I've got a new trick up my sleeve. It'll probably help if you have a couple of drinks with lunch to get you relaxed and then we can go back to the hotel for some sex that'll truly blow your mind."

Andy looked confused, but Ursi spoke up, obviously worried about where this could be leading. "I'm game enough, Georgie, but I'm really not into complex toys or wild SM scenarios. So, just let me know what's involved."

Georgie, somehow or other, managed to look wicked and bashful at the same time. "Okay, that's fair. Although I'd intended it as a surprise, I should have realised Andy would spot what I had in mind from my choice of clothes."

Andy looked even more confused. "I spotted that you might have something hermaphroditic in mind, but I'm buggered if I can work out what."

Her delighted giggles fit well with the schoolgirl theme. "Yes, buggering could well feature strongly in what I had in mind."

"But that was the problem last time. A normal strap-on just didn't work for you in that persona."

"Oh, you're thinking of strap-ons? I don't need those now. That's another technology gone the way of cryptocurrency and online privacy."

"Now I'm even more confused," Andy frowned, "I can't see what technology has to do with your sex life, weird and wonderful though it is."

"Yes, well I've been looking at further novel applications of the computing tools that we have. I can understand why you and the others are worried about the potential misuse of the power of this system, but I feel we need to find out just what the range of possibilities would be. For example, an obvious extension of the large spatial scale, multi-spectral, 4D tomographic scanning that we've used would be to look at smaller scales, specifically brain scanning."

Ursi sighed in relief. "That seems safe enough. I guess there'd be lots of medical applications for that."

Georgie looked surprised. "Oh, I suppose there would be. I'll need to remember to have a look from that perspective."

Now Ursi looked as confused as Andy. "But, if not medical, what applications would there be?"

"Sexual, of course. As I'm sure you know, there's no development of technology that hasn't been used for sex if it was at all possible."

Andy smiled as he thought of several good examples. "I suppose that's true. Who'd have thought when it was developing and expanding that porn would comprise almost half of the internet? So, is that it, some kind of hyper-porn?"

"No, not really. Well, kind of. Anyway, the main thing is that inversion of time-sequence, tomographic squid-scans allows a crude form of mind reading."

"I thought the scanning of buildings was bad enough, now we've got Big Brother mind reading. All aspects of privacy are now out the window." Ursi waved her arms for emphasis, almost knocking over her drink.

"Don't worry, I can't read thoughts." Ursi looked mollified until she continued. "Well, not yet anyway. But emotions and sensory nerve signals are much easier to pick up, which gives the input I needed. All I had to do then was reverse the process."

"Christ on a bike, mind control also! Where does this end?"

"No not mind control, although I suppose that it'd be possible if you needed it for another application."

Ursi and Andy looked at each other, both dreading what revelations were coming next, but Georgie clearly missed this. "No, for the sex that I was planning, I needed only stimulation of the tactile sensory nerve network. I could extend it to include other senses, of course, but that'd be a bit intrusive. We simply wear blade visors and everything that we feel will match what we view or hear in the simulation scenarios."

"So, it's a kind of immersive porn?" Andy seemed relieved by this explanation.

"You can think of it that way, but it's set up to be completely interactive. The three of us will have sex and the system will just enhance the experience for us."

"Enhance, in what way," asked Ursi suspiciously.

"Well, I'll need to do some calibration for the two of you first, but you'll be able to see me in full futanari form, as well-endowed as I feel fits me. But more than that, when I fuck you, you'll be able to feel everything exactly as you would in real life."

"Jesus, well I hope that you're like one of these little schoolgirl futanari with small dicks and not the humungous dongs that some of the more matronly types sport."

"Something in the middle," she smiled. "The great thing for me is that I'll also experience the insertion in full. As I mentioned before, this makes strap-on dildos completely redundant. Any woman who wants to experience what it's like to have a prick now has that option. It does take a while to get accustomed to, as this runs via the tactile nerves of the clitoris. Nevertheless, I find it an amazing experience."

"You've tried it already?" Ursi asked.

"Yes, but just with models to date. I'm sure it'll be great when we give it a go in real life. What about you, ever dreamed of being a hermaphrodite?"

Ursi took a moment to work out a response to this question. "No, it's not on my current bucket list. But I'm sure Andy would give it a go," she added mischievously.

"Not an option for him, as I'd need to simulate a vagina and he's got no existing nerves that I can

351

hack for that purpose. Unless, of course, he wouldn't mind a bit of surgery first. We can do so much more now with AI-controlled teleoperation technology."

Andy shuddered and then shook his head. "This looks like our food coming, so I propose we wait until we're back in the hotel and then give this a try to see what it's all about. I certainly support Georgie's proposal of getting some alcoholic relaxation organised first, so I guess we should have another round."

"Fine, but I'll go on to wine now," Ursi said. "I think we'll need a bottle."

"At the least," Andy nodded. "It just so happens that I think a cunning plan is emerging. Did you know that, in the US, the sex trade has a higher turnover than drugs and guns combined? Our main aim could be to eliminate associated human trafficking, but we could probably spin off a huge contribution to our global recovery fund."

"Minus one permil," Georgie added with a smile.

Andy nodded. *Well, I've no idea where this is all going, but it looks like a lot of fun and if we can do some good along the way, so much the better. The world is going to change very quickly in ways we can't predict at present. But, as it started up completely fucked, this's got to be a good thing.*

THE END